Enjoy!

Ellen Parry Lewis

Risking a Life

By Ellen Parry Lewis

D1238820

Also by Ellen Parry Lewis

Future Vision

An Unremarkable Girl

Avenging Her Father

Metal Lunchbox Publishing

Text copyright 2016 by Ellen Parry Lewis

Cover Design and Illustration copyright 2016 by SF Varney

www.metallunchboxpublishing.com
www.ellenparrylewis.com
www.sfvarney.com

Risking A Life

For my family

Chapter One

The midnight blue silk slid through my fingers.

"I cannot believe Mrs. White is letting dresses like this go to waste!" I exclaimed. "She really just keeps them in these trunks?"

"What else do you expect her to do with them?" Caroline, my friend and another one of Mrs. White's maids, asked.

"I don't know. Can't she give them away? She'll never fit in these anymore."

"Who exactly is she to give them to?" Caroline said as I made my way over to the standing mirror in the corner of the generally unused guest room.

"What about us?" I replied without thinking.

Caroline actually laughed. "And when exactly would we wear something like that?"

"I don't know. It would simply be nice to own something so beautiful," I said sheepishly, holding the dress up against my body by the mirror. The midnight blue made my skin look more even than usual, which was good as my face was almost always too flushed for my liking. It also somehow made my drab hair and dim eyes seem a deeper brown. I fingered the lace around the collar delicately, admiring the details that could only be afforded by a fine lady.

"It would probably fit me perfectly," I said quietly, eyeing the tiny waist above the voluminous skirt.

"Well, you can't try it on," Caroline said, beating me to my next thought.

"Why not? It isn't like Mrs. White would ever know. When is the last time she has even peeked inside these trunks?"

"It does not matter," Caroline insisted. "They belong to Mrs. White. I simply thought you would find them interesting, and that is the only reason I wanted to show them to you."

I reluctantly brought it back over to the guest bed and we folded it so that it could again be placed in one of Mrs. White's many trunks and forgotten.

We were just closing the trunk lid when the bedroom door opened.

"Louisa?" Laura, Mrs. White's third and only other maid, addressed me.

"Yes?"

"Amos is asking for help in the kitchen."

"Very well," I agreed, walking past her and out of the room as Caroline and Laura discussed who would dust where.

My employer, Mrs. Frances White, was a lively, though aging widow. She was somewhat short and increasingly stout. She had gray hair and blotchy skin with unavoidable age spots. She was kind and fun, though, and while she never made an effort to befriend us servants or learn the personal details of our lives, she treated us fairly.

Keeping in form with Mrs. White's personality, she enjoyed throwing lavish parties for her friends and acquaintances. She would have at least two a year, but often more. This particular night was to be one of her parties. It was to celebrate the New Year of 1854, though Mrs. White would throw a party even without an official excuse.

As I descended the velvet-lined staircase, there was a knock on the front door. I quickly, but professionally, walked past the empty parlor and answered it.

Before I could even greet the wild man before me, he raced into the house, grabbing my shoulders violently and shaking me as he shouted, "It's all over! I lost! It's because of me!"

I was quite frightened, even after identifying the man as Mr. James Snyder, an acquaintance of Mrs. White. Even though I knew who he was, he looked like a complete stranger. He was normally well put together and wore some of the finest hats I had ever seen in my life. In this instance, however, he was in a common cotton shirt, untucked from his pants. He was wearing no coat, despite the frigid temperature, and his mostly bald head was bare. The cold from his hands was soaking through the sleeves of my wool maid's dress, chilling me to my core.

"Mr. Snyder!" I exclaimed, hoping the man would stop shaking me.

He simply shouted in response, "What can I do? All is lost! I have lost!"

Fortunately, Frank, Mrs. White's servant and coachman, ran into the foyer at this point, separating Mr. Snyder from me.

"Sir," Frank began as calmly as possible. "What's the problem?" Then, "How can I assist you?"

Mr. Snyder stared at us with simultaneously terrified and angered eyes. He did not say anything for a few moments as he grew calmer. Then, a tear fell from one of his eyes as he whispered, "I have made a mistake in coming for help. It is true that all is lost."

Before Frank or I could say anything further, the man ran from the house and out into the cold. Frank and I looked out the front door after the man, only to see him run sideways across Mrs. White's yard and into the forest.

"Did he travel on foot all the way here?" I asked as Mr. Snyder disappeared.

"It would appear that way," Frank replied uncertainly. "How far does he live? A mile perhaps?"

"Perhaps, which is a long way barely dressed as he was and at his age."

Mrs. White's house was located in southern New Jersey, about ten miles from Philadelphia. It was positioned in a location primarily covered with woods, though there was still a fair amount of people in the surrounding area. As a result, there were many roads good enough for traveling via horse and carriage. While Mrs. White certainly had the money to live in an even more established area, she said she enjoyed the peace of the trees, but still appreciated the option of traveling to Philadelphia for occasional entertainment.

I tried to remember where Mr. Snyder lived in relation to Mrs. White. I had been to his house only once, but I thought I remembered it being in the opposite direction from which he had run. After Frank and I stood another minute in silence, I sneezed loudly, breaking us from our semi-trance.

"I am so sorry, Louisa. I entirely forgot myself, standing here with the door open," he said, and we backed into the foyer.

As we turned around, we saw several pairs of eyes staring at us. Caroline and Laura were fearfully watching from the top of the stairs. In the hall at the side of the staircase stood Amos, Mrs. White's cook, and Mrs. White herself.

Bravely coming forward, Mrs. White took my hands in hers. "Are you harmed, child?" she asked me tenderly, her pupils as big as saucers.

"No. Just shocked is all," I said quietly.

As she turned to look at Frank while still holding my hands, she asked if that was indeed Mr. Snyder.

"I believe so, but he looked perhaps very ill. He ran off that way," he said, indicating the man's direction with a nod of his head.

Mrs. White bit her bottom lip. "That is not the way toward his house at all," she said, confirming my earlier thoughts.

Dropping my hands then, she asked Frank to visit the Snyder residence to be sure that Mrs. Snyder was safe and aware of her husband's condition.

"I am sure Frank will take care of the situation," Mrs. White said after his immediate departure. "I am so sorry for the scare you received, Louisa. Caroline," she then said, catching the maid's eyes at the top of the stairs. "Do you think you can start a fire in the parlor?"

"Of course," Caroline answered, even giving a little curtsy.

"Well, then. Let us continue with preparations for the party," Mrs. White concluded, and she walked up the stairs while I went to the kitchen with Amos.

Obviously desiring not to upset me any further, Amos completely ignored the outlandish occurrence that just passed, instead only asking me to help with setting up trays and with preparing some of the simpler appetizers.

I remained silent the entire time I worked, anxious for Frank's return and for news of Mr. Snyder's malady.

Chapter Two

I worked in the kitchen for two full hours before Amos and I heard the stable door open and close. I tried not to fidget while Frank must have been taking the saddle and other riding equipment off the horse.

By the time he came through the back kitchen entrance, I was nearly ready to burst. "Frank!" I loudly exclaimed.

He normally had healthily tanned skin, even in the winter, though at this time his skin was ashen and his eyes were red. "Are you ill?" I asked as Amos ran to the stove to pour him a cup of hot tea.

"No," he responded hoarsely. "Just cold from the journey."

"You don't look well at all," I said, searching about frantically for something with which to wrap him, though he was still bundled up in his heaviest winter gear.

"Mr. Snyder?" Amos questioned simply as he brought him the cup of tea. Not finding a blanket or anything else useful in the immediate vicinity, I instead pulled out a kitchen chair.

Frank essentially collapsed into it, nearly spilling the hot tea on his lap. Finally, he answered, "I could not find him. I did find Mrs. Snyder, though."

"Was she aware of Mr. Snyder's absence?" I asked anxiously.

"She was dead."

All three of us fell silent.

"Was she ill?" I finally asked, growing slowly fearful as Frank would have surely been exposed to the deadly illness.

"She did not look it," he answered. "She was slouched in a seat in her parlor. She even had some biscuits and a cup of tea on the table next to her. She was dressed in a normal afternoon dress."

"What did their servants say?" Amos asked.

"There were none."

"What do you mean? How did you enter the house?" I pushed.

"When no one answered, I managed to break through their parlor window. Mrs. Snyder's chair was facing away from me and toward the fire. I called out to her several times, afraid I would terrify her if she were merely sleeping. She did not respond, though," Frank said, and he swallowed his own spit as the cup of tea remained untouched in his hands.

"And you are sure that the servants were nowhere?" I asked.

"I am sure. I searched the house," Frank said while he shivered. "There wasn't a soul in the place."

"Where could they have gone?" Amos wondered.

"Perhaps to alert someone?" I suggested.

"Perhaps," Frank agreed. "Either way, after I made sure that poor Mrs. Snyder was dead and alone, I traveled back here. I didn't know what else to do."

"You did a fine job," I said, laying a hand on his shoulder and trying to comfort him. Frank was twenty-four years old, and thus six years my senior, though I still felt motherly instincts kick in as he actually cried.

With only a few hours left until guests would begin to arrive, Amos returned to his work while Frank stayed in his seat in the kitchen. After stoking the kitchen fire, I went to find Mrs. White, who was sitting in the parlor with her journal. Seeing me enter the room, she pulled off her spectacles and asked if Frank had returned yet.

I relayed his story in as much detail as I could offer.

"Poor Mrs. Snyder. And now what will happen to Mr. Snyder?" she mumbled, utterly shocked.

Before I could offer my sympathies, there was a second knock on the front door for that day. Mrs. White grew paler as we heard the noise. I was almost afraid to answer it, though I knew that I must.

Rising from her seat, Mrs. White stood in the parlor doorway while I walked fully into the foyer.

With a deep breath, I opened the door.

"Miss West," the man on the other side politely addressed me, and I couldn't be happier to see such a familiar face.

"Mr. Graham," I gratefully responded, immediately stepping backward so that he could come in and out of the cold.

Mr. Graham was by far the most eccentric acquaintance of Mrs. White. Towering over all other men by a generous half foot, he had an enormous beard and wildly wavy hair. While he was well-off enough, he had not been born into money, but had fallen into it after his former employer died, generously and surprisingly leaving his entire estate to Mr. Graham. Though he could have been partially shunned due to his unorthodox rise to high society, his character was so charismatic and charming that despite his unkempt appearance, he was invited to every noteworthy social gathering in the area. He was also an amazing storyteller, often shocking his hosts with tales of his scandalous young adulthood. Rather than insult or disgust his listeners, his tales often secured an invitation to yet another party.

This day, however, Mr. Graham wore a serious expression on his face and moved his massive body with sad deliberation. "Mrs. White," he said solemnly as she too stepped into the foyer. "I have just come from the Snyder residence. Their servants summoned me to the house where I found that Mrs. Snyder has died."

"I have heard and was only just now debating what to do about it," Mrs. White replied, and Mr. Graham's bushy eyebrows rose in question. "I sent my servant, Frank, to see to Mrs. Snyder when her husband showed up at my front door in the most ill and frenzied of states."

"So you have seen James?" Mr. Graham asked anxiously.

"Yes, but I am afraid he ran off after frightening Miss West here."

"Did you see where he went?"

"Just off into the woods in the opposite direction from his house," Mrs. White answered with an unconscious flip of her hand.

Mr. Graham's mouth drew noticeably tight under his thick facial hair. "I see. Did he say anything to you, Miss West?"

"He just shook me hard and yelled about losing something. I was not quite following his words," I answered timidly.

Mr. Graham's lips drew even tighter. Turning back toward Mrs. White, he concluded, "Thank you. I came here to give you the news, assuming that you had not yet received it, and also to ask if you had seen James. Please, if you acquire additional news of the man, send word to his household at once. I will return to his staff to give further instructions on what is to be done for dear Mrs. Snyder."

"Of course," Mrs. White answered. Her hands then took the form of a strained butterfly, something she always did subconsciously when she was about to pry for information. "Did the servants happen to speak as to the circumstances of Mrs. Snyder's death?"

"They were not in the room when it happened," Mr. Graham responded. "They only said that she had been fine that morning, though Mr. Snyder had seemed slightly agitated. Then, while she and Mr. Snyder were alone together in the parlor, he started shouting and crying." Mr. Graham swallowed hard as uncharacteristic tears formed in his eyes.

Mrs. White appeared paler than usual once more and Mr. Graham quickly said, "I am so sorry. I fear I have upset you with my vulgar bluntness."

"No, no. It is fine," Mrs. White said, waving away the steadying hands of Mr. Graham. Then, more sure of herself, "Please see to the Snyder residence and I will of course send word if we hear from Mr. Snyder again."

"Thank you," he said, turning toward the front door.

"Will you still be at the party tonight?" Mrs. White asked as he was just about completely outside.

"I hope to never miss one of your marvelous parties, Mrs. White."

"And you'll be sure to bring Elbert? I have told a great many new guests about him."

"Of course," he responded, and for the first time since his arrival, a smile touched his lips before he walked out the door.

"Go finish in the kitchen and then come to my room to help me ready myself for the party," Mrs. White gently instructed me.

"Yes, Mrs. White."

Before I even entered the kitchen, I saw the warm glow of the fire's light dancing on the walls. The tantalizing smell of pies hit my nostrils and I felt once more secure as I walked in and saw a busy Amos and a much recovered Frank.

"Feeling better?" I asked him as I immediately fell in next to Amos to help with assembling the hors d'oeuvres.

"Much," Frank answered. "I was actually just about to head out to finish preparing the stable for the guests' horses before I go home to change."

"Will you tell Emily about what happened at the Snyders'?" I asked. Emily was his new wife of only one month.

"Of course," he answered. "She always knows just what to say, though I do thank you for comforting me as well."

"Please, don't mention it," I said politely, and I focused solely on the culinary task at hand while Frank went outside.

Smelling strongly like a cooking fire by the time I was finished, I finally went to help Mrs. White only an hour before guests were to arrive.

"Sorry I am running so behind," I said as I entered her room, only to find her already mostly assembled by Caroline and Laura. Though quite round, Mrs. White still appreciated the enormously large skirts that were in style. While it did not exactly give her the bell-shape of the younger women who would be at the party, it did take the focus off of her true figure a bit. Though I had never worn a dress of this nature, I could not help but like the look. It was bold and attention grabbing, but still classy. I, on the other hand, would wear a well-tailored but boringly modest black cotton dress, clearly differentiating the maids from the guests.

"You look lovely," I complimented Mrs. White as I stepped forward to help with her hair.

As I drew close, Mrs. White's nose wrinkled in disfavor. "Louisa, you smell like the kitchen. Go ready yourself now before the guests arrive. Laura and Caroline have this handled."

"Yes, Mrs. White." I said humbly, and I backed out of the room as Caroline threw me a look that begged me to trade places with her. I threw her a stealthy smile before walking out into the upstairs hall and racing to my room before Mrs. White could change her mind.

My room was small and on the third floor. I supposed I should have been thankful for my still above-average living situation, except that I found the constant, but unattainable wealth around me to be nauseating. I had been sent to live with and work for Mrs. White three years prior, when I was fifteen years old. I was the only child of my parents. Our lack of money made living uncomfortable, and so when I was of an appropriate age to work in the house of a fine lady, my mother managed to secure this job for me. Afterwards, I saw my family only twice, as they lived somewhat far away in the north of New Jersey, and a year after I started working for Mrs. White, my parents both grew ill and died. Despite the despair and depression that followed the discovery that I had no living family to my name, I expected that my physical life would remain comfortable due to my position as a maid. I would know reasonable luxury for the foreseeable future, and following Mrs. White's death, I would hopefully be able to find employment at a comparable household. Marriage was a dream, but not realistic at the time; Mrs.

White never mentioned the possibility to me, and it would be difficult to find someone without her help and support.

Caroline was the only other servant who lived in the house. At twenty years of age, she was more senior than me and lived on the second floor very close to Mrs. White in case our employer should need her assistance at an odd hour of the night. She too was without family, also finding herself an orphan at the age of sixteen. The other maid, Laura, was thirty-six, and she lived in a small, nearby house with her husband. Amos and Frank also had similar living situations.

When I was not serving Mrs. White, I was studying. I would read and practice my handwriting. My mother had managed to teach me the foundations of these skills, though I had been largely uninterested in them while living at home; they had seemed like pointless occupations at the time. However, upon moving in with Mrs. White, I saw her read in her spare time, and she seemed to enjoy herself immensely. Also, I loved to watch her engage in her morning correspondences. I often wondered how she had so many people to write to on such a consistent basis, but then I saw the large number of letters she would receive in turn. After only a short time in her house, I longed to hone these skills so that I too would be able to enjoy these fine things if the opportunity presented itself.

After I finished readying myself for the party, I looked in the mirror. I felt pretty in what Mrs. White referred to as my "party dress," but not radiant by any means. And radiant is most certainly what the women guests would be. It made me sick to think of the midnight blue dress in the trunk downstairs, never to be worn again. And also there was Mrs. White's new dress, with a flower pattern that was simply to die for.

Deliberately pushing these unspoken desires from my head as I always had to do immediately preceding a party, I fixed my hair and walked downstairs to the kitchen.

"Do you need any last minute help, Amos?" I asked the middle-aged cook.

He shook his head as he placed the last tray of hors d'oeuvres on the long counter for me and the other two girls to take out to the guests.

"I'll go check on the ballroom then. To make sure it's satisfactory," I said mostly to myself.

The ballroom was attached to the kitchen at the far end so as to make serving easier. Mrs. White also called this spacious ballroom the Emerald Room, as the walls and curtains were all green. It was not an original part of the house. Mrs. White had always been a fan of lavish evenings, though, and so she had this rectangular-shaped room designed to fit her needs perfectly. Its design was not typical to the best of my knowledge, but it was Mrs. White's treasure. It ran the whole width of the right side of the house. Near the front, set next to a large window, was a dining table with place settings, which looked especially perfect at that moment. In the far corner at the back of the house, a string ensemble was already set up and awaiting the appearance of the first guests. There was an incredibly large area for dancing, and decorative vases and paintings were squeezed into every free space along the walls. Aside from an opening to the kitchen and foyer, the Emerald Room contained a side door that led to beautifully manicured gardens, though I doubted anyone would make use of them on this particular, freezing night.

I strolled about the large room, hearing my footsteps echo off the high ceiling.

In a matter of minutes, Caroline and Laura had joined me, and before I knew it, we heard the heavy thudding of horses' hooves and the classy creaking of carriages out front. Mrs. White remained at the front door while guests poured inside. I immediately started my rounds with a tray of hors d'oeuvres that was difficult to balance due to its weight and huge size. I had had practice, though, and hadn't spilled anything for at least eight parties.

A half an hour into the official beginning of the night, I saw tall Mr. Graham enter the Emerald Room. Unmarried as he was, he always had several ladies around him the entire evening despite his rising age. Walking past me, he grabbed a snack from my tray while he inclined his head toward me. He was carrying a large, hooded cage, and I knew that Elbert would be inside.

With great theatricality, he took a vase off of a marble stand against the wall in the center of the room. He then gently placed the cage on top of the stand and removed the plaid, custom-made hood. Guests had already gathered round, waiting to catch a glimpse of Mr. Graham's exotic parrot. Elbert was not just any normal bird, though. Aside from having the most outlandish, bright green and red plumage I could have ever imagined, even on so fancy a bird, Elbert had a better vocabulary than half the guests at the party. He could carry on an in-depth conversation with anyone on just about anything from philosophy to books to politics. I personally did not like to speak with Elbert, as he actually managed to make me feel stupid. Perhaps he made others feel this way as well, though certainly no one with the exception of his eccentric owner would ever admit to feeling inferior to a small, winged animal.

As usual, when Elbert was revealed, there were claps and "oohs" and "ahhs." First-time guests gathered close to the cage, mesmerized by the way Elbert proudly stood before the onlookers.

"Greetings. Thank you for the gracious invite to this party," Elbert loudly squawked and the guests squealed in delight as people began to approach the bird to converse with him more personally.

"Where did you find him?" one of the female newcomers asked Mr. Graham, pulling at his arm in an attempt to capture his complete attention.

"A fellow in Philadelphia who had brought him from India," Mr. Graham responded.

"Did you teach him to speak like that?" a man asked.

"Partially, though I think he has a better vocabulary than I do," Mr. Graham answered, his usual reply to the usual question.

Eyeing my tray again, he walked over to me, people moving before him like the parting of the Red Sea.

"Good evening, Miss West," he jovially greeted me as he took more food from my now lighter tray.

"Good evening. I trust all is well at the Snyder estate," I said, trying to word my question as delicately as possible.

He grew more serious. "I have set all of her affairs in order and will begin to spread the news myself tomorrow, though I expect Mrs. White will make sure that everyone knows of the shocking tale in no less than an hour."

"Well, I do hope that at least for tonight you can enjoy the party as you have had to act under stressful circumstances today."

"Thank you," he said, obviously looking around for the refreshments.

Before he could head in their direction, though, Caroline came running up to me, her hands empty of any tray.

16

"Louisa!" she said loudly, though she whispered as she drew up next to me. Her actions had grabbed Mr. Graham's attention once more as well, and so he listened as she told me the horrifying news.

"It's Mr. Snyder," she quietly hissed. "He's hung himself behind the stable!"

Chapter Three

I nearly spilled the remaining contents of my tray as I ran outside. Fortunately, Mr. Graham was racing ahead of me, and so I was able to follow in his cleared path through the party guests.

Passing through the kitchen, I threw the hors d'oeuvres tray down on the table and flew out the back door with Caroline and Mr. Graham, not caring that we were without our coats.

There was a large number of guests' carriages gathered behind the house. Running in between them, we arrived behind the stable. Immediately, through some leafless trees, we could see the dangling form of Mr. Snyder, already surrounded by Frank and other coachmen.

While Mr. Graham ran forward to help with the task of taking Mr. Snyder down from the tree, I found that my feet would no longer move. My mouth opened involuntarily in shock, and though I couldn't make out the details of Mr. Snyder's body, I could not believe that what I was seeing actually existed. I knew Mr. Snyder had been unusually upset, presumably due to the unexpected loss of his wife, but I would never have pictured the normally dignified man hanging himself. It took Caroline saying my name and tugging on my elbow hard to pull me out of my stupor.

"We should go back inside and attend to the guests before we arouse suspicion."

"Of course," I said numbly, and we walked back inside just as Mr. Snyder was completely freed from the tree.

Amos had refilled my mostly empty tray, and so I picked it up and walked back into the bustling Emerald Room.

Soon afterwards, my tray was empty from the many hungry guests, and so I returned to the kitchen to retrieve more food. There, I found Mr. Graham sitting at the kitchen table, solemnly looking out the frosted window in the direction of the now pitch-black woods.

Setting my tray down for Amos at the opposite end of the kitchen, I retraced my steps to Mr. Graham and took a seat cattycorner to him. "Are you all right?" I asked.

"Humph…I suppose," he said sadly.

"Is Mr. Snyder's body in a safe place right now?" I continued in hushed tones.

"The coachmen are taking care of it."

"Should I alert Mrs. White or any others?"

"No," Mr. Graham replied, finally tearing his eyes away from the window so that he could look at me. "News of his madness earlier today will be rampant enough at this party, I'm sure. No need to add news of his...of his suicide just yet." Mr. Graham's large Adam's apple bobbed hard in his throat.

"Were you two close?" I asked, thinking the two men an odd pairing.

"In a way. It's just...." Mr. Graham paused for a second and looked me over, seemingly making up his mind about something. Meanwhile, Amos swiftly readied food at the opposite end of the kitchen, entirely absorbed in his job. At the same time, voices, music, and the sound of dancing bounced into the kitchen from the Emerald Room. Surrounded by all of this commotion, Mr. Graham's and my conversation seemed very out of place, and yet it also felt completely private.

"Please do not tell anyone this," Mr. Graham finally started again. "But I feel slightly responsible for James's death."

"How can that be, though? You certainly could not have pushed him toward killing himself, and you could not have had anything to do with poor Mrs. Snyder's death," I responded quickly.

"Not directly, no. But I told Mr. Snyder about the thing that, I believe, ultimately must have led to his wife's death and his despair."

"What could you have told him about?" I asked as Caroline raced past me with an empty tray.

Mr. Graham finally smiled a little as he looked at me. "You know, I have always liked you, Miss West. I suppose you remind me a little of myself from back in the day."

I smiled slightly, unsure of what this had to do with the Snyders, but happy to be in the good favor of so kind and wealthy a man.

"When I was your age, I was still working for old Mr. Wilcox. He was kind to me and treated me fairly, especially as he had no other living family members to speak of. I was more than just his servant; I was his companion. I was grateful for this, as I had always longed for something more than a mere servant's life." He stopped awkwardly here as if remembering that I was just a servant. "I see that same longing in

19

you," he finally decided on. "Were you with money at one time? It seems as if you are almost accustomed to the finer things in life."

"No," I answered, afraid that I would disappoint him. "My paternal great-grandfather knew wealth," I quickly added. "Not for long, though. He did not fight during the war, but remained on his estate. At some point during those years, he managed to lose most of his wealth to the British. He would never talk about the details, but by the time my father was born, his family was living quite modestly. My father grew even poorer, and my mother was poor to begin with."

Mr. Graham nodded thoughtfully. "Is this family history the reason you seem to pine for more?"

"I don't know, Mr. Graham," I responded, truly unsure of the answer to that question.

"Louisa, though you seem somewhat dissatisfied, I have never heard you speak out against your lot in life. You speak professionally and you seem to have a great deal of common sense. I tend to doubt that you would, even with the money and means, partake in some of the sillier fashions of today. Like those ridiculously large skirts," he said, looking out at the party, which we could see through the open door from our location. "I don't know how anyone can dance like that let alone have a personal conversation with someone while having to stand one hundred feet apart from one another," he said, shaking his head. I did not dare mention that just that evening I had found myself coveting Mrs. White's fashionable skirt.

Turning back toward me, he said, "It is because you seem to have a head on your shoulders that I tell you this. I expect that you will not act rashly, and that you will fully consider what I am to tell you. I do not want your soul on my conscience in addition to James's."

Under the table, I clutched my chair bottom with both hands, nervous and excited to learn about this dark secret.

"South of here there is a shallow, swampy area. I'm a hunter, as you may know, and I found myself deep in this wooded area about a year ago in the early spring. Some of the land was simply soggy while some of it was several inches deep in water, but I didn't care. I was perhaps careless as I moved along, searching for my quarry. Unfortunately, I never did find anything worth shooting, and as the afternoon grew late, I was just about to return northward when I stumbled into this paradise of sorts."

Mr. Graham grew immediately quiet as Laura passed by, who shot me a displeased look as I was not serving the guests as I should have been. Ignoring her, I returned my gaze to Mr. Graham as he continued with his tale. "There was an area with lush green grass, surrounding a tiny lake. There were no trees in this small opening with the exception of a beautiful willow tree. And on the opposite side of this small body of water was a random jumble of rocks in front of an area where the dirt rose up sharply. It seemed to be the mouth of a cave.

"Though the whole place had an odd, almost fearfully magical air about it, I was not one to spit in the face of adventure by ignoring my find. I walked right around that lake and poked my head inside the cave entrance. As soon as I did that, I remember a chill went through my body. I ignored this...haunting feeling, though, and stepped inside. Only a few feet inside, the cave split off to the left and to the right. I walked to the left, feeling my way down the passageway slowly as I could not see anything. Perhaps twenty feet down this passage I was about to turn back, for I did not wish to be needlessly reckless as opposed to simply adventurous. I only had the time to turn around, though, before I was sent flat on my back by a powerful force."

"What was it?" I asked, unable to contain myself.

"I don't know exactly."

"A bear maybe?" I suggested impatiently.

"No, no. When I said I don't know, I mean it isn't something I've come across before. You see...I think it is, well...maybe a demon. Or perhaps a monster. Either way, I felt immediately cold and truly terrified."

I made a skeptical face, my right cheek and side of my mouth pulling upward, scrunching my eye on that side. I could not help it. How did Mr. Graham expect me to believe such impossibilities?

"I see you think I am making this up," Mr. Graham said, and something about his tone brought a serious expression back to my own face. "Please, give me a minute to explain, for I know what I have experienced."

I decided to be fair, and as Mr. Graham was usually a jolly sort of man, his demeanor at least served to frighten me somewhat.

"As I was saying, I was terrified, thinking I was about to be eaten by whatever obviously large and strong thing was in front of me. But then it spoke. It said, 'Jasper—.'"

"It knew your name?" I interrupted.

"Yes. It knew much more than that too. It said, 'Jasper, why have you come here?'

"I was too scared to speak, and in the pause that followed, this thing laughed a harsh, cruel laugh. It then said, 'Jasper, I will not tell you who or what I am. Let it just suffice that it was destiny that has brought you to my home.' I asked what it meant by that. It said, 'If you had chosen the right path in the cave, I would have killed you then and there for that is where I dwell. But as you have chosen the left side, I am in a talking mood. I am not going to harm you right now. And if I harm you at all is up to you. What I offer you is a choice; if we come to an agreement, I can offer you treasures beyond your wildest dreams, or you could end up with unimaginable sorrow.'

"I again asked it what it meant, and the monster told me that it entertained itself by making bets. I asked what kind of bets. The thing said, 'I know your thoughts, Jasper. You are rich now, and you have enough money to live comfortably enough for the foreseeable future. But what of the social perks that come along with money? You are afraid that you will one day be an outcast, despite your money. After all, you are unrefined and have nothing but your vulgar ways to offer your more civilized hosts. For now, you keep them entertained with your scandalous and demeaning stories, but what will happen when your stories run out? Will they keep you around—you, with no ties to the society of the upper class?'"

Mr. Graham's voice sounded distant and chilling, and the music from the party seemed to fade from my hearing.

"He knew my thoughts and my fears," Mr. Graham said, looking even deeper into my eyes, as if he were trying to connect with me on the level of the soul. "I found myself shaking from the cold of this thing's presence, but also from the fearful reality of my life and my precarious position. I asked him what his offer was, but told him that I would not, under any circumstances, sell him my soul. He laughed at this stipulation and said he did not ask for my soul. He merely offered me the chance to secure an enjoyable and well-off life in exchange for a minor risk. He said that he had an unusual solution to my problem, as it was an unusual problem to begin with. He wanted to make a bet with me. If by noon the next day, I spoke to at least one person, I would win the bet. My prize would be a parrot, incomparable in beauty to any other bird and smarter than most men. It would be able to speak in full sentences and with a cognizance that was sure to leave a lasting impression on everyone who saw it. It would outlive even me, and it would ensure that, after all of my stories were used up, I would be invited to every party in the area, and perhaps even more as word of its existence spread."

I thought of Elbert and the non-detail-oriented way in which Mr. Graham always described his acquisition of such an incredible animal.

"It was a weird enough solution, and I thought that truly no one else would be able to rival me in this way. It was not like a fashion that would go out of style, and so I asked the monster what would happen if I lost. He said that if I lost, my youngest servant, Alex, would die."

I gasped, unwillingly pulled into the truth of his story. "You made that bet?" I asked, simultaneously in awe and disgusted. "You risked your servant's life for a parrot?"

"You have to bear in mind that this monster's presence was unnervingly powerful. Also, it was a life of comfortable security assuming I could simply have one human interaction in almost twenty-four hours' time. I was planning on heading home straightaway anyway. So, the thing explained some minor rules of the bet and asked me if I accepted. He said that once I accepted, there was no unaccepting. I told him that I understood and accepted, and with that, I could feel him move away. I slowly slid my way back down the tunnel and out of the cave and then made straight for home. I arrived back home late that night where Alex was waiting for me. He said hello to me, I said hello to him, and I went to bed. The next morning, a man arrived with Elbert in a cage, saying that it was addressed to me, but that it had no letter with it. I accepted the bird and asked him what name he would like. My parrot chose Elbert, noting that the name means noble and famous, and that's what he intended on becoming. And as a result, I've received more invitations to events than I know what to do with."

"What of Mr. Snyder, though?"

Mr. Graham's face fell, for it had lifted somewhat while he spoke of his feathered friend.

"Half a year ago, Mr. Snyder came to my house where he confided to me that he was starting to have money problems. He said he didn't know what to do, as he was growing too old to readjust his life or find a solution through labor. I took pity on the man, and so I shared this story with him."

"He made a bet with the demon too?" I asked, and shuddered.

"He never told me the details of it, but only a couple of days after our conversation, he thanked me and told me that he no longer had any money problems."

"Well then, why their deaths?"

"I obviously can't prove this for certain, but I think Mr. Snyder may have tried his luck for a second time. He told me he and Mrs. Snyder had always wanted children, but they had been unable to have any. He said he wondered how powerful this creature actually was."

"*Is* it that powerful?"

"I don't know. I thought it was a bit much to ask, but perhaps it really is that powerful if Mr. Snyder was able to make a deal with the promised reward as children. That seems like the only thing that could explain what just happened. He must have gone back to the cave to make this second bet. And he must have lost."

"And you think that it was his wife's life that he risked?" I asked, appalled by how anyone could do that.

"I believe so. It certainly explains Mrs. Snyder's sudden death and old James's snap from reality." Mr. Graham winced then, perhaps realizing his poor choice of words in describing Mr. Snyder's end. "Either way, it is too late for me to ask him, and I will have to forever wonder if I led him to his death."

"But it is not your fault," I said. "You did not tell him to go back a second time."

"Yes, but I opened his eyes to the possibility of the easy way out."

"You may have opened his eyes to the only possible way to achieve financial security, though," I said. "After all, he did have a point. What else was he supposed to do to fix that problem?"

"Perhaps," Mr. Graham admitted.

Uneasily, I pushed the conversation past the present. "Mr. Graham, how exactly do you arrive at this cave?"

Though Mr. Graham had almost been looking through me for part of our conversation as he recalled events past, he looked directly into my eyes at this point, a look of obvious fear opening them wide. "I am so sorry, Louisa. I should not have told you at all. This knowledge is a heavy burden to carry, and I tried to share it with you. It was very selfish of me, and now I've put your own life at risk," he started rambling.

"No, no, no," I tried to stop him. "I was just curious." I gave him what I intended to be a comforting smile, but it felt awkward in light of his immediate regret, reminding me that we were not nearly as close as we had just acted during our conversation, but that tragedy had simply pushed us momentarily together.

He sighed deeply. "You know Geresh's Glen?" he asked me.

While I had not had the opportunity to picnic there myself, I knew the area as it was a popular location with young people. "Yes."

"Directly south of there. Roughly a two hour walk."

"Ah," I said, storing that information in my memory.

"Please, use this information wisely, which should very well mean not using it at all. Also, I trust that you will not share it with anyone else. I don't want Elbert's origins being questioned so that he would be taken away from me."

"Of course," I said, and with an awkward, fatherly pat on my head, Mr. Graham stood from the table and rejoined the party.

Chapter Four

I glanced at the clock and noticed that it was almost three in the afternoon. Mrs. White's best friend would be arriving for tea soon, and as Mrs. White was incredibly rigid about having her tea at three o'clock every day, I dropped her summer bed sheets midway through making them up so that I could serve her at the proper time.

Rushing downstairs, Mrs. White and her friend, Mrs. Carter, could already be heard chatting away in the parlor. I hurried to the kitchen where Amos had finished placing the tea and cookies neatly on a serving platter.

"There you are, Louisa," he said.

"Thanks," I responded before carrying the platter calmly out of the kitchen and to the parlor.

As I entered the room, both Mrs. White and Mrs. Carter glanced in my direction.

"Thank you, Louisa," Mrs. White acknowledged me, and she went back to her conversation while I set down the tea and cookies on the small table between them. "As I was saying, when I heard that Adelade Sharp was going to be in Philadelphia, I decided to send her an invitation to my summer moonlight party next week."

"To perform?" Mrs. Carter squealed in delight.

"A few songs, yes. Of course, I do not yet have a response, but I am hoping for the best. I offered financial compensation for her presence here, as her performance would certainly up the quality of my party tenfold."

"Oh yes, yes. Oh, I do hope she comes. She is said to have the most heavenly voice despite her shocking upbringing with traveling performers."

"She is supposedly quite refined, though, having been trained socially by a rich benefactor who happened to hear her perform when she was still a child," Mrs. White said, defending the status of her star guest.

I left the room, wondering if Mr. Graham would be upset that Elbert might actually be upstaged at this next party.

I spent the rest of that summer day dusting and scrubbing parts of the second floor with Caroline, talking on the usual mundane topics, such as the new fashions that we could not partake in and our decreasing chances of finding a suitable husband.

Since the night of Mr. Snyder's death half a year before, I thought often of what Mr. Graham had told me about the supposed demon in the woods. At times I laughed aloud, amazed that I could have been so gullible. At other times I was fearful, imagining the creature to be just outside my bedroom window. And still at other times, I found myself longing for the story to be true and wondering what I would be willing to risk for the riches I so desired. When my thoughts went in this direction, the reality of my life seemed never-endingly dull. It was as if I were stuck in an unlived life, and slowly this began to scare me more than thoughts of the actual demon.

The next day was hotter than usual, even for June, and I wore my hair up off my neck higher than what was customary. Sweat trickled down my forehead as I scrubbed the kitchen floor, alone except for Amos, who was preparing Mrs. White's usual three o'clock tea. "Are you looking forward to Mrs. White's summer moonlight party?" he asked as I brushed myself off so I could look somewhat decent while bringing the tray to the parlor.

"I suppose. The garden will look splendid, I'm sure. I'm just not looking forward to setting up all of those chairs," I answered. Although we were not permitted to dance or truly socialize during Mrs. White's extravagant parties, I still generally looked forward to them for they offered a drastic change from the monotony of normal life.

"I'm sure *you're* looking forward to the next party. You relaxed and talked to Mr. Graham for half of the last one," Laura said sarcastically as she walked into the room.

"I told you that I am sorry about that. Mr. Graham was upset after finding Mr. Snyder's body. It would have been rude of me to leave."

"I know, I know," Laura said, not truly upset at me anymore, but enjoying the chance to be annoyed at something other than the usual housecleaning stains.

Following Mr. Snyder's death, there was much talk amongst the neighbors, but eventually the rumors and speculations died down, and the Snyder mansion remained empty.

"Tea time," I said, picking up the tray, the weight now quite familiar to me as I had been serving this daily to Mrs. White practically since my arrival as her maid.

Inside the parlor, Mrs. White was frowning at a letter she must have just opened.

"Bad news?" I asked cordially, setting the tea tray down.

"Unfortunately, Miss Adelade Sharp sends her regrets as she will be unable to attend my party. She will already be traveling south by that time for a different engagement. What a shame," she said, tossing the paper off to her side with an overly dramatic, distraught gesture.

"I am sure that your party will still be a fabulous success without such structured entertainment," I offered.

"I do hope so. I was looking forward to having such a renowned singer here. Singers hold such a mesmerizing, transcendent power over people, leaving them with a lasting impression of greatness," she sighed.

"Yes. Music can be quite soothing to one's soul."

No sooner had I returned to the kitchen than Laura stopped me. "Louisa, we just heard that Mrs. Carter will be joining Mrs. White for dinner tonight," she spoke while she hastily scribbled on a piece of paper. "However, that means that some extra items will be needed. I just checked with Amos and this should be sufficient. Could you run to the store and pick these up?"

Laura could also write, though not well, and she handed me a sloppy list with misspelled food items. "Of course," I answered.

Even though it was incredibly hot outside, I still decided that a nice walk would do me good as opposed to using one of the horses. And so with my small list in hand, I walked out the back door and into the muggy day.

The main cluster of stores was about a fifteen minute walk away. As I moved along, I started to sweat as I thought about Mrs. White sitting back home in the cool parlor with a fancy fan in her hand.

Reaching the first store in the area, I noticed that few people had ventured outside on this particularly blistering day. Passing by the second store, though, a group of young women with happy smiles on their faces emerged, each holding a parcel.

"It is going to look so lovely on you," one of them was saying to the tallest.

"Oh, thank you. And I do believe yours will complement your skin perfectly."

They walked by me with barely a glance in my direction. Stopping by the window of the store they had just exited, I saw the usual fine fabrics—something that I would probably never be able to purchase, and even if I could, I would have nowhere to wear a dress of such fine quality.

I sullenly made my way to pick up the items on the list for Mrs. White.

Passing by that same store with the fabrics once my task was complete, I found myself stopping again, despite the desire not to shame myself by drawing attention to my longing. As I stood there in the heat, my body sticking to the fabric of my average working dress, something inside me snapped. As the idea came to me, I was not shocked. I supposed, truthfully, that the idea had been building in me ever since New Year's. I would visit the devil or monster or whatever it was and at least hear his offer.

I raced back to Mrs. White's house.

Running to the back kitchen door, I nearly threw the food inside before dashing once more outside and into the stable.

Frank was there, as expected, and I only barked at him, "I need to borrow a horse immediately!"

Frank, understandably surprised by my tone, jumped up and began to ready a horse at once. "Is everyone all right?" he asked as he worked.

"Yes, yes," I responded, dismissing him.

As soon as the horse was equipped with the necessary riding gear, I hopped on and forced the animal as fast as I could stand toward Geresh's Glen.

I reached Geresh's Glen in what was surely less than an hour. The sun had not descended far in the sky. I would hopefully find the small lake and cave well before sundown and give myself enough time to return to Mrs. White's shortly after nightfall.

There was no one picnicking in the area at that time. The young people who would normally frequent Geresh's Glen were most assuredly in cool houses. Walking to the edge of the peaceful clearing, I tethered my horse to a tree.

Looking at the sun, I made sure that I was correct in my bearings, and I began to head due south.

As I walked through the forest, the trees grew thicker and the sun was often out of sight beyond the canopy of leaves. There were also many evergreen trees, and so I found myself walking on a mixture of soft dirt and old pine needles.

At first, I found the walk exhilarating—doing something for myself without having asked permission first. As the heat seemed to still find me in the shade of the trees, though, I eventually grew somewhat restless. I grew even more so as the land became soggy and mosquitoes buzzed in my ears and around my eyes. I could not fathom how Mr. Graham had found hunting in these parts to be enjoyable.

I walked and walked, and my irritation grew and grew.

What I figured by the slanted light and the fatigue in my legs, I must have been walking two and a half hours and there was still no sign of this fabled place. I began to wonder if Mr. Graham had merely told the story as a precautionary tale and there was no real monster after all. Either that, or Mr. Graham was a horrible estimator of time, or his long legs gave him an extreme traveling advantage.

By this point, I knew that I would definitely have to find my way back in the dark for part of the journey. Also, while I had tried to remain directly south, I didn't want to find myself lost without the sun to guide me for too long a stretch of time. Determining I would continue only a few more minutes, I sluggishly lifted my feet out of the water and mud and moved them forward.

Knowing that I was about to give up, the actual danger that I had already put myself in dawned on me. I was alone. No one knew where I was, and there was a very real chance that no one would find me for quite some time if I were to become injured or lost. Also, aside from the unfortunate ruining of my shoes, I never considered that perhaps I would catch an illness from all of this tromping through the beginnings of a swamp. Additionally, there were snakes in areas like this. A real jolt of fear struck me as I began scanning the shallow water for signs of twitching tails.

I was barely looking up when I realized that the sun was markedly brighter in front of me. Feeling as if I were dreaming, I lifted my head and beheld an out-of-place grassy area with a pond and a willow tree. Across from that, sure enough, was an opening to a cave surrounded by an incline in the earth.

Though the area was bright and warm, I shivered. I could tell then that part of me had surely not given consideration to what I was about to do. It had been one thing to merely daydream about improving my life through this demon, but this place was real, and when I was just about to give up on finding it, it was before me. It was almost as if I were fated to find this place, even at the last second.

I circled slowly around the tiny lake. It was hotter out from under the trees. Nearing the edge of the cave, though, I shivered yet again. It was physically cold there. "That is natural," I actually said aloud, trying to calm my suddenly racing heart. "A cave would be colder."

Only then thinking that I should have brought a candle with me, I prepared myself for the darkness of the cave. I took a deep breath of air before walking inside.

Just like Mr. Graham had described, there was a fork in the cave not far into it. I made sure to make a left, not desiring to become monster food, and I felt my way along the passage.

I shook from head to toe the farther I walked. "This is stupid," I whispered, though my voice seemed magnified by the cave walls. "Why did I come here?" I asked myself, and without warning, I started to cry.

"Why are you crying?" a voice behind me asked, and I nearly fainted from the fright of it. From what Mr. Graham had told me, I expected the demon to be able to speak quite well. Still, I had not been prepared for the low and gravelly tone of his voice. The tempo of his speech was too deliberate to be natural, and in combination with its dark quality, it sent instant shivers through my body.

I turned around out of fear rather than bravery. At this depth, the cave was pitch-black, and so I could not see the monster, though I could feel his presence before me. His mass pushed in on the cave around me, and I felt short of breath. At the same time, I felt his cold breathing hit me, reeking of rot.

"I will ask one more time," the voice said. "Why are you crying?"

"I am frightened," I said, my own voice sounding like the squeak of a mouse.

"Why are you frightened?" the voice asked, almost sounding proud.

31

"The cave is dark and cold," I said stupidly.

"Ah," the monster said and then paused before asking, "Surely you are not afraid of me? After all, you came here looking for me specifically. Did my friend Jasper Graham send you?"

"Yes," I said, unnerved by the thing's calm and controlled manner.

"And you desperately want to make a deal with me, do you not?"

"Yes."

"Very well," it said. "You seem to be a nice girl, Louisa," and it laughed a cruel laugh.

I shook all over, and my voice shook too while I asked, "How did you know my name?"

"There are things I simply know," the demon responded before moving his agenda forward. "I know what it is you desire."

"Money," I said, my overwhelming wish pushing from my mouth in the face of fear.

"No."

"No?"

"No. You know as well as I do that if you were to suddenly come into an extreme amount of money that its origin would be questioned. Also, you are unmarried. Do you anticipate buying a house on your own with your background as a mere maid? You might be able to afford the fine dresses, but would anyone invite you anywhere where you could wear them? Also, if you meet a man, you wouldn't know if he merely wants you for your money, and then you would be cast aside as soon as you were married and it was all under your husband's control. No, for now, you need something more secure than money."

"Well, I certainly do not want a talking parrot," I blurted, surprised by my frankness at such a time.

Much to my discomfort, the creature actually laughed as if I had made a most comical joke indeed.

"No. A young woman such as yourself does not need a parrot. What you need is a talent."

I remained silent, trying to soak in this suggestion, somehow managing to forget, or at least ignore, the fact that the thing conversing with me on such personal terms was not of heaven.

"If you had a talent, you could make your own money. You could wear the fancy dresses and always be ensured invitations to parties. A man would be attracted to you, not just your money." He then paused, and I could tell that it was for dramatic effect. "Mrs. White had desired that a singer be at her upcoming party. Would you like to be that singer?"

I considered his offer. I almost never sang, even to myself, for my natural voice was mediocre at best. To be able to sing with the voice of an angel, though? The thought unexpectedly hit me to the core, and I found myself suddenly longing for it as if nothing else in the world mattered except that I could bring people far beyond the realm of reality through the talent of a voice. I would wear a fancy dress, an eye-catching one as the star performer. Mrs. White would love me and sponsor me in my endeavors. I would perform in Philadelphia, and perhaps all over the world.

"Would you like to hear my offer?" he asked just as my thoughts were coming to a close.

"Yes," I answered breathlessly.

"Since you are so nice and in such a depressingly desperate situation, I shall make you an easy offer. Mrs. White is quite strict about her three o'clock tea, correct?"

"Yes."

"Then my offer is simple. Tomorrow, if Mrs. White has her tea at any time between two o'clock and four o'clock in the afternoon, then you shall gain the ability to sing more beautifully than anyone else in the world."

"That's it? That is so simple!" I responded, overjoyed. I could not recall even one occasion when Mrs. White had strayed from her tea outside of this allotted time.

"Let me explain the rest of the rules before you accept," the monster continued calmly. I could almost hear the smile in his voice, and I momentarily felt sick, though I could not consciously figure out why. "If Mrs. White does *not* have her tea within those two hours, she will die."

The thought of seeing Mrs. White's cold, lifeless body caused me to instinctually wrap my arms around my own body for warmth and protection. However, the chances of being responsible for this were so remote that I forced myself to drop my arms back to my sides as I quit considering the actual implications of such a statement. "Out of curiosity," I began instead, "why do you always pick the lives of others to be at stake?"

"Because I simply find it to be more interesting. After all, would you bet as much if your own life depended on it?"

The words "probably not" floated through my head, but I immediately pushed them aside. For such a simple bet with the chance of so incredible a reward, of course I would risk my own life. After all, it would certainly increase my quality of life beyond measure.

The demon continued, "Anyway, if Mrs. White were to lose her life, she would have exactly one minute from when the bet is lost to when she would die. It is only during this one minute that you could tell her of your bet, if you chose. You may not speak of this bet to anyone, even in the most subtle of ways, before the bet is fully complete. After it is complete, however, you are released from these stipulations and may tell anyone you wish, though I suggest not highly advertising it as people might come to think of you as not of a sound mind." Even this last, freeing part of his explanation came across more as a threat than a helpful suggestion.

"Of course," I answered seriously.

"Also, you may not do anything either way to change the outcome of the bet. If you are instructed to bring Mrs. White her tea at three o'clock and you would normally do so, then you may. If you are instructed to never bring Mrs. White tea ever again and you would normally listen, then you must obey," the monster said sternly.

"Yes," I responded.

"Now, if you break any of these conditions, there will be serious consequences. If you even hint of our deal before it is complete or attempt to change the outcome, *you* will be the one to die. And like the others, you will only have one minute between the breaking of our deal and your death."

I almost declined right then and there, but I told myself I was being silly. All I would have to do to avoid death is not tell anyone until after Mrs. White's tea tomorrow. It was not an overwhelming task, certainly.

"Do you accept?" the monster suddenly growled.

"Yes," I stated quickly, jumping into an instant answer following the demon's sudden demand for one.

"Good then," and I could feel the monster turn quickly.

"Wait!" I shouted.

"What?"

"Why do you do this at all?" I questioned.

The calmness never left the monster's voice. "I enjoy seeing how people react," he said, and I felt the rush of air as he raced back to his side of the cave.

Left alone in the dark, I shivered. I thought of the horrible reaction of Mr. Snyder and wondered if that was where the demon derived his true enjoyment.

Chapter Five

By the time I finally arrived at Mrs. White's house well after the sun had set, the whole house was anxiously waiting for news of me.

"Where were you?" Mrs. White exclaimed after I burst in through the back kitchen door.

I had had a long time to think of a lie. It was a bit outlandish, but I hoped that it would work. "I—I thought that I saw Mrs. Snyder. I followed her for a time, all the way through the woods, but in the end I lost sight of her."

Mrs. White actually turned white. "A ghost?" she said, drawing her hand to her mouth in fright.

"It looked like a real person. Perhaps it was only a case of mistaken identity on my part," I protested, but I knew that my lie had worked. My sudden disappearance in pursuit of Mrs. Snyder's ghost would not only explain my mysterious absence, but it would thrill Mrs. White with a new tale to tell.

Due to my troubles, Mrs. White gave me permission to sleep in the next day.

When I awoke, my bedroom was full of light, giving my small space a luxurious, happy appearance. It was also very hot, though, and despite my original good mood, I quickly grew annoyed as I felt my nightgown sticking to my body. Almost never having the chance to sleep in, I had forgotten that my room became unbearably scorching after the sun had fully risen in the summertime.

After spending a few minutes readying myself and fixing my hair, I walked downstairs, trying to ignore the fact that that day would be the day my life would change forever.

Mrs. White was in the parlor reading when I arrived on the bottom floor.

"Louisa," she greeted me pleasantly. "How are you feeling, child?" she asked and she actually motioned for me to take the seat next to her.

"Much better. Thank you for allowing me some extra rest."

"Of course. After all, you had quite a scare yesterday."

"Thank you for your compassion," I added, and I once more stood so that I could begin my daily duties.

I glanced at the clock. It was already eleven thirty. I began to walk out of the room when Mrs. White spoke once more. "Louisa."

I stopped and looked at her. Her pale blue eyes seemed to penetrate my brown ones with a tender look that made me feel strangely weak.

"I just wanted to let you know that I'm glad you're safe. I do care about you, and I appreciate the job you have done for me so dutifully and faithfully. If there is anything I can ever do for you, please let me know," she said, and she smiled at me. The wrinkles around her eyes grew more noticeable as she did so, and I felt compelled to drop my gaze to the floor.

"Thank you," I said in a tone that could have been taken for humility. In actuality, it was a tone of guilt. How could I look at the woman or speak to her with any sort of sincerity after I had agreed to risk her life just the day before?

I practically ran out of the parlor as my heart began to race. Inside the Emerald Room, I found Caroline and Laura.

"How are you doing today?" Caroline asked, walking forward and giving me a hug.

"Are you feeling all right? Your face is quite flushed," Laura said, putting her hand to my forehead.

"I'm fine. It was just a bit hot in my bedroom is all," I answered, trying to act normal.

"Do you really believe that you saw Mrs. Snyder's ghost?" Caroline asked, her eyes wide with wonder.

"I'm honestly not sure," I answered. After a night's rest, I somewhat regretted this particular lie; I did not wish to dishonor Mrs. Snyder's memory, after all.

"I don't believe in ghosts," Laura stated firmly. "Probably just a look-alike."

"Probably," I agreed. "So, what are we doing right now?" I asked, hoping to change the subject.

"Dusting for the party. Frank and Amos are setting up the chairs outside right now. We've already finished with the curtains." I visually examined the curtains, which looked a brighter green than usual.

I was helping the girls dust the artwork and golden trim around the edges of the room when we heard the prance of horses' hooves out front. I walked to the front window and saw a carriage stopped in the driveway. Setting my dust rag down, I hurried to the front door in anticipation of the knock.

When it happened, I answered slowly, and before me stood Mrs. Campbell. "Good day, Mrs. Campbell," I said, stepping back so that she could enter while her coachman brought her carriage and horse around the side of Mrs. White's house toward the stable.

"Good day," she said. "Is Mrs. White available?"

"Yes. Please wait here while I let her know of your arrival."

"Thank you."

Though Mrs. White was surely already aware that Mrs. Campbell had arrived, the parlor situated near the front door as it was, I tried to be as formal as possible. Mrs. Campbell was easily one of the richest women in the area, as she was both from old money and married into old money. She had visited the house before, but only a couple of times during my three years under Mrs. White's employment.

Stepping into the parlor, I moved around the corner and out of sight. The chair Mrs. White was sitting in was facing away from the front door, and I saw Mrs. White's eyes staring at me excitedly as I stepped into their line of sight. Seeing them, I immediately grew guilty again, and found myself examining my shoes. "Mrs. Campbell is here for you, Mrs. White."

"Thank you," she responded as calmly and regally as possible. Standing up, she walked to the foyer with me.

"Mrs. Campbell," Mrs. White greeted her warmly.

"Mrs. White, so good to see you," Mrs. Campbell responded as the two walked arm in arm back to the parlor.

I followed several steps behind as the two sat together on the loveseat. "What brings you here?" Mrs. White asked.

"I am very much looking forward to your party in a few days, and I have come now simply for a little visit. After all, I am sure you will be quite busy during the actual night of the event. Also, I heard that you have invited Miss Adelade Sharp."

"Yes, but she will unfortunately no longer be in this area the night of my party," Mrs. White answered.

"Mrs. White. Mrs. Campbell," I cut in as politely as possible before they could continue with their conversation. "Can I bring you anything in particular?" I asked.

"Yes," Mrs. White answered. Then, turning to Mrs. Campbell, she said, "I normally don't have my tea for another few hours, but if you are interested, I would gladly make an exception."

"Tea sounds lovely actually," Mrs. Campbell responded pleasantly.

"Please bring us some tea, Louisa," Mrs. White said, and she then focused all of her attention on her guest once more.

My feet remained momentarily frozen to the spot. My breath caught in my throat and I actually felt all of the blood drain from my face.

Sensing that I was still there, Mrs. White turned and looked once more at me. "Are you all right?"

"Yes. I'm fine," I said quietly, and I turned and walked out of the room. Perhaps tea would not be ready before three o'clock anyway, I told myself as I walked down the hall toward the kitchen. Or perhaps Amos would not yet be ready to make it. Entering the kitchen, I remembered that he was outside setting up the chairs. I walked out the back door and around the side of the house, praying that he would not be there for some reason. He was, though.

"Amos," I said, and he wiped his brow on his shirt sleeve and looked at me. "Mrs. Campbell is here for a visit, and Mrs. White requests that they have tea at this time."

"Well, that's early," Amos said as he put down the chair he was holding. "In all of my years working for Mrs. White I can count on one hand the times that she has changed her three o'clock tea time."

I was shaking visibly while Amos walked past me and into the kitchen.

As Amos readied the tea kettle, I tried to act as natural as possible while I arranged the tray with cups and saucers.

Mrs. White was going to die, and it was all my fault. I had been selfish in my attempt to obtain a better life, less dependent on others. And because of that, my kind employer was going to perish simply because she drank a cup of tea at the wrong time! I thought I was going to vomit, upset as I was. As I continued preparing the tea tray, I thought I could not bear to bring it to her, knowing that this action on my part would secure her death. I then thought of what the demon had said. If I spoke of the bet or acted on it unnaturally before it could be fulfilled then I would be the one to die instead. So, if I stopped everything and told Mrs. White what I had done, I would save her life.

Could I do that, though? It would mean saving Mrs. White's life, but mine would be lost in the process. And only because I wanted to have a singular talent—not any evil desire. Mrs. White was old and I was young. I had my whole life ahead of me, I tried to reason.

I could hear the water beginning to boil, or perhaps that was only the sound of my own beating heart.

Just as I was finishing arranging the teacups, Laura walked into the kitchen. "Never mind about the tea. A messenger just came with an urgent message for Mrs. Campbell. Her son has grown ill, and so she has left at once to see him. Mrs. White told me that she will have her tea at her normal time now that Mrs. Campbell is not here."

I was so relieved that I fainted.

I opened my eyes slowly and found that I was lying on the bed in the main guest room on the second floor. The curtains were drawn tight, so the room was quite dark. In the shadows, though, I thought that I could make out Mrs. White's form.

"Mrs. White?" I asked hoarsely.

"Yes, Louisa. It's me. Are you all right?" she asked.

"Yes. It was—it was the heat," I lied.

"Poor girl," she said. "You just rest here for a while. I will send Caroline to come and check on you in a bit.

"Thank you," I said, and there was a burst of light as Mrs. White opened the bedroom door leading to the upstairs hallway.

I actually fell asleep for a little, worn out as I was. When I awoke, I stayed in bed for a time before Caroline entered. By the time she came in, I was feeling much better, though my nerves were still on edge.

"How are you feeling?" Caroline asked me. "I came in before now, but you were still sleeping."

"I'm feeling better," I answered. "What time is it?" I asked, not able to see the clock from my position in the bed.

"It's a little after three," Caroline answered. Much to her surprise, I sat up straight with incredible speed.

"Did Mrs. White have her tea?" I practically shouted.

"Yes, of course," Caroline answered. Then, in the dim light, I saw the white of her teeth as she smiled. "You're not the only one who knows how to fix a tea tray and take it to her. The whole house didn't fall apart just because you weren't feeling well."

"Thank you," I simply responded, choosing not to share the true reasons for my concern.

We talked for a little bit, and while we did, I continued to feel even better each second. Mrs. White had had her tea at the proper time. The danger was passed and I could relax. And not only could I relax, but I would reap outstanding benefits!

After perhaps a half an hour of politely conversing, I informed Caroline, "I feel that I can return to the day now."

"Very well," she said kindly.

She held my arm as I climbed out of bed, but I felt quite steady by that point. Walking downstairs with a considerable bounce to my step, I entered the parlor while Caroline turned to the left to continue with party preparations.

"Mrs. White," I said happily, looking directly into her bright eyes. The tea had been consumed and the cookies eaten.

"Louisa! Do I need to call a doctor? I wanted to give you a chance to rest first," she tried to explain.

"It is fine. I am feeling much better. I believe it was just the heat."

"Of course. Please, take it easy today."

"Thank you," I said, and I practically skipped out of the room, my worn shoes clacking lightly on the wooden floor of the foyer.

The rest of that day, I felt as free as a bird. I dusted with an unusual amount of vigor and though my mind was joyfully preoccupied, I conversed lightheartedly with Caroline and Laura. I was anxious for the end of the day, though, when I could actually discover in the safety of my own bedroom if the monster had kept his end of the deal.

Following an especially hearty meal prepared by Amos according to Mrs. White's instructions, I walked up the creaking stairway at the back of the house, which led to my room on one side and the spacious attic on the other.

Lighting a candle, I undressed and slipped on my nightgown. Then, I moved to my mirror and stood in front of it. I had almost expected to look different, but my hair was still just as frizzy and lifeless as it always was and my skin was still imperfect. And so ignoring my physical appearance, I took a deep breath and let out a few musical notes.

They were perfect, rich and complete. I tried singing a few more notes, higher and higher, and found that I had an amazing range, previously unknown to me. Thinking back to the lullabies my mother used to sing to me, I chose my favorite, a haunting and strangely sad song. As I sang, I grew louder and louder as my confidence soared with my voice. As I made my way through the simple lullaby, it's almost as if my voice knew exactly where to expand on the given notes of the song, and I knew how complex to make it without taking away from the true melody.

I found that I was actually having fun, and the rest of my room seemed to disappear as I watched myself singing in my mirror. It was strange, but I felt more beautiful as I sang too, for my cheeks took on a wonderfully natural rosy color and my posture became regal yet carefree.

As I was finishing the lullaby for the third time, I heard a knock on my door and immediately stopped singing as I was pulled back to my surroundings.

Expecting to see Caroline, I was surprised when I instead found Mrs. White on the other side of my door. She had only ever been up to my room the time she originally showed it to me when I moved in.

"Mrs. White," I said sheepishly. "Can I bring you anything?" I asked, and I wondered how much of my singing she might have heard if she had been in her bedroom, located primarily below mine.

"Louisa!" she cried. She was dressed in her nightgown, and I hoped that I had not woken her. "You have a voice beyond that of any other woman in the world!" she exclaimed, and to my shock, she actually stumbled forward and hugged me excitedly. "I never knew you had such a talent! Such perfection inside of you," she said, and she actually touched my throat gently in awe.

Despite a bit of embarrassment at being this highly praised by my employer, I could not help but smile.

"Louisa, please, I beg of you, sing again," Mrs. White said, and she unceremoniously plopped herself down on my bed.

Standing up straight and tall, I began the lullaby once more. By the time I had finished, Mrs. White was covering her mouth reverently with one hand, her eyes not shifting their focus from me. "That was the most beautiful sound I have ever heard," she said. Standing up, she took my hands in hers. "I promise you, I shall hire you a teacher, and you shall perform anywhere your heart desires. Before long, I just know that you shall give concerts in grand theaters, your talent is so incredible. And, oh! Would you like your first performance to be at my party in a couple of days?"

I remembered the demon had mentioned Mrs. White's upcoming party when discussing the reward of a singing voice, so I was prepared for this offer. "Of course, but I don't know many songs."

"Do you know more lullabies like that one?" she asked.

"A few more," I answered.

"Perfect! Tomorrow, do nothing but practice them. I will look into finding you a teacher to help you perfect your skills and teach you songs. For now, be ready for your first fabulous performance!"

And with that Mrs. White gave me a kiss on the cheek, threw open my door with strength I did not know she had, and hurried downstairs.

I sat on my bed, still staring at myself in my mirror. I was talented and desirable, and my voice would carry me to new heights.

I cried myself to sleep that night, so extremely happy that I could not contain myself.

Chapter Six

I woke up early as usual and went downstairs to eat my breakfast in the kitchen.

Caroline was already sitting at the table. "The water's still hot," she informed me.

"Great," I simply said, turning my back to her to hide the smile that was plastered across my face. I had planned on keeping calm and normal before telling my friend the good news.

Her fork made a light tink behind me as she set it against the side of her plate. "You don't have to try to hide your happiness. I was still awake when Mrs. White went up to your room last night. She told me about the whole thing."

Though I was looking at the tea kettle while she spoke, I could hear the smile in her own voice, and I spun around happily. "Isn't it wonderful?" I asked.

"Yes! I never knew you could sing."

"I didn't either," I said.

"Well, I'm so happy for you. This might very well change everything for you now," Caroline said as she stood up and started clearing her place at the table. "I'm going to ready Mrs. White's breakfast now. Have fun practicing today."

"Thank you," I said, and we remained silent as she readied Mrs. White's breakfast and left with it.

After I finished my own breakfast, I headed to my bedroom. It felt strange as I passed by a table in the hallway that I would have normally been dusting that day.

As I climbed the stairs, feeling extraordinarily liberated, Mrs. White met me. "Good morning, Louisa."

"Good morning, Mrs. White," I said with a slight curtsy.

"Heading off to practice I presume?"

"Yes."

"Where are you going to practice?"

"In my room," I answered.

"Nonsense! You'll pass out from the heat again. No. If it's relative privacy you desire, at least use the main spare bedroom."

44

"Thank you," I accepted, and I made a right down the hall instead of heading up the next flight of stairs.

I rarely found myself in this beautiful spare bedroom, as it was primarily Caroline's duty to clean. It was dark at that moment, the curtains having been closed for me the day before. Stepping confidently inside, I tied back the curtains and opened the window to allow a bit of air to circulate. I then walked back to the bedroom door and shut it before turning around and scanning the luxurious room.

The wood of the furniture had a rich, dark stain to it, yet the light blue carpets made the place look relaxing and airy. Almost all of the furniture had feet like a lion on the bottom of them. I particularly liked the look of the mirror in the corner, though, with carved flowers climbing up the outside edges of the frame.

I stepped toward it and looked at myself. I once again appeared normal, but I quickly forgot my looks as I spotted a trunk's reflection, placed at the foot of the bed. Remembering the lovely dresses inside, particularly the blue one I had held up half a year before, I walked over to it and knelt before the box. The trunk creaked a little as I opened it, and I was half-afraid that Mrs. White would walk in and ask me what I was doing.

On top where I expected it, lay the midnight blue silk dress that had once been worn by Mrs. White to lavish parties.

I simply ran my fingers over the top of the dress, wondering how such material would feel all over one's skin.

Outside, a hawk squawked, bringing me out of my peaceful daydreaming. It was time to be busy and practice. I sat quietly for a few minutes, weighing the pros and cons of the different lullabies that I knew. I felt a little deflated the longer I thought; how would such simple songs impress those guests with such fine tastes? Still, for the time being, I had no better material with which to work, and so I chose my five favorites and began to sing.

I still could not believe that it was my own voice singing the lovely melodies that I could have only dreamt about before. And as I sang, my confidence even in my choice of songs grew. I also found that my voice did not tire as I practiced, and indeed I was enjoying myself so thoroughly that I did not particularly notice the passage of time.

Risking A Life

Three light knocks on the bedroom door interrupted the chorus of a lullaby about mischievous kittens. "Yes?" I called, and it seemed that even this spoken word had a musical quality to it.

The door opened and in came Caroline, supporting a tray with food. "You sound absolutely amazing," she complimented me. "I do hope you're not embarrassed, but we can hear you through most parts of the house. It has been quite soothing to work to."

"I'm glad you've been enjoying it," I said as politely and refinedly as possible.

"Anyway, I brought you some lunch," Caroline continued. "Also, Mrs. White requests that you join her for her three o'clock tea."

"Oh, wonderful! Please tell her that I will definitely meet her in the parlor at that time."

"Certainly," Caroline said, and she walked out of the room.

I sat in the light green silk cushioned seat in the corner of the room and ate my lunch while the birds took a turn singing to me through the open window. The lunch was excellent, and I noticed that Amos or Caroline had even placed a flower on the corner of the tray, like they would do for Mrs. White.

Feeling full, I sat for a while, still listening to the birds. Finally glancing at the clock, I saw that I only had an hour until tea time. I determined to practice for a bit more, especially since Mrs. White would apparently be able to hear if I had been singing or not.

The hour flew by and I was almost disappointed to leave the guest room, absorbed in my new talent as I was. I was greatly intrigued by my tea invite, though, so I left to arrive in the parlor promptly at three.

"You sound absolutely lovely, my dear," were the first words Mrs. White said to me as I walked into the room. "I have simply been sitting here, listening all morning," she continued.

"Surely, you compliment me too much," I said, trying to echo the sorts of words I had often heard her guests use over the years.

"No, my words are true. Please, take a seat." Her old hand moved forward to indicate the other high-backed chair with flowered fabric. With only the small tea table between us and in identical seats, I felt very much like an equal to Mrs. White, which shamed me only a little to think.

46

Before Mrs. White could move the conversation forward, we heard the light tapping of Caroline's feet on the foyer floor, and a second later she came forward with the tea tray.

"Thank you, Caroline," Mrs. White said, and Caroline exited immediately after placing the tray on the table.

"So, Louisa, I have written to several people who reside in Philadelphia, asking for references for a music teacher. A teacher should be able to expand your repertoire for future performances, though I daresay your voice is so perfect I do not believe you have anything left to learn about singing."

"Thank you," I said, taking up one of the delicate cups with three of my fingers. I realized as I brought the thin china to my mouth that I had never once taken a sip from these cups; I had only filled them day after day.

"Do you feel prepared for tomorrow? I know it's last minute for you."

"Yes. I feel fine in anticipation of tomorrow."

"Very good," Mrs. White responded, picking up a cookie with all of her fingers. "I thought that you might want to give your voice a rest for the remainder of the day. I would love your company for a while here, and then perhaps you would like to take a walk. It is not nearly as hot today as it has been recently."

"Thank you. That sounds lovely."

We spent a couple of hours talking, Mrs. White asking most of the questions. She wanted to know if my mother or father could sing, if I had ever thought about being a singer when I was younger, if I had any experience giving performances. While my answers to most of her questions about my talent were unilluminating, they often led to tales of my humble childhood, which Mrs. White thankfully found fascinating as opposed to distasteful.

Mrs. White, finally having the good manners to excuse herself so that I might have a break from her questioning, went upstairs to rest in her room for a bit. This gave me the opportunity to go for the suggested walk around the grounds. I was pleased when I did not pass any of the other servants, as I felt increasingly awkward about my newly acquired favoritism while they continued with life as usual. Stepping outside through the back kitchen entrance, I did not even see Amos or Frank. I

47

then remembered that everyone would probably be setting up for the summer moonlight party.

Keeping well away from the side of the house where they might spot me, I walked into the woods behind the stable. Though I did not often have the chance to roam aimlessly around Mrs. White's grounds, I knew that there was a stream and pond located only a few minutes into the woods in this direction.

The cool breeze whipped some strands of my hair out of their proper position and around my face. No one could see me, though, and so I did not fix them as I soaked in the smells of summer and the tingly feel of the shaded heat on my skin.

Soon enough, I reached the stream, which bubbled excitedly over the rocks and branches in its way. Lightly skipping along next to it, I followed its flow out to the open pond. The pond was quite large and could more accurately be described as a lake. Nevertheless, it was always referred to as the pond by the people in the area. Though I had been there only a few times, each time I was alone. This time, however, I saw a young man and three women on the opposite bank. I could not make out their features, though they were sitting on a blanket, laughing and talking loudly, but still with an air of refinement. Once I saw them, I kept somewhat behind a tree, not wishing to interrupt them by making my presence known. The ladies were holding light parasols which coordinated in color with their dresses. They laughed and lazed about with such indulgence that I suddenly felt jealous inside. They were all perhaps my age, and these people appeared as if they had never known even one day of work in their lives.

I had felt like a queen that day, being brought my lunch and invited to tea with the lady of the house. Listening to the laughter across the pond, though, I longed to join this younger generation of aristocrats. They had it all, and I wanted it all too.

Chapter Seven

The morning of the party, I woke up at my normal, early hour. Still feeling sleepy, though, I allowed myself to fall once more into my dreams.

Finally rousing myself late in the morning, I dressed in my usual maid's clothing and descended both staircases. Passing through the foyer, I noticed Laura rushing about the Emerald Room out of the corner of my eye. When I entered the parlor, I saw that Mrs. Carter was sitting there with Mrs. White.

"There is the woman of the day," Mrs. Carter spoke to me as I entered. Though she was over frequently as she was Mrs. White's best friend, I could recall only a handful of words that she had ever spoken to me in the past.

I politely bowed my head in her direction in thanks.

"Did you sleep well?" Mrs. White asked me, saying nothing of the late hour to which I slept.

"Very, thank you."

"Good. Now Mrs. Carter and I were just discussing what you should wear for the party tonight. Obviously, as an honored performer, you cannot be wearing your maid's uniform," Mrs. White continued.

I nearly jumped with joy, but while my hands began to fidget, I at least managed to force my feet still.

"Unfortunately, I do not have time to purchase you a dress tailor-made for your figure. However, Mrs. Carter was reminding me of some of the party dresses I used to wear in my younger days. Believe it or not, I was once as thin as you."

I did not say anything as I did not know the proper protocol for responding to self-deprecating remarks about one's weight.

Mrs. White continued, "Upstairs in the guest bedroom there are several trunks containing dresses. Have Laura help you try them on and choose a dress that is to your liking. If something simple on it needs to be fixed or hemmed, have Laura busy herself to that task at once."

"Thank you," I said, and I raced into the Emerald Room to grab Laura.

"Laura," I said, and she poked her head out from behind a statue that she was dusting for the millionth time.

"Yes?"

"Mrs. White requests that you help me choose a dress to wear for tonight's party out of the trunks in the guest room. She also requests that you make minor repairs to it if needed since you are skilled in this way."

Laura simply nodded, and, laying down her dust rag, she rigidly led the way upstairs.

Ignoring Laura's stiff attitude, I pranced around from trunk to trunk, holding up the many dresses and examining them. Though they were all fine, I could not rid my mind of thoughts of the midnight blue dress. Still, I was not about to choose so quickly, and so I had Laura help me try on practically every other dress.

Leaving the best for last, I could not help smiling as I slipped on the blue dress. It was not entirely up to the day's current fashion standards, but it was so elegant and wonderful, I truly didn't care. Also, it was only too big for me in the waist just slightly, and the matching sash to be tied around me would surely help with that, as well as some minor tailoring to be done by Laura. After I told her that this was to be the dress, I stood in front of the mirror while Laura examined exactly what needed to be fixed and what could realistically be fixed in so short a time.

After she saw what needed to be done, I went upstairs to my own room to wipe myself off and do my hair. No sooner had I finished combing my long hair than Caroline entered my bedroom. Like the day before, she had a tray in her hand. On it was some lunch. "Did you want to eat together?" she offered.

"That sounds wonderful," I said, and Caroline set the tray down. As she did so, I noticed that there were hair pins and powder on the edge of the tray. "What are those?" I asked, giddy over the anticipated answer.

"Mrs. White had me bring them for you. I'll help you with your hair and makeup after lunch," she said.

Though I chatted quite animatedly about how wonderful the party would surely be, I noticed that Caroline remained quieter than usual. Eventually, I slowed down too until the two of us were finishing our lunches in silence.

After lunch, she parted my hair down the middle and pinned it back in a low bun. She then began powdering my face, angling me toward the limited sunlight trickling through the singular window in my stuffy bedroom.

"You're finished. Have fun tonight," Caroline said as she gathered up the remaining items and left.

Following awkwardly in her footsteps, I turned away from her and toward the guest bedroom at the bottom of the stairs. Inside, Laura was still sewing away. As I had gained confidence in my singing voice from the day before, I simply began to practice my songs as if Laura were not there.

After perhaps a half an hour, Laura actually interrupted one of my songs to tell me that the alterations were complete.

I walked over to her and slid out of my maid's dress once more as Laura helped me pull the blue one on over my head. Once situated properly on my body, it fit like a glove. Despite Laura's somewhat sullen attitude, she had at least done a dutiful job at her assigned task.

I stepped in front of the full-length mirror. There, Laura tied the matching ribbon around my waist, giving my petite figure the appearance of having more womanly hips. The skirt portion of the dress was not very wide, though it still had a basic triangular look. I moved my gaze to the short sleeves, which weren't extraordinarily poofy, but were tied in a way that made them appear slightly bunched. As I had guessed it would when Caroline had originally shown me the dress, the midnight blue went perfectly with my skin, taking away some of the harsh redness in my cheeks. The lace around the top of the low and wide-spaced sleeves also helped to temper my complexion. This lace went up to my neck, almost like a second, see-through layer to the dress.

I moved my gaze up to my brown hair, a few loose strands breaking free from the low, loose bun. Unlike the mellowing effect on my skin, the blue of the dress seemed to make my hair stand out as a healthy walnut brown. At the same time, my brown eyes seemed to pop with life.

Laura then handed me matching slippers that I must have missed during my own rummaging through the trunk. I put them on my feet, finding that they were only a tad too small, and so they would do for just the one night.

Finally ready, I saw that the afternoon sun was beginning its slow descent. It would soon be time for the party and for my debut performance. I walked down the stairs where Mrs. White was already waiting in the parlor, wearing a new dress with the largest skirt I had yet seen on her.

"Wonderful choice, Louisa. Granted it is a bit dated since that has to be…oh…around twenty years old! It looks lovely on you, though, and Laura did a good job altering it in all the right places."

"Thank you," I said while I mentally compared the sizes of our skirts.

Mrs. White and I ate a little snack, and before I knew it, guests started to arrive.

I stood with Mrs. White at the front door at her request, the warm air rushing inside and filling the foyer with the smells of summer. More intoxicating than the night air, though, were the flowery perfumes of the ladies. These ladies came in wearing silk dresses that hung off their shoulders. They also had the tiniest waists I had ever seen, and I doubted that I portrayed this same regal appearance. The men also looked rather splendid, most of them dressed in stiff black and white.

Fortunately, the men and women all greeted me politely after Mrs. White explained who I was. Even those who immediately recognized me as one of her maids spent the time to take my hand and make a formal introduction. I was being treated as an actual lady, and the resulting feeling was one that I swore I would never grow tired of.

After spending a while by the front door, Mrs. White suggested that we move on to the actual party. We stepped into the Emerald Room where some of her guests had stayed. We walked straight for the side door, though. It was closed despite the warm air, presumably to keep out bugs. Rushing forward, I opened the door for Mrs. White before following her out into the side yard.

Immediately, my eyes met the light of dancing fires in dozens of lanterns hung about the garden. The yard smelled of freshly cut grass, and the night flowers had begun to open to reveal their soothing blue blooms. Chairs had been set up around tables, and they were as clean as if they had been inside. Though there was no dance floor, Mrs. White had hired a stringed ensemble to play just outside of the seating area, closer to the woods but where there was the largest empty, grass area. The earth was also rather even in that location, and so while dancing would not be as ideal as in the Emerald Room, it would still be more than possible.

The music was already going strong when we stepped outside, and many guests were dancing as the last of the evening's pink light faded and the stars became more noticeable. "Miss West," a booming male voice came from directly behind me. Transfixed as I had been on the scene before me, I had not been aware of the man's approach or the fact that Mrs. White had walked away from me to mingle with some of her guests.

Turning around, I saw the large figure of Mr. Graham. "How are you doing, sir?"

"I'm doing fine," he said, though he was eyeing me quizzically. "I heard a rumor that you will be performing tonight."

"What will you sing?" Elbert squawked in his cage, still held by Mr. Graham.

"Just some simple songs from my childhood. Mrs. White tried to obtain Miss Adelade Sharp, but she was unavailable."

"Mrs. White has been bragging that your voice is far superior to that of *any* other person, though. Have you always had the ability to sing, Miss West?"

The question was out there. Did I go to visit the demon in the woods? I had no choice but to answer.

"No, I did not always have the ability to sing, Mr. Graham. I expect discretion on your part."

"Of course," he said seriously. "And I do hope that you will not revere this new talent of yours in a way that will destroy you. However, I see that you have at least not yet given into today's frivolous fashion styles when you chose your attire for tonight."

Mr. Graham said the statement innocently enough, and though he obviously meant it as a compliment to my common sense, as I would be able to easily sit unlike the ladies with the largest skirts, I felt my face flush red with embarrassment. "I am only wearing this old thing because I was not able to have anything else made in time. I must go now," I said, and I marched through the crowd away from a puzzled Mr. Graham.

Trying to brush off my growing embarrassment, I engaged in conversations with several people, some of whom I remembered greeting in the foyer and some of whom must have entered after Mrs. White and I had joined the party.

I was speaking to Mr. Knight, definitively the wealthiest man in the area, when Caroline came over with a tray of food.

"Hors d'oeuvres?" she offered, and Mr. Knight and I each reached for something.

"Thanks, Caroline," I said, and catching Mr. Knight's disapproving look, I remembered that I should probably try to hide the fact that I was still technically a maid while conversing with such high-class society.

Caroline, having the good taste to not embarrass me further, simply nodded her head politely and offered food to the next group.

I moved through the crowd, overhearing everything from pointless, yet polite compliments to a heated political debate. When pulled into a conversation, I found that they all went rather similarly: an exchange of compliments, questions about my vocal training, questions about the evening's songs. By the end of conversation number six, my answers felt fully prepared and largely mechanical.

During a conversation with several young women my age, I caught Mrs. White's eyes from a few feet away. She gave a nod of the head, and I decided to excuse myself; it was finally time for my performance. I opened my mouth to say so when one of the women I had been conversing with asked, "How old is that dress? You do wear it so well despite its somewhat matronly look."

I shut my mouth as my face grew hot for the second time that night. "Excuse me, but it is time for my performance," I simply said, though I knew that had I been well-bred, I would have had the perfect response. Then again, if I had been well-bred, I would not have been wearing old clothing belonging to my employer.

Meeting Mrs. White, she instructed me to stand in the center of what was currently the dance area as soon as the musicians finished the current song. She then signaled them, and when their lively waltz ended, they set down their instruments and the young people cleared the area.

I was not given an introduction, as everyone already knew who I was and why I was there.

I felt my skin prickle with red blotches due to nerves and frustration at what that woman had just said to me. As all eyes were on me, though, I knew that it was time to begin. Pulling all of my emotional strength to the forefront, I opened my mouth and began the saddest sounding lullaby.

As my confidence had grown during my practice, so my confidence swelled during the actual performance. I sang a cappella, though my voice sounded so full that it swallowed up the silence of my attentive listeners. I proceeded flawlessly from one song to the next, and though my music was from a simpler life than those of Mrs. White's guests, everyone remained incredibly still, not moving even a finger. The only movement was that of the dancing shadows from the lanterns, swaying ever so slightly on their posts in the light breeze. In the middle of the fourth song, I noticed just a bit of movement as some of the coachmen peeked out from around the back of the house where they had been waiting with their employers' horses and carriages.

As the end of the fifth song approached, I wished that I was not almost finished with my performance. I wanted to keep going, but I was out of songs that I knew in their entirety. Choosing to sing a higher note than what was traditional to end the song, I held it as long as possible before finishing off strong.

The guests remained completely silent while I sank into a deep curtsy, but as I rose again, they erupted into the loudest applause and cheers I had ever heard or could have ever hoped for. Taking up their instruments once more, the musicians began playing a song that sounded far off and weak compared to the congratulatory remarks that reached my ears as a flood of people approached me. Their congratulations were all a blur: "That was the most beautiful thing I have ever heard and surely ever *will* hear." "You have talent beyond compare." "I feel honored to have been present at such an inspired performance."

Mrs. White finally managed to squeeze through the mixture of faces. "Absolutely brilliant!" she yelled at me. "I loved it! And I just heard from several people about potential music teachers so that you can learn even more music!" She was then whisked away as many people also crowded around her in order to congratulate her on finding me and recognizing my talent.

In the midst of my well-wishers, there were a bunch of young men. I was invited to dance several times, which is when the only negative emotions managed to find a way inside me during so happy a time. In reality, I did not know how to dance, but each time I made up an excuse rather than admit this shameful fact. "I'm a bit tired right now by my performance, but I'm flattered by your offer."

"I'll bring you a drink of water!" was one eager young man's specific response, and despite my unwillingness to dance, I found that six men stayed close by me, flattering me with every ridiculous phrase they could think of and attending to my every need. Despite common sense imploring me to feel just a bit foolish by this extreme amount of attention, I could not help but like it.

After some time with this handsome crowd, Mr. Graham politely forced his way through to me. "Miss West," he said courteously.

"Mr. Graham."

"I just desired to say that your talent is truly incredible, and I wish you the best of luck with it. I simply hope that you use it wisely and to the best of your abilities. Also, I fear that I offended you earlier, and I can promise you that offense was not my intention."

I smiled, not wanting to hold a grudge against so kind a man. "Thank you," I accepted, and Mr. Graham smiled and walked away, leaving me with my many admirers.

The conversation eventually moved to the subject of the young men before me. They each tried to impress me with their manly hunting hobbies or the number of places they had visited in Europe. I was actually beginning to feel poor once more when something distracted me. It was yet another young man, but there was something exceptionally regal about his appearance.

He was walking toward me as if meeting me were his ultimate objective. Like a painting that had freed itself from its framed prison, his parted, wavy hair stayed perfectly still and respectable though he moved with a certain amount of confident vigor. He was strongly built, but unlike Mr. Graham, not intimidatingly so. His black coat seemed a shade darker than the coats of all the other male guests, and his dark eyes shone in the lantern light.

More impressive than his mere appearance, though, was the way the other young men around me became reverently subdued upon his arrival. "Miss West," he said, taking my hand and bringing it to his lips. I felt the nerve-induced, red blotches returning to the skin on my chest, and I was newly thankful for the lace covering that part of my body.

"I wished to tell you that I found your performance to be of the highest quality."

"Thank you," I said, my voice sounding far away to my own ears.

"But please, allow me to introduce myself. I am William Knight, son of Mr. and Mrs. Theodore Knight."

I recalled talking to the stiff, older Mr. Knight earlier that evening. I had also seen him a couple of times before then, but I had never laid eyes on his son.

"It is a pleasure to meet you, Mr. Knight," I responded, feeling rather small. "I am Miss Louisa West." There was no point in adding the names of my parents to my introduction, as he would obviously have no idea who they were.

"Would you like to dance?" he then invited me.

"I would love to except that I am so tired from my performance," I stated regrettably.

"I completely understand. I do hope to stay in touch with you," he said.

"That would be splendid," I responded too eagerly, and William Knight took my hand in his once more, kissed it and bowed to me slightly, and then retraced his footsteps into the crowd.

I continued talking to the young men in front of me, but I could not rid my mind of the introduction between me and the impressive William Knight. My heart nearly broke then when I spotted him dancing with a young woman who far surpassed me in beauty. Her pale skin went beautifully with her golden blonde hair and the elegant green of her dress. Her lips were bright red and she was curvy in all of the right places. My body felt utterly normal then, and I am afraid that I frowned visibly during one young man's tale of attending an opera in Italy.

The evening wore on, and though my demeanor took on what I hoped was the expected, natural grace of a woman at a party, my mind kept racing. William Knight. He was the richest of all of these young men, so surely he was merely flattering me with his kind words. But what if he were actually interested in me? Or worse, what if he *had* been interested in me, and he took my refusal to dance as my rejection?

I worried and worried until I realized that I had been unconsciously picking at my fingernails. None of the young men mentioned anything about my distracted presence, though, and when the end of the night came, several asked if they might call on me in the near future. I politely accepted and made my way into the house. Mrs. White was standing at the front door bidding farewell to her guests. When she saw me, she exclaimed, "You must be exhausted following your performance! Go upstairs and go to bed!"

"Thank you," I said, for I felt dizzy following the night's whirlwind events. I took a step toward the stairs when Mrs. White reached out and took me by the arm and whispered in my ear, "The guest room is yours, my dear. No need to sleep in such a hot, cramped space. It cannot be good for your voice."

"Thank you," I said with more vitality, and I walked up the stairs and into my new, luxurious room. I would ask Mrs. White about William Knight in the morning.

Chapter Eight

I must not have shut my curtains entirely before collapsing into my new bed the night before. As such, a narrow beam of light was shining into my room, highlighting tiny dust particles in the air.

I yawned and rolled over onto my side to try to continue sleeping. My mind was awake, though, and so after a few minutes, I chose to climb out of bed.

Dressing in my normal maid's clothing, I walked downstairs and to the parlor where Mrs. White was already sitting with her breakfast.

"Good morning," she said cheerily.

"Good morning," I responded. I stood there for a moment then, unsure of what I should do next. After all, I had spent the last couple of days as a performer. Now that it was over, should I resume my usual maid duties? I was still standing in front of Mrs. White awkwardly, trying to figure out my next move, when she fortunately motioned me toward the seat next to her.

"As soon as Caroline comes in, we'll have to ask her to bring you your breakfast," Mrs. White said.

"Thank you," I said, beginning to relax in knowing that my time of importance was not finished.

"Anyway, last night was absolutely perfect. The party was an incredible success and your voice truly enchanted everyone!"

"Thank you. You are too kind."

"Not at all! You are simply being too modest. So, I'd like to start several things with you. First, today a music teacher will be coming to the house, and if you like him, he shall come every day in order to teach you new music. Second, we'll take a little trip into town together so that we can have some new clothes made for you. If you're not going to be a maid any longer, you have no need to wear the clothing of one."

"I'm not to be a maid any longer?" It slipped from my mouth in shock. I had already pieced together that my daily schedule would not be like it once was, but I thought that in my spare time I would still be expected to clean and tidy.

"Of course not. With a talent like yours, I plan on investing in it fully. Your life will be completely different from how you had probably imagined it from here on out. I only ask that you allow me to sponsor you, and as such I will reap some of the monetary and social benefits of your performances."

"Of course. Thank you," I said, the high level of happiness from the night before fully returning to me.

"Now, before we begin all of the things that must be done today, is there anything else that I should be made aware of? Anything I can do for you?"

I almost did not speak, flattered as I was by having my former employer offer me her assistance. "Actually, there is something. And perhaps it is too soon, but I could not help but notice a particularly striking young man from last night."

Mrs. White's eyes sparkled as they always did when she was learning or sharing a juicy bit of gossip. "Who was it? Arthur Hunt? Elliott Gray? Oo! No! I bet it was Evan Stone!"

"William Knight, actually."

Mrs. White's face fell while her eyes simultaneously glittered even more. "William Knight! Why, Louisa, you poor dear. The Knights are probably the most respected family in the area. Unfortunately, while you should have a decent choice of men due to your talent and your presumed future position, you will never be able to achieve a match with someone like William Knight. You would have had to come from extreme wealth with a classy upbringing that I'm afraid you have not had. Not that I believe you are of poor manners or anything of the sort; you're just not of the same type of material that the Knights are of. If it makes you feel better, even I would not be able to marry William Knight were I your young age."

As she spoke, I felt the feeling rush out of my soul. "Thank you for your honesty."

"Of course, Louisa. Now, if any of the other young men struck your fancy, I would be more than pleased to speak on your behalf."

"Not just yet, thank you."

Breakfast was a blur and even being fitted for new dresses did not thrill me as I had hoped. I had already achieved such greatness, and yet there were still things, and particularly people, that would forever be out of my grasp. I conjured up an image in my mind of a woman fit for William Knight, twirling her lilac parasol, her creamy milk skin glowing as she descended gracefully from her family's brand new carriage. I found myself oddly jealous of this figment of my imagination. However,

I realized that while I may have made up this particular girl, there had to be real people out there just like her. I was simply not one of them.

Back at Mrs. White's house, something did happen to raise my spirits somewhat, though. There was a pile of letters waiting on the small table in the foyer. Mrs. White began flipping through them, pulling almost half of them out and replacing them on the table. "Those are for you, Louisa. Do you need me to read them to you?" she asked.

My heart was pounding in my chest. During my years with Mrs. White, I had only once received a letter, informing me of my parents' deaths.

"No, thank you. I can read," I stated, and Mrs. White politely nodded.

Following her lead, I took my letters to the parlor.

"It is very nice of my guests to send me thank you notes after each party," she said as she took her seat.

I sat in the chair next to hers and began opening the letters:

Dear Miss Louisa West,

I wished to inform you that hearing your performance last night was a rare treat.

Indeed, I wish you the best as you continue to hone your talent and perform on an even

greater scale.

Your grateful listener,

Mrs. Charlotte Newman

I didn't even remember a Charlotte Newman from the party, there had been so many people there.

The next one had a fancy wax seal on the back, and I opened it eagerly:

Dear Miss Louisa West,

I am writing separately to your employer, but wished to write you directly as well. I enjoyed your performance immensely, and I was hoping that you might be interested in performing at a party I plan to host in December. I have written

61

*to Mrs. White about the issue of appropriate compensation. I do
hope that you might be willing to join me as the honored guest at
what should be a wonderfully festive occasion.*

> *Yours,*
> *Mr. Daniel*
Rodgers

My fingers tingled as I placed the letter on the table next to me. I
was already receiving offers for paid performances! I eagerly opened the
next letter:

To Miss Louisa West,
> *I found myself truly enchanted by not only your voice, but
by your company last*
> *night. I pray that you do not find me too eager when I request
your permission to call on*
> *you at your earliest convenience. I do hope to hear from you
soon.*

> *Your humble*
servant,
> *Elliott Gray*

Unfortunately, this letter only served to remind me of the young
man I could not have, and I opened the next letter with slightly less
enthusiasm. My mood deflated further when I found yet another letter
from a young man. I continued opening, feeling good as I found another
performance offer, and finally wonderful as I opened several
complimentary letters in a row. The last was a third note from an
admirer, though, and so I finished with a sense of loss.

As I was silently consoling myself, there was a knock at the front
door. I sprang from my chair instinctually, only then remembering that I
no longer needed to do that sort of thing.

Sitting back down as nonchalantly as possible, I waited for one
of the others to answer it. In just a few moments, I heard the light
pattering of Caroline.

"Good day," she greeted the guest, and I wanted badly to turn and see who it was.

"Good day," a young man's voice greeted Caroline. "Is Miss West available?"

"Yes. Please come in," she said, and I heard the front door shut after heavier footsteps could be heard in the foyer. "May I ask your name?"

"Thomas Parks," he answered.

"Miss West," Caroline said only a few seconds later as she approached my left side. My cheeks burned as I heard her address me in such a formal way, but I was afraid to protest in front of Mrs. White and with the guest standing just outside the parlor. "A Mr. Thomas Parks is here to see you."

"Thank you," I said, and I stood up, straightening out the wrinkles in my maid's dress as well as I could.

Walking around my chair and toward the foyer, I was most surprised to receive a look at my caller. The young man before me was certainly not one of the wealthy young men from the night before whom I had expected. He was tall and thin with brown hair as brittle as mine. He even had a few faded pockmarks on his face underneath his bright blue eyes, which were fortunately strikingly beautiful as arguably nothing else about him was. He had large hands, which had the look of someone who was used to hard work. In one of them was a letter, the only crisp thing about him. He wore a plain pair of pants and a gray-blue shirt—simple work clothes.

When I had first begun walking toward him, I immediately noticed that he seemed nervous and fidgety, with his fingers twitching as if he were playing the piano. As I came closer, though, he smiled as he looked me over. It was then that I remembered that my own ensemble was that of a maid, and so I appeared on a similar level to the young man before me. I determined to try to act in accordance with my new status, however.

"Good day," I greeted the young man. "I am Miss Louisa West."

I offered my hand, which the young man took. This action finally quieted the restless motion of his fingers.

Releasing my hand, he said, "It is a pleasure to meet you, Miss West. I am Thomas Parks. I come to you for two reasons. First, I have a letter for you from my employer, Mr. William Knight."

It was my turn to become the nervous one. My hands trembled as William Knight's servant handed me the letter. "Thank you," I said as my eyes locked upon the fine handwriting on the envelope, with my name on it.

"Secondly," Thomas Parks said, rudely interrupting me from my thoughts, "I was hoping that you might enjoy just a short walk with me on this fine day. The weather is nice. Not too hot or anything. And there is a slight breeze. And, you see, I saw you perform last night. I heard that you were a maid—."

"I'm not any longer," I cut in. "Mrs. White has been kind enough to help me with my vocal talents."

"Oh, I see," he said nervously, and his eyes flashed toward my clothing again briefly before he continued. "I apologize for the mistake. I—uh—I heard your story, though, and I was inspired by it. I was hoping that you would enjoy just a short walk."

His fingers twitched uncomfortably again as he stopped speaking, awaiting my response. His eyes, however, remained direct and unflinching.

I honestly did not know what the proper response was. Walking with the young man might send the wrong message—that I was still on the level of a maid, spending my time with other servants instead of pursuing the men who had just sent me letters that morning. Still, there was something wonderfully hopeful in the face of the young man before me, and I struggled with bringing myself to fully turn him down. Also, if he stayed, I could read William Knight's letter and give this man a verbal response to bring to his impressively handsome employer.

"A short walk," I agreed, and Thomas Parks smiled. "In the back," I added, hoping that no one but Mrs. White's servants would spot us among the trees.

I led him through the house, past Amos in the kitchen.

"Thank you for taking a bit of time out of your schedule," he said awkwardly as I walked forward, toward the trees.

"Of course. Thank you for the invitation," I said politely. Then, "Before we talk, do you mind if I read this in case it contains something of an urgent nature?"

"Of course not," Thomas Parks said, a slight frown on his thin lips.

I broke the elaborate wax seal on the back and pulled out the thick paper.

Dear Miss West,

    It was a pleasure meeting you last night. Your performance was truly inspiring,

    and I hope I might hear more of your beautiful voice in the future. You had a passion for

    music that was evident, and a passion for life that was delightful to behold.

                           William Knight

"How very kind of him," I said aloud. I was absolutely giddy inside. Turning to look at Thomas Parks, I said, "Please thank him for sending such a kind note, and so quickly. I will of course send Mr. Knight a more formal reply as soon as possible."

Thomas Parks merely nodded his head. We passed the time in silence until we reached the little stream and started to walk along it.

"So, I wanted to come myself and talk to you and meet you. I know I should have remained directly next to Mr. Knight's carriage and horses last night, but I kept catching pieces of your music, and so I snuck around the side of the house to hear you sing the last couple of songs. You have the most beautiful voice I have ever heard."

"Thank you," I said, already used to the compliments from the previous night and from the letters I had received.

"You looked so wonderful too. I was shocked to hear that you are—were—a maid."

"Yes. Mrs. White hired me when I was fifteen, shortly before my parents both died."

"My mother died a few years ago too," Thomas Parks said seriously. I was sixteen at the time."

"I am sorry to hear that," I said, and we reached an awkward lull in the conversation.

"So, Mr. Parks," I finally began.

"Thomas," he corrected me.

"Thomas," I continued, "how do you feel about working for the Knights?"

"They are fine employers. My main responsibility is taking care of their horses. I grew up in a small farming community in Pennsylvania. There were a few horses there, so I was used to them. When I went searching for a job, my knowledge of horses helped me. What about you? Where are you from?"

As Thomas talked, he seemed to be overcoming his nervousness. This was almost bad for me, though, because I was hoping to keep the subject on his employers. Now that he was obviously feeling more comfortable, he was proceeding as if this were a normal conversation between the two of us.

"I am from New Jersey, though much farther north in the state," I answered.

"Do you have siblings?"

"No, I'm an only child."

"So, do you have family to visit now that your parents are dead?"

"No."

"That is a shame, though I suppose Mrs. White is like your family?"

"I guess you could say that to a certain degree," I said as I broke off a twig from a bush that we passed. I thought about my life at Mrs. White's, and before I knew what I was saying, a rush of words and emotions burst from my mouth. "Mrs. White has always been very kind to me, but not like family. I was her maid through and through. I would do everything for her. I'm friends with one of the other maids, Caroline, though it has already become a bit uncomfortable with my new status. Also, if Mrs. White were my family, she would have taken an interest in my interests. As it is, all I ever do is daydream and talk with Caroline. I write, but only about my boring day-to-day life. I have no real hobbies with the exception of reading, for I do not have time for them. Also, Mrs. White should have taken an interest in finding me a suitable husband, which she hasn't until today."

Thomas smiled at me lightly. His eyes were opened wide, probably surprised by my sudden outburst.

"I am sorry," I stuttered. "I should not have spoken so plainly."

"No, please. Don't be sorry," he said, and as he spoke, we reached the lake. I had planned on turning back immediately upon reaching it, but no one was there. Instead, I walked forward and sat down on its bank.

Thomas followed my lead, stretching his long legs out in front of him.

"I know what it's like to work for someone for so long, but not really have a connection with them. The Knights are...at times...harsh," Thomas said, and he grimaced slightly.

I could not picture William as harsh, though I could see his older, stiff father in such a light.

"Please do not repeat that," Thomas continued.

"Of course not," I said.

"So, you said that Mrs. White has not taken an interest in finding you a husband until today?"

"She asked me if I was interested in anyone whom she might approach for me. However, when I named someone, she told me that it was impossible."

"Who?" Thomas asked, not seeming to care that such a question was incredibly personal.

"I cannot tell you!" I protested.

"I'm sorry," Thomas responded sheepishly, and he directed his eyes toward the lake.

Following his gaze to the calm waters, I finally allowed myself to speak his name with a sigh. "William Knight."

"William!" Thomas exclaimed, jerking his head to look at me.

"He was so wonderful at the party last night."

"You are not William's type at all!" he said, and a smile actually started to form on his lips once more, stirring up a bit of anger in me.

"And why not?"

"William is overly polite to a nauseating degree, hence the note that he sent you today. However, he is self-serving and cruel behind closed doors. He likes the most fashionable women who will agree with his every word."

"I will be fashionable, though. My new clothing has simply not arrived yet!"

"Even if he found your personality engaging, he is too set in his ways. He will not go for someone like you. You are without money too, which is obviously not desirable for him."

"I will make money, though."

"I mean old money. And a family to further boost his own image."

My face grew hot, and I could feel my eyes become glassy with tears. "You do not know what you are talking about!" I shouted at him in an unladylike way.

I stood then and flew off in the direction of Mrs. White's house, not even bothering to wipe the dirt from my dress.

"Miss West! Wait!" Thomas called as he raced after me.

"No!" I said, stopping and turning toward him at the edge of the woods. "Leave me alone now!"

Thomas looked pained, though he complied with my wishes as I ran toward the house, tears streaming down my face and my dress catching on a few branches.

When I reached Mrs. White's backyard, behind the stable, I stopped myself. I could not believe I had let a servant bother me in such a way. I had started out so polished, but had made the mistake of letting my defenses down because he was not someone of high rank. Perhaps that was one of the things that separated me from a woman of a more privileged birth. For me, being polished and poised was something observed and then copied. Was it natural for women born into it? I began to grow angry all over again, realizing that even the way I constantly watched my language and tone around the upper class was something that a real woman of quality might not do, and thus Thomas was probably correct about me not having a chance with William Knight.

I wiped my tears on my sleeve and took deep breaths. I could not allow Mrs. White to know I had been crying. Then I straightened my dress, noticing a tiny tear in the side that I hoped would not be too noticeable to anyone else.

Finally feeling calm, I walked into the house through the back door. "Louisa," Laura said to me from her knees as she scrubbed the kitchen floor. "Mrs. White and that music teacher are waiting for you in the parlor."

"Thank you," I said, standing tall as I walked to the front of the house.

"There you are, Louisa," Mrs. White said calmly as I entered the room. "This is Mr. Covington. He will be teaching you additional songs to expand your repertoire."

"It is a pleasure, Miss West," he said, coming over and taking my hand.

Then, thinking of something else I needed to learn for future parties, I asked, "You do not know how to dance too, by any chance?"

Chapter Nine

The next morning I awoke to still more letters. Thumbing through them, I was intrigued by one without an official seal and bearing incredibly messy letters.

Pulling out the note, written on the plainest of stationery, I would have thought a child had written it.

> *Dear Miss Louisa West,*
>
> *I am most sory for my insult of you yesterday. Please take no ofens as I regretable spoke quickly and out of turn. You are a butiful and talented yung woman and I remain your humble servant*
>
> *Mr. Thomas Parks*
>
> *P.S. I regret that I am not skilled as you are with pen and paper and so I had to receeve*
> *help in the riting of this note.*

I could not help but smile at the Knights' servant's attempt at a formal note.

After reading the remaining complimentary letters, I sat down in the parlor to write back to people. I started with the letter to Thomas Parks.

> *Dear Mr. Thomas Parks,*
> *Thank you for your sincere apology.*

I stared at the paper, unsure of what else to write. After a long while, I simply added:

> *Also, thank you for your company yesterday.*
>
> *Yours,*
> *Miss Louisa*

West

I then started in on my note to William Knight. I pulled a crisp sheet of stationery out of the middle of the pile that Mrs. White had given me.

Dear Mr. William Knight,

Thank you for your complimentary and lovely letter. Your kind words have made me incredibly happy. I do hope to see you again soon, as it was truly a pleasure to meet such an impressive man as yourself.

Yours,

Louisa West

I used Mrs. White's materials to place a wax seal on the back, and set the letter on the side table next to me.

I went to pick up the next clean piece of paper when there was a knock on the door. My legs twitched with the urge to answer it, but I remained seated. A moment later, Caroline came into the parlor and announced that a Mr. Elliott Gray was there to see me.

I rose and walked to the door where a blonde-haired young man stood before me.

"Hello, Miss West," he began as his pale cheeks turned slightly rosy.

"Hello, Mr. Gray. It is good to see you again," I said, remembering him from among the young men at the party.

"You need not call me, Mr. Gray. Elliott is fine."

"Then you must call me Louisa."

"Very well," he said with a smile on his face. "Did you receive my letter?"

"Oh, yes. Yesterday. I was actually just about to write you back when you knocked."

"Fancy that!" he said loudly. Then, more rigidly, he inquired, "I was wondering if I might enjoy your company for a brief time."

"Of course," I said, and I invited him into the parlor. Mrs. White was taking a nap, and so I had the ability to play hostess fully.

He sat on the loveseat while I chose the nearest of the two high-backed, light blue, flower-patterned chairs.

"So, are you planning other performances?" Elliott asked.

"Yes. Several people have already invited me to perform at their private functions. Hopefully, I shall give large-scale performances soon too."

"I am sure that you will," he said seriously.

I smiled at him, for here was a kind man before me, but I found no true excitement in his presence. I supposed that having just been a mere maid only a week ago with no hope for a better life, I should have been thrilled that such a man was giving me attention. I had seen the type of elevated person that existed in William Knight's form, though, and so now the man before me paled in comparison. Elliott was excitable as opposed to regally calm. He also did not have that almost mystical command of respect that William Knight boasted. Furthermore, Elliott's fine clothing seemed to be worn with an air of necessity rather than with a sense of pride and style.

As the young man before me jabbered on, I was not surprised to find my mind still stuck on William Knight.

Chapter Ten

"It is absolutely gorgeous!" Caroline gushed as she pulled my brand new dress out of its box.

The windows of my spacious bedroom were open, though the breeze was nonexistent and it was sweltering—even hotter than usual for the end of July. I felt a drop of sweat drip down the back of my neck, wetting the bottom of my hair, which had already been pinned up.

"Hold it up so I can see!" I said excitedly.

The bright blue dress with off-the-shoulder sleeves made me giddy with excitement. As she continued to free it from its box, the large skirt nearly took my breath away.

"You will look absolutely enchanting!" Caroline announced, and she set to work putting it on me.

Finally, I was able to step in front of the mirror to examine the finished product. Though the dress had some similarities to Mrs. White's old blue dress, this new one, specifically made for me, was clearly much more up-to-date. With the off-the-shoulder sleeves, I felt quite exposed, but delightfully seductive. The lace ribbon around my center decorated me like a piece of fine jewelry. The large skirt gave me the illusion of having the world's most petite waist, and I daydreamed about men holding it while they danced with me.

"Beautiful!" Caroline announced, and I smiled at her.

"Thank you."

"You are quite welcome," Caroline said, and she abruptly walked out the door.

I put on my new shoes by myself, feeling awkward as I could not easily sit in my dress in order to do so.

Finally, I took one last look in the mirror before I stepped lightly down the velvet-lined main stairs where Mrs. White was already waiting for me.

"Splendid!" she proclaimed, and I believed I would never grow tired of hearing such nice things said to me.

I would be giving my first private performance that night outside the home of Mrs. White. It would be for the respected Rice couple, almost an hour away.

Mr. Covington had been a wonderful music teacher, introducing me to new types of music, even in multiple languages. He had already spoken with the musicians who would be performing at the Rice residence this night. They had the accompanying music for my performance, which would consist of one rather fun and folksy song and several pieces from Italian operas. I still had no idea what I was actually saying in Italian, though Mr. Covington was always praising my pronunciation.

The carriage ride was uncomfortable in my new, stylish dress, but I didn't care. I thought to myself over and over how happy I was.

When the carriage finally came to a stop, Frank walked around to the side of it to help me and Mrs. White out. Despite the setting sun, the humid air still held all of the day's heat. I was thankful when I noticed through a front window with pulled back curtains that the party would be indoors and not outside with the humidity and bugs.

The Rice home was about the same size as Mrs. White's, though it had many more European paintings and statues inside, giving the house the feel of a museum. As I entered through the front doors, my eyes immediately became glued to a lively painting at the top of the foyer stairs where naked nymphs danced in a circle.

"Mrs. White," Mrs. Rice greeted her, and the two women pecked each other lightly on the cheek.

"And Miss West," Mrs. Rice then said, taking my hand in hers. "It is a pleasure to have you here. Mr. Covington has arranged everything with the musicians, so you should have no problems when it comes time for your performance. We are really all so very excited. I have invited an especially large group of guests so that they might have the pleasure of hearing your voice."

"Thank you," I said, and I followed Mrs. White into the ballroom where the party was being held. Unfortunately, there was a slight lip on the floor dividing the ballroom from the foyer, and I tripped slightly on my way in, the action looking much more serious than it was due to the sway of my enormous skirt.

Henry, one of several men who had come to visit me following my original performance, rushed up to me and grabbed hold of my elbow. "Are you all right?"

"Oh, yes. Thank you," I said as I blushed. I had hoped no one had seen.

Necessarily, I exchanged a few polite words with Henry and Elliott, who ran up behind him. While I tried not to be obvious about it, though, I kept my eyes and ears open for William Knight. I had not seen him or heard from him since his letter immediately following Mrs. White's party, and I sincerely hoped that he might be in attendance this night, especially as my performance was to be rather impressive compared to my last, somewhat shameful choice of songs.

It took ten minutes of obligatory small talk with several guests, including Mr. Graham and Elbert, but I finally spotted him, standing straight and tall as he entered the ballroom. My heart began beating wildly as his dark brown hair shone healthily in the light and his almost black eyes seemed to connect with mine. I thought he was walking straight for me, and I touched my hair anxiously with my hand, which stuck to it somewhat with nervous sweat. He was only five feet from me when he suddenly smiled and veered to the right, taking the arm of a young woman standing there. She giggled instantly, and before I knew it, there were three more girls surrounding him. Apparently I was not the only one drawn to Mr. Knight as if he were a magnet.

I had to wait an unbearable fifteen minutes while he chatted with his growing group of admirers. Finally, though, his eyes truly caught mine, and I looked away in embarrassment. My body involuntarily shivered with excitement, though, when I heard my name uttered by his masculine voice behind me.

"Miss West." I turned around, all too glad to be out of a particularly boring, one-sided conversation I was having with a man named Clark all about his father's business.

"Mr. Knight," I said, putting out my hand for him. As he kissed it, I soaked in the feeling of his lips on my hand, wishing it were on my lips instead.

"Will you be performing tonight?"

"Yes," I answered. "I do hope that you enjoy my selection. It contains quite a bit of Italian."

"Wonderful," he responded, and I noticed that his teeth were whiter and straighter than anyone's I had ever seen.

He turned ever so slightly in a position so that he could easily walk away, and so I nervously shot at him, "How have you been doing?"

"Outstanding," he answered calmly, without missing a beat. "I have been enjoying my summer with my parents, but I am looking forward to continuing with my study of law in a couple of weeks."

"Law? Very impressive," I said, picturing him studying over his books by candlelight, his piercing eyes taking in every detail of the words before him.

"Yes. I study in Philadelphia under the supervision of a highly respected attorney."

"Truly impressive."

"Thank you. I must return to some people, but I wished to say hello to you."

"Thank you," I said, and I hoped that he would look down at my fashionable dress, but he walked away with his neck as straight as ever.

"Anyway," Clark continued the second William Knight left, but I was not listening at all. My eyes were glued to the girls around William Knight and the way that they practically threw themselves at him. Though I had tried to push Thomas Parks' words from my memory, I thought then of what the Knights' servant had told me. William Knight liked only the most fashionable and richest girls who would agree with everything he told them.

As William Knight's eyes did not wander over to mine at all for the next couple of hours, my happiness began to shut down and my smile began to fade. I did not even enjoy showing off my new dancing capabilities as I thought I might. Instead, during these lifeless waltzes, I found myself constantly checking on how near I was to William Knight and his dance partners.

All in all, I was not enjoying the party in the slightest. Elliott, Henry, Clark, and others continued to take turns talking to me, but when I actually tried to listen, I found myself bored within a matter of minutes. It was true that they were all polite, kind, and attentive to me, evidenced by the dozen drinks brought to me throughout the course of the night without my having requested them. However, they were also boring. They droned on and on about their fathers' occupations, tedious hobbies, and the trips they had been on that I hadn't. I told myself that if William Knight were talking to me, he would be interested in everything about me. He would not simply speak of his past, but he would speak of the possibilities of the future, where I was included. The men before me were good, but not good enough.

By the time of my performance, my soul felt heavy and I did not step to the front of the group of people with the grace that I had been practicing in my bedroom. Instead, I automatically looked around for William Knight. Only after I spotted him in the back of the crowd did I begin to sing. My eyes remained focused on his general vicinity as I did not even think on the words coming out of my mouth. Then, halfway through my first song, a blonde girl whose dress was lower cut than mine whispered in William Knight's ear. He smiled and stealthily escaped out through the back of the room with her. An incredible sense of loss weighed down on me, but I mechanically made my way through the rest of the songs.

The night was ruined despite the prize that I had won from the demon in the woods.

Chapter Eleven

I quickly grew into the routine of a performer as opposed to a maid. Each day I would wake up and write and respond to letters and eat my breakfast. Mrs. White would often join me while I did so. Then, Mr. Covington would come over and I would learn new songs and practice for a couple of hours. Afterwards, I would take a solitary walk through the woods to clear my head, after which I would have tea with Mrs. White. We would talk, often about her privileged childhood, until dinnertime. Finally, I would retire to my room to read or write.

A couple of weeks following the party at the Rice residence, though, my thoughts were consumed by too much emotional turmoil to read or write. I sat on a padded bench, staring out my window at Mrs. White's manicured backyard and stable. William Knight would surely be leaving around this time to return to Philadelphia where he would continue with his studies. I wondered how long it might be before I should see him at another party.

Granted, I would be in Philadelphia myself in a few days; Mrs. White had arranged for me to sing in front of several people who were interested in my talents for purposes of a concert in the city. I knew Mrs. White, though. Although she liked to socialize, she enjoyed the familiar atmosphere of her house; we would surely only remain in the city for the day, and then we would return home.

Aside from William and my dying hope of seeing him in the near future, I most definitely still had other young men interested in me, and men with a decent amount of money too. But nothing about them sparked anything to life inside of me, and I found that I continued to be bored with their well-bred, but unstriking personalities. I also had the awkward feeling that I was, in a sense, being hunted by them, and there was something definitively unappealing in that notion.

With my emotional distress reaching its peak, I could not fall asleep that night despite the comforting hoots of an owl outside my window. I tossed and turned in my newest nightgown, afraid that I would forever be unhappy, unable to attract the man I most desired.

After a sleepless night, I rose and dressed myself in a simple, dark-colored dress. I slinked downstairs when a knock on the front door rang throughout the whole house. I had not answered the door even once since I had acquired my new talent, but I was standing literally in front of it, so I made an exception.

I nearly cried in shock when I saw William Knight on the other side of the door.

"Mr. Knight!" I exclaimed loudly. "I thought you would have left for Philadelphia by now," I said. I rubbed my hands on the sides of my dress, attempting to still them and keep them smooth and not sweaty despite my extreme anxiousness.

"I am leaving this afternoon," he said as calm as ever. "This morning I am making my rounds, visiting certain people in order to say good-bye."

"Well, thank you for choosing me," I said while I silently cursed my plain choice of dress.

"You are quite welcome. You performed fabulously at the last party, and I do hope that my father will have you perform at one of his future functions."

The blood burned in my cheeks for I knew that he had not stayed for even most of my performance. I knew that I should have kept politely quiet, but after a sleepless night, something inside me snapped. "I thought I saw you slip out the back with some woman."

For the first time, I saw William Knight's calm demeanor falter slightly, though he regained it after only a split second. "The young lady was in distress and required that I speak with her, though I still heard the majority of your performance from the hall."

"And I suppose it did not hurt that she was fashionable and beautiful," I said before I could stop myself. My hands were twisting the sides of my dress into a terrible ball, but I did not care.

At my much more insulting outburst, William Knight actually smiled. "Do I detect a bit of jealousy, Miss West?"

"Well, even my voice could not keep you in the same room as me!" I shout-whispered, hoping that no one was listening to our conversation, though I could almost be certain of the fact that Caroline and Laura were nearby.

"Miss West," he said, losing the agonizingly playful tone and switching to light-hearted sincerity. "I am flattered that you have obviously become so attached to me after our brief meetings, but, as I am sure you know, you are a plain girl with a poor background, despite your blessed talent. I am positive that you will find a suitable husband with a fine background, but I'm afraid that my particular tastes lean more toward the visually striking."

I actually gagged slightly as all words became entangled in my constricted throat.

"I do hope you understand," he continued.

I still could not speak, so I only nodded. My hands tingled as the blood rushed from my head downwards.

"I hope to see you again in the future, Miss West," William Knight continued as if nothing awkward had passed between us at all. "You have an incredible gift, which I find quite mesmerizing." And with that, he walked back toward his carriage, which was waiting out front. As his servant opened the carriage door for him, my tears blurred the scene before me and I shut the door.

As I turned around, I heard the sound of footsteps scurrying away. I was so insulted and upset, though, that I did not care if it had been Caroline, Laura, or even Mrs. White. I was alone, embarrassed, and ashamed. As I actually shook by the front door, anger, sadness, and the effects of a sleepless night took over once more. "I'll show him visually striking," I actually said aloud, and I raced through the house toward the stable, shouting to anyone who could hear that my presence was requested for the day on the other side of town.

Chapter Twelve

My hands slipped along the damp cave wall as I walked to the left. It smelled just as stale as it had the first time I had gone to the demon in the woods, but I was not afraid as I had been during my original visit. I not only knew what to expect, but my mind was totally consumed with both frustration and longing for the happiness that would come with an even better life.

As I moved recklessly along, I did not hear the monster approach me from behind. "Back so soon, Miss West?" his voice said deeply, but politely, and I thought of William Knight's polite manner.

"Yes," I said, turning to face the monster, despite being able to see nothing in the dark. "You convinced me that I needed a talent. That singing would give me everything. That I would be happy if I could just sing." As I shot my anger-fueled accusation at the monster, I tried to recall the exact words he had used when suggesting a talent, and I truthfully could not remember "happiness" being among his promises. Still, I had thought that was implied.

"And is your new voice not yielding the results you expected?" he asked slowly and calmly, and the stench of his breath nearly knocked me over.

"It is yielding much praise and newfound power, but there is something more that I have found without which I do not believe I will ever be happy again!"

"Oh dear. And what is that?"

"A young man. Mr. William Knight."

"The Knight family is a highly respected one. And how do you think you might obtain this young man as your own?"

"I must be beautiful!" I shouted, and my voice actually echoed off the cave walls.

"But you have won the attention of other suitable men, have you not?"

"They are kind, but painfully boring. None of them carry the charisma of Mr. Knight."

"I see," the monster said happily, and I shivered all over as my mind finally began to process where I was and what I was doing. "Well, I must agree with Mr. Knight that your looks are not all that they could be, and in some ways I would expect that they are holding you back. Your coloring is not at all even and your hair tends toward the frizzy side. There is no life to it, and if you were to wake up next to Mr. Knight one day, he would find you immediately plain. Your eyes are bland, and their shape is boring and not exotic in the slightest. Your womanly curves are almost like those of a child, and your hands still manage to maintain the look of work where they are bony. Perhaps your appearance could be improved upon. What do you think?"

"Yes," I said, feeling the joints of my hands and contemplating their boniness, something I had never even considered before.

"For the prize of beauty, though, a fair wager must be made—."

"Please not William Knight!" I shouted.

Without light, I would not have originally thought this possible, but I could actually *hear* the demon-creature smile at my outburst. "No," he growled. "That would be cruel, and you are such a nice girl. I will not allow you to risk Mrs. White's life again either. I will give you an easy one. You are to risk the life of Mr. Thomas Parks."

"Who is Thomas—oh," I said, putting the name to the face. "William Knight's servant? The man who visited me and told me that I was not William Knight's type?"

"The same. It seems only fitting for you to risk the life of the young man who originally told you such devastating news. You shall prove him wrong once and for all."

I remained silent, remembering the nervous way that the young man had introduced himself to me and his kind letter of apology following our heated discussion.

"Here are the conditions," the demon quickly continued, jerking me from my thoughts. "Mr. William Knight will be studying in Philadelphia. I happen to know that he will have a very difficult written test in about one month's time, on the fourteenth of September. During his time in Philadelphia, Mr. Knight will keep his three favorite horses at a stable in Pennsylvania, outside of the city. While he may visit and ride any of these at his leisure up until then, the day of the actual test, he may not come for them at all. If he leaves the city and comes to see them for any reason on the day of the test, you will have lost the bet and Mr. Parks will die. If, however, he does not come for any of them, you will awaken the next day of a visually striking nature that will be sure to stop Mr. Knight dead in his tracks, for you will then be talented, soon-to-be well-off, and gorgeous. Also, the normal rules apply where you cannot purposefully alter the outcome or speak of this before the bet is complete or you will die." He left a dramatic pause. "Do you accept?"

I didn't pause. "Yes."

Chapter Thirteen

"Well, that sounds particularly promising," Mrs. White announced as we walked out of the Philadelphia concert hall arm in arm.

"Yes, though it's disappointing to hear that they're taking fewer chances on previously unknown performers simply because of the political climate," I said.

"Simply because of the political climate? Why, Louisa, politics affect almost everything, and right now turmoil is building, which makes people afraid," she said, and I blushed hard for I had thought my previous observation sounded intelligent enough.

"So, you think they will schedule something in the spring?" I asked as we turned left next to the bustling main street.

"It certainly sounds that way. Just keep your fingers crossed, my dear," Mrs. White responded.

Though it had only been a couple of days since I had seen William Knight and had consequently made my second bet, part of me longed to see him despite his embarrassing rejection of me. After all, in only a month's time I would be beautiful to behold, and he would surely want me then.

Thinking about him, I fixed my hair under my maroon cap as I heard a loud, girly laugh. Looking across the street in its direction, I was shocked to actually see the object of my desire, William Knight, with a girl hanging off of his arm.

"Oh, look! It's young Mr. Knight," Mrs. White said, fixing her grayish-white hair under her own cap. "Come, let's cross the street and say hello to him." As our arms were still linked, she used her larger weight to pull me across, and so I truly had no say in the matter.

"Mr. Knight," Mrs. White said when we were at an appropriate distance.

Turning around to look at us, William Knight smiled in a genuine way as he said, "Mrs. White. Miss West. What brings you to the city?" He had to speak loudly for just at that moment several carriages passed by, making a great deal of noise between the horses' hooves and the carriage wheels.

"Miss West had a meeting with some people in the concert hall. She will give a performance there in the spring we hope."

"Marvelous," William Knight said, and he looked at me without an ounce of awkwardness. "This is a dear friend of mine, Miss Melanie Burges," he said, introducing his companion who simply nodded at us politely, though she allowed her eyes to linger on me, as if evaluating me.

"How are your studies going?" Mrs. White inquired.

"Well, I have only just returned, but they seem to be going well. I just found out that on the fourteenth of September, the attorney whom I have been studying under has created a rather rigorous written exam for me. He says that he believes I have learned much, but he desires to test my skills in this way. I am sure I shall have my nose in books until that day."

"Do take time to have some fun, though," Mrs. White said, her plump cheeks puffing up to the sides as she smiled.

William Knight laughed lightly. "Well, I must work hard so that I might reap great rewards."

I eyed the girl next to him who was obviously bored with the current conversation. I wondered if she was one of the rewards he sought.

Mrs. White continued to smile. "Very admirable of you, indeed."

"Thank you," William Knight accepted. "Well, I should be going, but I do hope to see you both again soon," he said, patting the girl on the arm, which caused her neck to snap up straight as she focused again on the present.

"Nice meeting you," she finally spoke. Mrs. White and I nodded our heads, said some polite parting words, and watched them walk off.

"Such an impressive young man. I can see why you were so taken with him," Mrs. White said in a hushed, mischievous tone as we turned and walked in the opposite direction.

I had planned on remaining quiet on the subject, but thoughts continued to swirl around in my head, causing me to actually grow physically dizzy. I found the weight of my secrets heavy on my soul, and so right then I determined that I would tell a confidant my secrets and save me from some of the inner turmoil of dealing with everything by myself. But then I struggled with who I could actually trust with that information. Caroline and I had taken on a strange relationship ever since my wonderful change from maid to performer. There was no one, but...

"Mrs. White?"

"Yes?" she said, looking over at me as we were almost identical heights.

"Mrs. White, I do indeed believe that I still have a chance at winning the heart of William Knight."

"And how do you figure that?"

I was disappointed when she asked that, even though I had already known that I wouldn't be able to tell her *everything*.

"I sincerely believe he might find me even more appealing in the near future. However, if I leave Philadelphia...well, I fear that I will be out of sight and thus out of mind."

"So you wish to stay in Philadelphia?" she actually stopped walking at this and turned my shoulders so that I faced her.

"Perhaps," I said, and I bit my teeth down lightly on my lower lip.

"Well, he's not going to be attracted to you if you do things like *that*," she said, staring at my mouth, and I immediately stopped.

"What do you think?" I asked.

"I think that you wish to make an attempt that will surely end in failure. As I have said, my dear, William Knight would not have even picked *me* in my younger days."

Under the long skirt of my dress, I twirled my one ankle about anxiously in replacement of biting my lip.

Seeming to sense my anxiety and discomfort, Mrs. White finally smiled lightly and asked, "How long do you believe you need?"

"Just slightly more than a month," I answered promptly. Only one more month until I would be radiantly beautiful, and then perhaps a couple of weeks to be sure he had fallen in love with me so that even were I to return to Mrs. White, he would pine for me.

"Very well," Mrs. White said, and I stopped twirling my ankle.

"Really?" I asked in happy shock.

"Yes, though I expect frequent correspondence letting me know how you are doing and that you are safe."

"Of course!" I exclaimed.

"Also, in exchange for my generosity in allowing not only your absence, but in paying for your expenses, I ask that you meet with people in this area who might be interested in hiring you for performances. In this way, perhaps you might end up paying largely for yourself, which would be most helpful. Do we have a deal?" she asked.

I had a sudden flashback to the demon asking me if I accepted his deal, but it did not last long as Mrs. White's kind face was reflecting the bright setting sun, and her dress that day was a lively green.

"Yes," I said, and with that, she set out to procure a place where I could stay.

Chapter Fourteen

During my first week on my own, I had immediate success in finding patrons. I had managed to arrange five future performances at private parties, the earliest one taking place in three months. Mrs. White would be thrilled as these parties would not only pay for my stay in Philadelphia, but they would also secure Mrs. White invitations to these events.

I spent my spare time walking the streets of the city, and I had already treated myself to two new dresses during my wanderings. The city was loud, especially compared with the woodsy quiet of Mrs. White's residence. At first, I found my new environment intoxicating, and I felt wonderfully out of place. However, I soon found myself longing for the simple peace of the forest and the hoots of the owls. I had not realized how attached I had grown to these things until I lay in bed at the end of that first week, hearing the loud discussions of men drinking and dining on the floor below.

Often a quiet person, I had not previously realized how comforting it was to have the option of conversation open to me. In Philadelphia, though I spent time with potential patrons, the majority of these meetings were business-related. There was no one I could truly just have a conversation with if I desired such a thing. And so, due to its absence, I longed for company. Still, if I left the city, I risked losing William Knight.

That was yet another problem, though. I had not again bumped into him accidentally in the streets, and at this rate, he was likely to forget about me, even with our being in the same city. So, the next morning, I awoke early, put on my new, flower-print, mustard yellow dress, and walked straight out of the city. Rather than return to New Jersey, though, I had a different destination in mind.

It was a typical, hot August day, though I was not prepared for how hot it would seem after an extended time outdoors. I kept walking and walking while the sun beat down on my brown hair, which seemed to absorb its heat like a sponge. More than two hours after I had left my lodgings, I finally reached my destination, utterly exhausted.

Ahead of me was a farm, vegetables growing on one side and on the other a spacious area in front of some woods where a stable and fenced-in field were located.

On the way, I had stopped at some other farms to inquire as to where William Knight's horses might be kept. I was finally pointed in this direction, and so I knocked confidently on the farm's front door.

The door opened noiselessly, and a stately-looking woman appeared, staring at my eyes well below hers as she wiped her hands dry on a towel. "Can I help you?" she asked and her friendly voice immediately put me at ease despite her stature.

"I do hope so. Is this where Mr. William Knight keeps his horses?" I asked, standing as tall as possible.

"Yes, it is," she answered.

"I have come in the hopes that he might be riding today."

"If he's come, he's gone right to the stable. You are more than welcome to check. Also, his servant, a man by the name of Thomas, is staying there. He can probably help you if you're looking for Mr. Knight."

"Thank you," I said, turning away in order to walk to the stable.

My hands began shaking on the way, and I could not figure why. I was simply going to see if William Knight were there so he might keep me in mind. If not, I would leave. That was all. I would ask Thomas Parks—and a whole new shiver went through me. There it was. How on earth was I supposed to look the man whose life I was risking in the eyes and talk to him like he was any other human being to me? In front of the closed stable door, I lifted my hand, which then dropped back down to my side like a lead weight. I could not see Thomas Parks, I determined, and I certainly could not speak to the man. But what if William were inside, perhaps readying his horses for a healthy stroll? I knocked before I could lose the strength to do so again.

The door swung open wide, and much to my displeasure, Thomas Parks stood before me, towering over me in his somewhat gawky way. "Miss West?" he said, clearly shocked. "What can I do for you?"

"Hello, Thomas. I was just looking for Mr. William Knight. He isn't here by any chance, is he?"

Thomas cocked his head as he looked down at me. "No, he's not. Is he expecting you?"

"No. I just—I don't know where he's staying in the city, and I was hoping to catch him here during one of his excursions to see his horses."

Thomas actually laughed slightly.

"What is so funny?" I asked, feeling completely uncomfortable with every part of my current situation.

"Mr. Knight hasn't been here at all. He almost *never* takes an interest in his horses."

"Oh. I see." I was disappointed on one hand, as I had truly hoped to find him there based on what the demon had said about William Knight being permitted to ride any of his horses up until the day of his examination. On the other hand, I was rather relieved and excited. After all, if William Knight never took an interest in his horses, the wager I had made would be even easier to win than I had initially thought.

I suddenly realized that Thomas was staring at me awkwardly, clearly unsure of what to say or do next. It then hit me that I was also being rather awkward, standing there staring at him while my mind wandered.

"I—um, would let you know where he is staying, but I truly don't know the answer to that question. I was told to just remain here and take care of the horses until directed otherwise," Thomas finally offered.

"I see. Well…thank you for your time." I took a deep breath and turned around, not looking forward to another two-hour trek to return to the city.

"Do you have transportation?" Thomas called out to me.

I reluctantly turned back around to face him, now some five feet from him. "No. I'm staying in the city and I walked here."

"All the way here?" he asked. "Depending on where you're staying in the city, that could be over a two-hour walk! And in this heat!"

"Yes," I answered, feeling somewhat foolish and not at all of the elevated social rank which I tried so hard to be a part of.

There was another awkward silence between us. Finally he spoke, "Do you want to rest here for a while? I can bring you some water and later take you back into the city using the Knights' horses. I'm sure they wouldn't mind."

He looked directly into my eyes, and despite my good chances of winning the bet, I felt shame wash over me again at having decided to risk his life for my personal gain. "No, I really couldn't, but thank you for your offer," I said as sweat trickled down the back of my neck.

"Really," he said. "Please accept. You look so hot as it is. I could not in good conscience send you back to Philadelphia in this extreme heat without so much as a beverage."

"Fine then," I said, marching toward him somewhat angrily since I had given in despite my guilt.

"Excellent," he said, his mouth creating deep lines on his cheeks as he smiled. "You can just wait in the stable while I pour you a glass of water."

"Thank you," I said, and we unfortunately brushed arms slightly as we passed each other.

Inside the stable, I was greeted warmly by the smell of hay and horses. "Neigh!" one of the horses verbally welcomed me while another poked his head over the door of his stall to see who was there.

"Hello," I said to them. I walked down the stable's center aisle, peeking into each stall. All in all, there were five horses: two midnight black ones, one dapple, one brown with a tan mane, and one brown with a black mane.

The stable was practically spotless aside from the usual bits of horse-related debris, and even the equipment was placed neatly. It was obvious that Thomas took pride in his performance as a coachman and servant.

I had enough experience with horses thanks to Mrs. White's moderately-sized stable to feel quite comfortable with them. Walking over to one of the black ones, I pet his large nose as he sniffed the front of my new dress. As the horse seemed quite happy, I remained with him for a couple of minutes.

"Making friends with Midnight, I see," Thomas's voice eventually sounded from the doorway where he stood holding two glasses of water.

"Yes. They're quite lovely. Are they all the Knights'?" I asked, accepting one of the glasses from him and bringing the refreshing beverage to my lips.

"No. Midnight is the Knights' and so are Commander and Violet," Thomas said, pointing out the brown horse with the black mane and the other black horse. "The other two are Mrs. MacIntosh's."

"And it's usually your job to take care of them?"

"Yes, though this is the first time that I've been sent here to do so. Normally they stay at the Knights' estate."

"Why are they here then?"

"I believe the younger Mr. Knight is attempting to assert his independence by separating his possessions from his parents to make a future transition easier. You see, nothing has been written in stone yet, but if I had to guess, Mr. Knight is looking to stay in Philadelphia as he anticipates that his time studying under his mentor is coming to a close. I suspect he will go into business with the older gentleman and buy property out here. Then these horses will be moved to this new property."

"I see," I said, wondering what would become of my living situation, assuming that I would capture William's heart with my impending beauty. "Would you still stay with the younger Mr. Knight then?" I asked.

"I suppose so. I'm really just waiting to see what happens," Thomas said before downing the last gulp of his water.

"Would you be happy for the move?"

"Yes and no. I did enjoy the wooded location of the Knights' estate, as where city living is not in line with my particular tastes. However, I would be closer to my family here."

"What family, and where do they live?" I asked. I tried to recall our first conversation, and though I remembered telling him that I was without family, I could not recall inquiring about his.

"My father is still alive as are all six of my siblings."

"Oh my goodness! That is quite the large family."

"Yes, and I really enjoyed growing up with a group that large. I am the sixth of us seven children. They all still live here in Pennsylvania, about three to four hours west of here. When I left, most of the family was still living on our tiny family farm. There was not enough farm for all of our hands, though, so I figured I could make a better living away from home and be one less mouth to feed with our limited resources."

"I see. And are you happy with that decision?"

"Yes and no. It's quite complicated. My living conditions with the Knights are largely improved compared with the conditions back home. I lack true relationships, though, and I miss my family."

"I know what you mean," I said quietly. "I had Caroline, another servant, but we were only friends on a surface level. And I do miss having family, even though I only ever had my two parents."

"Yes. It can be very lonely at times," Thomas said, and I miserably thought back to how I had not even wanted to go for a walk with the young man when he had visited me at Mrs. White's house.

"Would you like a seat?" Thomas suddenly said. "Give your legs a rest. Unfortunately, I can't offer you anything classy, but there are a couple bales of hay that can do the trick."

"That sounds fine," I said cheerily as we switched tones, and I walked to the back of the stable with him where there were several bales of hay.

"So, you learned about horses on your family's farm?" I asked as I smoothed out my dress around the hay and tried to keep the fabric from catching on the sharper pieces that jutted outward at odd angles.

"Yes, though we only owned two at a time, and for most of my childhood we only had the one. Still, I was naturally good with them and so this experience helped immensely when it came time to be considered as a servant by the Knights."

"Yes, I suppose having a skill like that would be useful."

"Well, you have skills too. Aside from the obvious talent of your voice, you can read and write. Speaking of which, I am very sorry that I was not able to correspond with you on my own. I had to dictate to the Knights' cook who wrote the letter for me."

"That is completely understandable. I only learned because my parents stressed its importance. I mean—well, my family knew richer times at one point. I suppose my parents were still attached to the hope of it."

"They were poor and not satisfied with their lot in life?" Thomas asked.

"Yes, and I really can't blame them. I grew up in the tiniest and barest of houses."

"Yes," Thomas simply said, but he was clearly holding something back.

I remembered yelling at him when he spoke his mind before, and my cheeks reddened. "You may speak your mind," I said quietly.

"It's just—I can understand hoping for better things to come your way and being thankful if and when they do. But if you refuse joy until that day, you'll never find it. After all, there will always be something bigger and better to obtain, and so you need to embrace happiness in the present."

I was silent. My conscience nagged me quite loudly that I was repeating the same, unhappy mistake that my parents had made. Inside, though, I screamed even louder than my conscience that I would indeed be happy as soon as I was beautiful. It had to be true, or I was risking Thomas's life for literally no good reason.

"I'm not sure that I agree, but I suppose we should leave it at that for now," I said.

"Fair enough," Thomas responded, and he looked at my face with his blue eyes, bright even in the cool shadows of the stable. "So, what brings you to Philadelphia?" Thomas asked, changing the subject to what he had probably figured was a neutral topic.

"Uh…I'm setting up future performances with people who live in the city."

"I see. Any success?"

"A lot."

"I can understand why," he said. "While I didn't actually receive the chance to see your last performance, I heard that it was excellent from people talking about it."

"Yes, and I suppose one of those people was *not* William Knight," I said before I could evaluate my words.

"What do you mean?"

"Mr. Knight left with a young woman in the beginning of my performance," I said, feeling hot again despite the shade in which we sat.

"I apologize for his behavior," Thomas said seriously. "How long are you staying in Philadelphia?" he continued in a happier tone, once again working to change the topic.

"About a month more."

"A full month?" he asked, his brown eyebrows rising upward. "Do you really have enough to keep you busy here for that long?"

"Well, I—you see—um…I'm…I'm not *just* here because of my music."

Thomas leaned back, resting partially on stacked bales of hay behind him. He had a slightly smug look on his face as if he knew what I was about to admit to, but his eyes looked so mischievously pleasant that I couldn't be mad at him for his know-it-all demeanor.

"I came here because I'm hoping that if I stay around, I will not leave William Knight's mind."

"I see," he said, leaning back even further. "And do you have reason to believe that this endeavor will end in success?"

"Yes."

"Well, then, I wish you the best of luck. Unfortunately, though, like I already said, William very rarely takes an interest in his horses, so you could almost always bet that you will not find him here."

"Yes. Thank you for the information," I said, growing more relaxed as I looked directly in Thomas's eyes now. While I had originally felt quite uncomfortable, this double reassurance that I would win the bet against the demon allowed me to drop some of the guilt at having to risk Thomas's life. After all, it seemed that he would be in essentially no danger.

As I felt freer, I moved the conversation forward. "So, where are you staying while you're here?"

"There is a small room with a separate entrance attached to the back of the farmhouse. I'm staying there, though I spend most of my time here in the stable."

"You don't sleep here, though?"

"Sometimes."

"Where?" I asked. "Not in one of the empty stalls?"

"No. Up there," he said, motioning to the discreet ladder attached to the wall behind him and a couple bales of hay. "Do you want to see?"

"All right," I said, and he took my hand as he helped me climb the bales of hay until I could reach the ladder. Before setting a foot on one of the rungs, I kicked my shoes off, figuring it would be easier to navigate barefoot.

I only had to climb four rungs before the top of my head poked through the hole in the ceiling, cut out for access to the shadowed second story. "Do you need help?" Thomas called from below.

"No," I said, grabbing hold of the hay-strewn floor above and pulled myself up onto it. I quickly slid back away from the opening so Thomas could climb up too. I felt my dress catch on a piece of wood in the floor and tear very slightly, but while disappointed, I figured I would tend to it later.

Thomas was up the ladder the next second, and he offered me his hand to help me up. Standing, my head almost touched the low ceiling, and Thomas had to remain bent over.

It was incredibly dark as there was only a sliver of light coming in from the front of the stable.

"Stay here for one second while I open the door," Thomas said, and he shuffled forward in the dark. I heard his feet crunching down straw in his path, and then all at once light shot into the room as he pushed open a small, door-shaped area that seemed to serve more as a window as there was no way to the ground through the opening except by jumping.

Stacked on both sides of this space, under the gently-sloped ceiling, were more bales of hay. A few semi-rusted tools lay in a pile on one of them near the ladder. "You sleep up here?"

"Sometimes," he repeated. He pointed to an extra-thick pile of loose hay to the side of the open window.

I stepped forward to look outside, and though we were not incredibly high, we had a nice view of the farms in front of us from our vantage point.

Thomas sat down with his legs dangling over the edge of the open space, and I followed his lead. The sun was bright, and I shielded my eyes for a moment as I once more soaked in the sun's light.

"So, what do you like to do for enjoyment?" Thomas asked brightly as he looked at me.

"Well, I read a lot in my spare time."

"I remember you mentioning that briefly before. What do you like to read about?"

"Oh, whatever Mrs. White has lying about."

"She must have some selection to choose from, though. Are there any of her books that you favor?"

"I suppose books about travel and animals, especially exotic ones that you cannot find here."

Thomas smiled. "Like what?"

"Hippopotami, for example. They are absolutely fascinating." I smiled back, feeling shockingly comfortable with my semi-new acquaintance and cozy despite the heat. "You don't suppose I might acquire one as a pet in the future?"

He laughed. "I do doubt it."

"What a pity," I said, puffing out my bottom lip in fake disappointment. "What about you? What are your interests?"

"Well, as you are already painfully aware, I cannot read or write. I do, however, play the fiddle."

"Really? Why didn't you tell me before, while we were discussing my voice, that you play a musical instrument?"

"I don't know. I can be clumsy with my playing at times, and in comparison to the beauty of your voice, my skills are nothing."

"Please don't think that," I said, picturing Thomas learning to play the fiddle at a young age and then comparing it to me coming by my talent overnight. "Do you play for the Knights?"

"No. I generally play folk music on it, which they consider too unrefined for their tastes. I often take my instrument and play out in the woods at night where they can't hear it."

I then pictured the dark forest around him and owls hooting nearby while he played exuberantly for an audience of nighttime forest creatures. "I wish I had stumbled across that," I admitted. "That would have been quite the spectacular find, I'm sure."

"Well, thank you," he said, and he smiled again, showing surprisingly straight teeth.

At this point, an exceptionally puffy white cloud came into view over our heads. "Wow! That looks exactly like a horse!" Thomas exclaimed, staring at the floating pillow.

"Really? I see a hippopotamus," I said, and I actually winked at Thomas playfully. Immediately regretting using such a familiar gesture with Mr. Knight's servant, though, I grew momentarily serious.

However, Thomas continued as if nothing bad had happened. "No, it is *definitely* a horse. See, that other cloud next to him even looks like a saddle."

I squinted at the adjacent cloud, trying to see from where he could possibly be finding a saddle. Finally, I saw it. "I know what you're saying!" I said excitedly. "Wow! I would have never thought that clouds could take on such lifelike shapes."

"You mean you have never tried to pull out pictures from clouds before?" Thomas asked in disbelief.

"No. Is this a common pastime?"

Thomas laughed good-naturedly. "Yes. How about we look for some more?" he suggested, and we started pointing out the numerous clouds as we laughed and debated over what we saw. I spotted a castle once, and talked about how my ideal castle would be decorated with white and pink pearls. Thomas saw a dragon and wondered aloud if the creatures could have actually been real at one point. It was all a wonderful fantasy, and I happily stayed in the stable and away from what I perceived as the harsher realities of my life.

I didn't notice the change at first, absorbed as I was in our game. But eventually the clouds became harder to pull shapes out of as their edges blurred together and their color changed from a bright white to an off-white to a yellow and eventually to a yellow-gray.

"I think it might storm," I said, also finally noticing that the sun had sunk quite a bit.

"You're right," Thomas said, the blissful expression disappearing from his face. "Um…," he said before exhaling out the side of his mouth. "I'm just trying to think about how to take you back to the city while keeping you dry and out of harm's way."

The phrase "out of harm's way" brought back my feeling of guilt at risking Thomas's life that I had tried so hard to suppress.

"Um…do you have a carriage?" I probed, though I had not seen one.

"No. The carriage was returned to the Knights' residence, and even if I did have access to one, it looks like it's shaping up to be a nasty storm," he said, craning his neck far out of the stable loft's open space. "The sky isn't just dark. It's strange colors."

He was right. Aside from the sick-colored yellow, a bit of menacing red began to swirl through the thickening sky as well. A gust of wind suddenly caught my hair, and I shivered, finally sensing the temperature drop that had occurred.

"What do we do?" I asked, turning to face him.

"Well, you're welcome to stay here with me until the storm passes," he offered. And with the weather, I had no choice but to agree.

The storm was upon us in no more than a half hour. We remained down in the main portion of the stable with a lantern lit against the darkness. At times the horses let out whinnies to tell us that they were frightened by the wind and the thunder and lightning. Thomas and I spent a large portion of the time soothing the horses, assuring them we were there in case something should happen.

It was odd—I was standing in a stable in the middle of a horrendous thunderstorm with a mere stable boy. And yet, I found myself feeling more alive than I could ever remember feeling. Even my recent singing performances and the resulting social interactions I had enjoyed paled in comparison. In the stable, I was a part of something bigger than myself, and I could feel it. The excitement of the lightning raced through my blood and the thunder struck fear into my heart that I relished with gladness. There was an element of real danger; at any moment the all-wooden stable might catch fire by a rogue lightning bolt. The thought exhilarated me, and I felt strangely equal to the task. That night I was also a comforter, calming the frightened horses with my presence. And then there was Thomas. We were engaged in the same tasks, and though I had recently considered myself well above him, I could not comprehend how I had ever thought that. He whispered to a horse next to me, and I lost track of time.

Eventually, as the horses grew used to the noise, my eyes began to droop as the lightning-feeling took a healthy toll on my body. Before I knew it, I was lying on a patch of hay in the aisle between the horses and their stalls, and I fell asleep.

Chapter Fifteen

The hay crinkled loudly as I rolled over onto my back, waking me from a peaceful and deep sleep. Light snuck into the stable at odd angles, alerting me that it was morning. There was not a sound outside, and the horses were resting. Gently, I pushed myself into a seated position. A few steps below my feet, Thomas lay in the hay as well, his brown hair partially covering his eyes as he slept on his back, but with his head turned to the side. I sat watching him and the horses for a few minutes. I could not tell for certain in the shelter of the stable, but it felt refreshingly cool, and I wondered if it might not be a typical, blistering summer day. The barn actually creaked then, under the pressure of a cool breeze, and I smiled.

At the slight creak, Thomas awoke slowly. Like I had, he gently pushed himself up and saw me. He smiled sheepishly, his face reddening very slightly. "Good morning," I said, and my voice sounded loud to my own ears in the quiet of the morning.

"Good morning," he said. "Thank you for your help last night."

"Of course. It was honestly a pleasure."

He smiled at me for another moment before scanning the horses to take in their condition after such an eventful night.

"Well," he finally said after looking over the whole scene, "I suppose I can take you back into Philadelphia now."

"Oh," I said, feeling my mouth involuntarily pull downward into a frown.

"What is it?" Thomas asked, sliding his long legs under him so that he was sitting on his knees.

"Oh, nothing."

"No, really. What is it?"

"I'm just—I guess I'm just not looking forward to returning to Philadelphia."

Thomas sat and stared at me expectantly, so I was forced to continue.

"I was only there for a week, and I had already grown to feel so unnatural and lonely," I said quietly. "And then yesterday and last night…well, I guess I had fun. I enjoyed myself."

Thomas smiled again, appearing like a happy child who had just been given a piece of candy. Despite the fact that I had previously considered Thomas to have an awkward appearance, I found the smile adorable as he obviously could not help but show his thoughts on his face.

"Well, you don't have to go back, you know. You are more than welcome to stay here as long as you wish."

Logic told me that it made absolutely no sense to stay on the farm with Thomas. Not only would I not see William Knight since he never checked on his horses, but I would be staying with the person whose life I was currently risking. I then quickly reminded myself that it wasn't even a risk since I would surely win, once again quieting my guilt on the matter. And as I quieted this thought, other ones in support of staying on the farm popped into my mind. I hadn't run into William Knight at all while in Philadelphia thus far, and I had truly enjoyed myself the day before. I found Thomas's presence soothing yet fun, and I had felt something that I experienced more and more infrequently—happiness. I didn't allow myself to think on it any further before I spoke. "I think I might like that actually. I have a full month before I should return home to Mrs. White."

"Very well, then. We'll just make a quick trip into Philadelphia."

"What for?" I asked.

"Your clothing and belongings, of course," he answered, and so I helped him ready two horses, and we rode off into the pleasant breezes of the morning.

As we rode, we noticed large branches that had fallen from trees during the storm in the night, and all the earth was still and hushed. The closer we drew to the city, however, the busier and more congested things became until we had to carefully watch where we were going to avoid other travelers and business people in the packed streets. Arriving at the inn, I informed the owner that I would no longer be staying there, and to please forward any mail that I might receive to the MacIntosh Farm. The woman was obviously surprised by this drastic change of venues, but she was very polite about it.

Outside once more, we were attaching my bulky items to the horses as well as we could when I was shocked to see a familiar face walking straight toward us. "Thomas? Miss West?" the flawless male voice said as he approached us.

101

"Mr. Knight," I spoke aloud, my tone suggesting that I had been caught with my hand in a cookie jar.

"What are you two doing here?" he asked, trying to be casually polite, but obviously incredibly confused and intrigued.

"I am helping Miss West with some arrangements as far as staying near the city," Thomas said ambiguously, clearly unsure of what he should share and what he shouldn't. "I do hope you do not mind the use of your horses in performing such a task."

"Of course not," William Knight said with a gallant wave of his hand. "And if I might ask, Miss West, what brings you to Philadelphia at this time?" he inquired, his dark eyes locking on mine and creating in me a sensation of pure ecstasy.

"Booking some more singing engagements. I have had quite a bit of success," I said, and I found that my voice sounded odd to me. I then realized that I had practiced using a sophisticated and measured tone for so many years. And yet, the day before, I had quickly grown so comfortable and casual in my speech with Thomas. It suddenly sounded strange to go back to the way things usually were. I glanced at Thomas, afraid that he would now see right through my act. And it was true—his eyes held a hint of sadness, or confusion perhaps. He said nothing, though, and he instead threw me a small, comforting smile.

"I'm glad things are going well for you," William said, glancing back and forth from me to Thomas and, I feared, catching something unusual in our eyes. I immediately told myself that I must maintain better eye contact with William Knight before he should think that I were a suitable match for Thomas and not for someone of his position.

"Thank you. Things are going very well for me, and I am enjoying quite a bit of attention from new acquaintances," I said, drawing my spine up straight and proud.

"That's wonderful to hear. I might flatter myself that I know such an accomplished woman," he said, embracing the lock of my eyes. "Might you consider coming to a little get-together that I am co-hosting at my mentor's residence?" he asked. I bit my tongue for a second lest I should shriek in excitement.

"Thank you. I would absolutely love to attend."

"Wonderful. It will be on September the twelfth. Will you still be in the area, or still be able to make it in any case?"

"Yes," I said.

"Very good. I shall send you the specific information as to the time and address. Where should I send it?"

"You may send it to me and I shall make sure that she receives it," Thomas spoke up.

"Very well, then. Good day, Miss West," William Knight finished, and he continued strolling purposefully down the street.

I glanced at Thomas who was looking at me with his head cocked to the side very slightly. I was too afraid to ask him what he was thinking, so I simply climbed atop my horse. Fortunately, he took the lead, and we left at once for the farm.

As we rode and talked of the city, I sincerely wondered if I had made the right decision, going with Thomas instead of staying in the city in the hope of seeing William Knight again. After all, that had been my true reason for staying away from Mrs. White's. The twelfth of September I would definitely see him, though, and that was only a couple of days before I would be beautiful. It was a perfect time to remind him of me so that I would be fresh in his mind. In the meantime, I would enjoy my time in the solitude of the farm. Also, it helped that Thomas was being a perfect gentleman about the whole meeting in Philadelphia. He continued to not bring it up even though I could tell that he had detected my sudden change in demeanor.

At the farm, Thomas immediately fetched us some food.

"So, what do you wish to do during your stay here?" he asked as he handed me a plain plate with some biscuits and gravy.

"I simply wish to help you with the horses," I oversimplified.

"Sounds fine," he said, dipping one of the biscuits on the edge of his plate into the delicious goo in the center. "We'll start with cleaning up the horse manure," he said, and he smirked playfully into his plate.

"Deal," I said strongly. Now that I was fully in it, I was not about to shy away from the temporary life I had chosen. My determination seemed to please Thomas, and we set to work the second the last bite of biscuit touched my lips.

That first day was exhausting. We worked hard taking care of the horses—harder than normal, I speculated, and I wondered if Thomas were merely having fun shocking me into farm life. Even as a maid, I had almost always helped with usual indoors tasks, and so I was not at all used to this new type of labor.

I had chosen a simple, navy blue dress to wear that day, but it was still fancy when held up against the task of farm work. After all, I had originally planned on dressing to impress in case I should see William Knight, and so I had not requested any work-worthy clothing when Mrs. White had asked which of my belongings she should send to the city. Now, my wardrobe choice seemed silly, and I had picks and even a minor tear in my dress by the end of the day.

As the sun started to set, we sat in the meadow outside of the stable area. We each had a glass of water in our hands, and we sat facing the woods behind the farm. The grass was cool beneath us and fortunately dry after a whole day in the pleasant sun. I sat with my legs pulled up and crossed in front of me, allowing my dress to simply cover my unladylike position.

"So how do you feel?" Thomas asked, his brown hair matted very slightly in the back from sweat.

"Tired," I replied, taking a gulp of water.

"You ask for the temporary life of a groom, it's yours."

I laughed as the stars began to pop out in front of us, over the tall trees.

"Sorry about your dress," he said, poking the tiny tear, which was located at my right thigh.

"No worries," I said, casually dismissing it. As I spoke, an owl hooted in the trees.

"I love owls," Thomas said, reclining backward partially with his elbows supporting his weight.

"They are interesting creatures. They used to scare me as a little kid. I thought they sounded like what a ghost would sound like. But as I grew older and could hear them from my bedroom, I actually found them comforting. If I can't sleep, it feels like they're talking to me."

Thomas nodded his head in approval. "My favorite nighttime creature is the lightning bug, though," he said, pointing in front of us where a few were glowing. As the dark continued to deepen, it seemed that dozens were appearing each second, and before I knew it there were easily thousands of lightning bugs dancing in the twilight on the edge of the woods.

We were silent as we stared at them. The sight was too mesmerizing and beautiful to immediately ruin with words. Eventually, and very quietly, I whispered, "I've never seen so many in one place. Even at Mrs. White's."

"Me neither. I thought you'd enjoy the lightshow I discovered here."

"Very much so," I said, and we watched them until they drifted back into the safety of the woods.

Chapter Sixteen

I felt like a new person on MacIntosh Farm with Thomas, safe and secure and as if I had someone in the world whom I could finally talk to. I could not remember ever feeling that way, and was grief-filled for a bit as I dwelled on Mrs. White's usual position as an employer rather than a friend and how Caroline and I had not been close on an emotional level. I had not even, truly, felt entirely comfortable with my parents. I talked with Thomas about this, and he had listened with patience and compassion. I told him how, when I thought about it deeply, I worried that I had merely been another mouth to feed in my mother and father's eyes. How I simply made their dreams of being rich seem even farther away and unattainable. I cried at the end of that conversation, and Thomas wrapped his long arms around me, embracing me in the first time I could ever remember feeling true human warmth.

Thomas also shared his feelings with me. He said that when he would feel lonely working at the Knights', he wondered if he had made the correct decision by leaving his family's farm and taking the different life path of a servant. He took pride in his work, though, and tried his best, but he sometimes worried nonetheless that he was sacrificing the more important human side of life and relationships. I knew what he was talking about from my life as a maid, and yet I told myself that I had found a way out of this lonely life of servitude through my voice. I came within an inch of telling Thomas about the demon and the cave, but I stopped myself. It wasn't that I was afraid of breaking the bet—of course I would not yet tell him of my current bet—but I stopped because something about sharing this information didn't seem right. After all, I could not, under any circumstances, picture Thomas going to the evil creature in an attempt to make his life better. If he decided that he was definitely meant to leave the Knights and pursue other paths, I believed he would. He would not approve of this demon option, and I felt shameful as I thought of what he might say if he knew about my decisions. I guessed he would say I had taken the easy way out, and I told myself over and over that there had been no other way to improve my life.

As the days passed, our conversations varied from the playful to the serious. We discussed clothing, horses, and even politics and the slavery issue. I discovered that Thomas was extremely anti-slavery, and while I had been unsure of my feelings on the topic originally, his arguments were quite convincing, and I found myself drawing toward his sympathetic point of view.

We also discovered odd little facts about each other. I had never learned to whistle, though after Thomas spent an entire hour trying to teach me, I was able to emit a sort of musical noise that might pass as whistling. I then tried to teach Thomas how to curl his tongue like I could, but to no avail. When he tried to do so, his tongue just became flatter, so that it looked like a miniature pancake. I did, however, teach him the basics of dancing as they had been recently taught to me, and though we had no music and I had not felt like singing, we danced to the chirps of crickets and the hoots of owls one night.

Time seemed to fly by, its passage only made apparent due to my increased knowledge of both horses and Thomas, and I wished I could pause it and savor my days even more. Still, by September the twelfth, I could not help but be a little excited to leave the farm after nearly three full weeks of rewarding farm life. After all, I would be a guest of William Knight that evening.

As the hour of the party approached, I climbed up into the loft area and changed there, putting on the one dress I had spared from farm work, and thus I found it free of little tears and pulls. It was all white and lightweight like a cloud.

Even though it was September, it was not cool just yet, and so I didn't think twice about the summertime dress as I slipped it on over my newly washed body. I worried momentarily that it would smell like hay, but Thomas had kindly kept it in his room at the farmhouse. Even though he had this room available to him, my dress was one of the only things that stayed there as I usually slept in the stable loft and Thomas slept downstairs between the horses' stalls.

After slipping on the dress, I quickly fixed my hair despite the absence of a mirror. Hurrying outside, I found Thomas already waiting with two horses. Behind them, the brilliant sun was starting to set, spraying streams of pink and orange across the sky.

"You look gorgeous, Louisa," Thomas said, and his ever-transparent face proved that he meant it.

"Thank you," I said, my cheeks growing hot as I blushed.

Thomas did not say anything about his young employer as we made our way to William Knight's mentor's enormous house on the outskirts of the city. Instead, Thomas commented on the very slightly changing colors of the tree leaves, pointing out just a couple of bright red and orange ones that he could spot in the semi-darkness that slowly wrapped around us.

Upon arrival, I was a little out of place, having arrived actually on top of a horse and not from within a carriage drawn by one. Nevertheless, I tried to climb down with an extreme amount of dignity. Thomas came over to me and awkwardly wished that I might have a good time. He said he would take the horses around to the stable at the back and wait for me there.

As he hurried off with the other coachmen, I felt sick to my stomach to see him go and take his proper place as a servant. Pushing my nausea aside, I ascended the wide-spaced front steps leading to the open double doors.

As I entered, I found William Knight standing in the foyer. "Miss West," he said, taking my hand and kissing it. "I am so honored that you might share your presence with me tonight."

"I am honored to have received an invitation," I responded.

"This is my mentor, Mr. George Hall," William introduced me, and the man regally took my hand in his as he spoke words of welcome.

"I hope I might be honored by a dance at some point tonight," William then said to me.

"Of course, Mr. Knight," I answered as I felt myself shake with excitement. The time was finally approaching when I might once and for all win this impressive man's heart.

As others crowded behind me in the open doorframe, I politely tore myself from William Knight and entered the heart of the party in a grand ballroom accented with gold and cream-colored velvet.

Most of the girls wore stylishly large skirts. Though my dress was otherwise very fashionable, I had not chosen a rigid skirt due to the necessity of arriving at the party on horseback. While I might have previously felt self-conscious about this decision, standing among other young women with the tiniest waists you could imagine, I dwelled on Thomas's sincere compliment and I felt confident in my choice.

The music was superb, and several young men introduced themselves to me and asked for a dance. I obliged, but there was really only one person I was waiting to dance with that night.

Finally, after at least two hours, William Knight pried himself away from the women with whom he had been conversing. I recognized one among them as the woman he had been with the day I originally saw him in the city.

"Miss West," he said as he stepped over to me.

"Hello, Mr. Knight. Thank you again for the invitation. This is proving to be such a wonderful party. Not that I had expected anything less from such an attentive man as yourself," I said, feeling as if I were stumbling over my words.

"Thank you," he simply accepted. "Might I have the dance now that I requested earlier?"

"Of course," I said, and I gave him my hand as the next song started up. It was a little livelier than I had imagined a song I would dance to with William Knight might be, but it was still wonderful as he held my waist and twirled me around the dance floor. He moved with a grace that seemed to go beyond anything I had thought possible. I felt clumsy in comparison, but I strove to do my best.

At the end of the song, William Knight bowed to me and I curtsied in response. Another girl tapped coquettishly on his shoulder then, and he turned to her. No sooner had he turned than I felt a tap on my own shoulder. It was distinctly feminine, and when I turned I saw that woman-friend of William's whom I had met on the street.

"Hello, Louisa West. Do you happen to remember me?"

I searched my mind for a name, and I was embarrassed when none came to mind. "I do remember a face as captivating as yours, but I am ashamed to admit that I cannot recall your name," I said.

"Melanie Burges," she said flatly. She pulled down tensely on one of her bright blonde, tight curls before smoothing out the already perfect fabric of her poofy, red skirt. Drawing my eyes back up from her skirt, I caught sight of her monstrous cleavage sitting in what I considered a rather revealing dress. I assumed it had already caught William Knight's eye that night too. I self-consciously wondered if my own body might be improved upon in that specific way in a few days' time.

As I once more met her eyes, she said, "That's a pretty dress you're wearing, even if it is rather past the more appropriate summer season."

"Thank you," I said, fighting to ignore the obviously cutting remark. She looked over my shoulder then as William Knight whisked the girl who had tapped him on the shoulder off at the beginning of the next song.

"Louisa," she said, drawing me to the side by the elbow. "I noticed the way you were looking at William, and I felt obliged to have a little chat, woman to woman."

I did not like where this was going, but I remained silent.

"You must know, surely, that you don't stand a chance with a man like William. I asked about you. You have a recent background as a maid," she said, and she stared at me with pitying eyes.

"I have a talent," I said defensively, feeling my cheeks turn a color that was surely similar to that of her dress.

"And I'm very happy for you," she said, shaking her head from side to side as she spoke. "However, I just do not want to see a sweet girl like you become disillusioned by any fanciful notions that are sure to disappoint in the end."

"I understand perfectly," I said through gritted teeth, and my voice came out almost like a growl.

She laughed a high-pitched, girly laugh and walked suddenly away. I stood fuming against the wall until the song ended. Once it did, though, I was pulled abruptly back to my surroundings through an unwelcome announcement.

"May I have everyone's attention, please?" the somewhat nasally voice of Melanie Burges rang across the room. People quieted down and looked in her direction. "I just finished talking with the delightful Miss Louisa West. After much prodding on my part, she has agreed to regale us with a song since she is such a renowned singer. So everyone, let's take a moment to listen to a song by Miss West."

Everyone applauded as I burned with anger inside. I was supposed to be a guest for once, and now she was forcing me to show what I really was still—a worker. I had no choice as all eyes were pulled from Melanie's chest to my face. I walked proudly to the front of the room. As I leaned in to the musicians to tell them which song to play, one of the men with a violin spoke up, "Miss Burges already told us which song to play."

Without hesitating any further, the band started to play one of the simpler, folksier songs I had performed at Mrs. White's, and so I could not even choose one of my more refined, Italian opera pieces.

As I sang, my fists shook and I found myself holding back from racing at a smiling Melanie Burges in front of me. I was humiliated, and my fairy tale night was crashing down around me. With one quick announcement I had been officially reduced from a guest at the party to Elbert the talking parrot. After I finished, I was met with exuberant applause, but I took no joy in it. William Knight had been reminded of my status, if he had ever even forgotten it. I was not simply a maid, but how could I fool myself into thinking that I was good enough for him?

After my song ended, I did not politely talk with others, dance, or even say good-bye to my hosts. I walked out the front door and raced around the back of the house to the stable.

The servants were sitting in a group talking, but as soon as they saw me hurrying toward them, Thomas stood up and ran to me. "Are you all right?" he whispered urgently, drawing me close by my arms.

"No," I said as tears streamed down my face.

"Would you like to go back to the farm?" he asked, and I nodded my head. He was ready to leave in under a minute.

We did not talk the entire ride back to the farm, and we kept our horses moving at a quick pace. When we arrived, Thomas took the job of settling the horses in for the night while I went upstairs to the loft and threw myself down on a pile of hay.

The loft was very dark, but in a few minutes, I could hear Thomas climbing carefully up to me. Kneeling down, he shyly touched his large hand to my back and head, stroking my hair soothingly.

"A woman there humiliated me," I said into the hay. "She insulted my dress and then had me sing a folk song, just to embarrass me and put me in my place."

"I am sorry, Louisa," Thomas said gently. Then, after a pause, "Don't you like singing at least?"

"No. It was just the convenient talent. It puts me in people's minds. That's all it is to me," I said furiously. "It was an awful night," I concluded, and Thomas stayed by my side as I cried myself to sleep.

111

Chapter Seventeen

When I awoke, I was alone. I was still in my white dress from the night before, though I no longer cared about the damage the straw might inflict upon it. Not even pushing myself all the way upright, I crawled sloppily on hands and knees to the miniature door at the front of the stable loft. I pushed it open and blinked furiously at the early morning sunlight.

I heard noises below me, and so as soon as my eyes were adjusted, I thrust my head outside and looked down. The stable entrance was open and the heads of two horses were poking outside as I could hear Thomas readying them with riding equipment. As he finally focused on their bridles, Thomas came into view below me. I did not call out to him immediately, figuring that he would look up himself momentarily, and also because I was actually enjoying watching him go about his work.

He was wearing a plain, off-white, button-up shirt rolled up to his elbows and gray trousers. His brown hair appeared slightly tousled. From my vantage point, I could not see his eyes, but I could see his nose, normal-sized for his oval-shaped face and set above his thin lips. All in all, he was not a physically striking man, but that's part of what I liked about him. He had a soothing presence and I realized that I actually liked his appearance more than I did the picturesque, artwork-look of William Knight. This realization, though the thought came naturally, still shocked me to my core. I used to daydream about William Knight professing his love for me and embracing me passionately. It was Thomas's strong arms that I was currently picturing wrapped around me, though.

I withdrew fully away from the window so he couldn't see me. I was breathing hard. I had to stop myself from feeling and thinking that way. Thomas was a mere servant. I had already risked Mrs. White's life so that I might have more than just the basics. Thomas would hold me back, I told myself. I cried silently, but forcefully, at that thought, for I no longer wanted to believe it. My memory pushed Thomas's seemingly wise words on the subject of "joy" into my mind. He truly believed you could have joy without having things, and while it seemed true enough in his life, I had never even tried to embrace this. Then again, had I? I had been happier than I had ever been during my few weeks on the farm with Thomas, where I had had even less than I did as a servant at Mrs. White's. It was possible, then. So was it worth the trade? I might hope for Thomas and a life of little, or I could hope for William Knight and the many things that would come with him—material and even the intangible, such as respect. Then again, was it really little that would come with Thomas? Or was it true joy?

My thoughts were bouncing around wildly in my head, and I peeked out the window once more. As I did so, the movement caught Thomas's attention below. Shading his face with his hand, he looked up and smiled. I felt a warmth curl up inside of me, and the wildness of my thoughts calmed at once. "Good morning," he said gently. "How are you feeling today?"

"Better, thank you."

"Good," he said. "I was thinking, after the…um…disastrous events of last night, I thought you might like to attend a *real* party tonight."

"What do you mean?"

"Why don't you come down here and eat some breakfast with me, and then you can find out?"

I shut the window and flew down the back ladder.

Less than an hour later, our stomachs were full and we were each on horseback, riding to the west, farther into Pennsylvania.

Prior to our departure, I had told Thomas that I was afraid I did not have any more suitable clothing to wear to a party after my time on the farm with him. He had told me any dress would do, though, and so I had slid on a flower-printed dress with minor picks and tears and tied my hair back in a simple bun.

The day was hot, but not excruciating. Nevertheless, Thomas tried to keep us in shade when possible as we rode along.

It took what had to have been at least three hours, but Thomas finally declared that our destination was in sight. We had been passing small farmhouses surrounded by acres of farmland for quite some time, so our trip was all starting to look like one big blur to me.

"Can you tell me where we are heading now?" I asked.

"To my home," he answered. "Each year, my family and our neighbors have a little celebration at the beginning of the fall season. I was recently sent word that it would be today."

I smiled straight ahead of me, my eyes focused on the little farmhouse before us.

As soon as we reached the front door, Thomas hopped off of his horse and called "hello." In seemingly no time at all, a girl perhaps a few years younger than me burst through the door, rushing at Thomas with a force that made him stumble backward slightly despite his height advantage. "I'm so glad you could come," she squealed, not letting go of him.

"I'm glad I could come too," he said down into her mousy brown hair. "This is Louisa," he introduced me, and the girl finally let go of him in order to examine me.

"Nice to meet you," she said, and she curtsied slightly.

"This is my little sister, Sarah," Thomas said.

"Nice to meet you too," I said, and I curtsied back to her. Looking at her, I felt a little foolish that I had only brought nice clothing with me to Philadelphia in the hope of running into William Knight multiple times. Sarah was before me in a plain, olive green dress that buttoned up the front.

"Come in and see everyone," she then said, racing into the house before us.

We immediately entered a tiny kitchen, appearing even tinier due to the number of people inside. There must have been at least ten people, all crammed against one another.

"Hello!" Thomas called over the hustle and bustle.

People turned and hurried over to him. I smiled at the scene, cramped as it was.

Thomas's father was the first to come over, giving his son a hearty hug and then me a strong handshake. I then met three older brothers and their wives. I also met a few small children to whom Thomas was an uncle. I tried to remember names with faces, but there were so many of them that the task seemed impossible: Ben, Carter, Robert, Ellen, Harriet, Mina.

"Where are the rest?" Thomas asked, and at the thought that there were yet more people to meet, I became happily overwhelmed, and I allowed myself to simply be taken up by the excitement as opposed to worrying about proper social protocol with introductions. This was obviously going to be an informal event.

Some of the women pulled me aside at this point, asking questions about me while they cut up fresh apples to place into pies. Though I had not been Mrs. White's cook, I did have basic cooking knowledge, and so I offered my help as we talked.

"So, you're a…friend of Thomas's?" the oldest one asked, whom I was finally able to remember as Ellen.

"Yes," I answered.

Another one with the brightest blonde hair I had ever seen asked, "Just a friend?"

I blushed. "I suppose so," I answered, and Ellen laughed quietly next to me for a few seconds.

"Stop making her feel uncomfortable now," Ellen eventually play-scolded the others, and she turned the conversation to basic questions of my background. I asked questions of theirs as well, and soon our conversation became quite natural as they took me under their wings while the men went elsewhere to prepare for that night.

I worked all day with the women, passing Thomas only occasionally as he was busy readying other things, such as the beginnings of what would be a bonfire out in the field to the west.

As the sun started to set, I, along with the other women, picked up a few dishes to take to the field where everyone would gather that night. There, a table was set up for the food, which I helped arrange as I noticed other people making their way to the large, outside clearing. On one side of this particular field, a wooden fence bordered the area where the horses were kept.

The sun set quickly that evening, and so while I was introduced to even more siblings, their families, and many neighbors, the bonfire was set ablaze in order to provide light aside from that of the only quarter-full moon.

As the fire grew in intensity, I looked around to see how many people had arrived; there were about fifty. Even though we were surrounded only by more fields and sparsely placed farmhouses, the people moved close together, giving the party a pleasantly packed ambiance.

I had lost track of Thomas after he helped to light the bonfire, and I finally found him only after I heard the high notes of a fiddle pierce the night air with a lively tune. I turned toward the wooden fence, which he was sitting on top of, playing the fiddle with a content expression on his face. People started clapping and dancing. Thomas's slightly older brother grabbed me unexpectedly and began dancing me around with the others in an exciting, clumsy fashion. It was fun, though every time I could in between spins, I looked at Thomas, who was soon happily accompanied by his dad and another man who had also taken up fiddles. A couple of songs deep, Thomas laid down his fiddle, leaving the music up to the other two men. He made a show of taking me away from his brother, bowing extravagantly and then taking my hand. Some of the girls nearby laughed as his brother threw up his hands exasperatedly, playing along.

My hand felt small in Thomas's. We danced around and around, and I found myself not worrying in the slightest about where to place my feet next. It was not a chance to show off one's talents to the rest of the guests, but an exhilarating form of entertainment, which I had not imagined dancing to ever be after my first experiences with the more formal styles.

Taking a break, Thomas and I talked to his other sister and her husband, both of them several years older than us. Others continued to dance behind us, as there was no formal start or stop to any of the festivities.

As we talked, my stomach gurgled loudly, and I asked Thomas if we might eat. Walking there with Thomas, his sister, and brother-in-law, I found even more dishes packed on the food table than there had been earlier.

We served ourselves and filled our plates. I thought back to the tiny hors d'oeuvres at Mrs. White's parties; these pies and dishes seemed much more inviting.

Walking to the far side of the horse fence together, close to the group, but not sitting directly next to the fiddle players, Thomas set his plate down before placing his hands on my hips and lifting me up on top of the fence. He then picked up his own dinner and took a seat next to me. The fence's sharp, axed ridges were not exactly comfortable, but the whole experience was so relaxed and fun that I did not care in the slightest.

"So, are you having a good time?" Thomas asked as he hastily swallowed a bite of food.

"Yes," I said, beaming at him, and I hoped that he could read the sincerity on my face like I always could on his.

"I told you this would be a real party," he responded, proudly surveying the scene before us.

After we finished our meals, we let the plates drop to the ground while we remained sitting on the fence, watching the dancers. I was still watching them joyfully hop to and fro when I felt Thomas's eyes resting on me. I looked back over at him, and I saw fireflies dancing in the distance behind him.

We were silent for a moment, and then he quietly asked, "So, did you have fun with my sisters-in-law all day?"

I smiled lightly, feeling extremely aware of Thomas's presence next to me. "Yes. They were fun. Also, they had a little fun at my expense, at first," I said, feeling my body temperature rise even though the bonfire was too far away to really experience its heat.

"How so?" he asked, smirking mischievously, which endeared me to him even more.

"Just probing into…um…whether or not we were simply friends." I knew I was blushing bright red, and my eyes dipped from his for a split second.

"What did you say?" Thomas asked, smiling broadly as he was clearly having fun watching me squirm slightly under such playful circumstances.

"I don't know," I said, and I actually looked back at the fire, too embarrassed to maintain eye contact.

"You didn't tell them about William Knight?" he asked.

"I don't care about him anymore," I stated immediately, turning my head back to face Thomas.

All at once, he brought his calloused hand up to my soft cheek and leaned in and kissed me. Though the action took me somewhat by surprise, I did not try to pull away in the slightest.

Time was blissfully nonexistent, and then I heard the hoots and claps grow louder, and I knew it was not just the intensity of the song making the party-goers do that. We reluctantly parted and turned in the direction of the bonfire where a large percentage of the dancers had stopped twirling and started making a scene in our direction.

Thomas and I laughed, and though his skin usually remained a lightly tanned hue, I was pleased to see that his cheeks were as red as I assumed mine were.

117

He reached over and contentedly took my hand in his as the dancers shifted their focus back to the music and the bonfire.

"Do you know how absolutely breathtaking you are?" he asked quietly.

"You really think that?" I asked, again turning my head back in his direction.

"Of course. Just look at you. You have the most delicate, rosy cheeks I have ever seen. And your eyes—so deep."

"My—my cheeks are always too flushed, and my eyes are so drab, though," I sputtered.

"No," Thomas said calmly. "That isn't true. You are the most beautiful woman I have ever laid eyes on."

He said it with such absolute certainty that I could tell he meant it; Thomas actually believed I was beautiful.

Chapter Eighteen

"Thank you so much," I said again as I hugged the women who had stepped forward to say good-bye to me and Thomas the next morning.

"Please come again soon," they each said to me.

It was late in the morning. Everyone had slept in following a full night of festivities. I had slept surprisingly well after I finally did go to sleep, despite being bunked with Sarah who had the disturbing tendency to mumble nonsense in her sleep.

With full stomachs from a hearty breakfast, Thomas and I rode back eastward toward the MacIntosh Farm.

"I had a great time. Your family is so much fun," I said as our horses trotted along.

"I'm glad you had fun," Thomas said proudly.

After the kiss from the night before, there was no awkwardness at all. Conversely, things were as comfortable between us as they had ever been, even with a lingering, wonderfully pleasant fire feeling still dancing over my skin and through my veins.

"So, I was thinking," Thomas finally began after a natural silence in the conversation. "Your time in...uh...Philadelphia is more than halfway over."

I swallowed hard, actually causing my throat to hurt with the sharp action. "What day is today?"

"It's the fourteenth."

"Of September?"

"Of course."

The fire feeling vanished. I instead broke out in a cold sweat. *Today was the day.* The devil's bet was for *this* particular day. William Knight would be taking a test. If he came for one of his horses Thomas would—I couldn't finish the thought. If he did not come for one of his horses, by the next morning, I would be beautiful. That did not sound nearly as appealing as it had when I was in the cave, making the deal with the demon. After all, I felt immeasurably better about life, and Thomas thought I was beautiful. What would it matter if William Knight would also suddenly find me beautiful?

"So, anyway, I wanted to talk about what you would like to do next," Thomas said.

119

"Not just now," I said too quickly.

Thomas cocked his head, his bright blue eyes flashing confusion. "It's not you. It's just—let's wait until tomorrow."

"All right," he hesitantly agreed, though he was not a stupid man, and he surely knew me better than anyone else I had ever met. He knew something was seriously wrong.

Thomas tried to talk to me of normal things, but my mind was only half-focused on what we were discussing. I kept glancing at him to see if he showed any signs of a rapid demise. After all, William Knight could be at the farm that second, and I would only know that I had lost the bet if I saw Thomas die before me. I was shaking by the time we reached the farm.

"Thomas, could you go and ask to be sure that we didn't miss anyone who might have come looking for either of us while we were gone?"

"Um, all right," he said, and he walked off at once for the farmhouse.

I kicked at the dirt while he was gone, too nervous to even take the riding equipment off of the horses. I tried to calm myself with reassuring thoughts. William Knight would not come that day to ride one of his horses. He hadn't come at all the entire time I had been staying at the farm. Why would he come this day?

In what seemed like ages, Thomas returned to me at the stable.

"No one came for us or left any messages. What's wrong, Louisa?" he asked, taking me in his arms where I quaked like a dead leaf dangling from a tree in the wind.

"I can't tell you now. I will later," I said, wishing I could tell him everything right then. No other part of my life was off limits to him any longer, and keeping this single secret, even if just for one more day, felt sickening and unnatural.

I stayed upstairs in the stable's loft, pretending to rest after a long night while Thomas tended to the horses. I tried to recapture the confidence I had felt in discovering that William Knight never took an interest in his horses. But so many things had changed both within myself and with Thomas that risking his life for such a shallow, unimportant reason, regardless of the level of the actual risk, now seemed completely detestable.

I watched the sun crawl back down toward the horizon. Perhaps only an hour or so of light until darkness would arrive, and William Knight surely wouldn't wish to come then. So with the danger all but past, I climbed downstairs and walked outside, shaking now from a weakness that had come upon me during my hours of isolation.

Thomas was sitting against the side of the stable opposite the forest while the horses frolicked in the field around him. I focused on his face as I walked toward him, examining his healthy skin tone.

Looking up at me, a smile touched his lips. "Feeling better?" he asked.

"Perhaps," I said, and I casually raised my head to look in the direction of the city, invisible as it was from this location. I stopped then, frozen in my tracks. In the distance, a man and woman were walking toward us, dressed as if they were ready for a fabulous night out on the town, stumbling a little.

Thomas followed my gaze. "That isn't William Knight, is it?" he asked, squinting in the direction of the couple. As they grew closer, we could hear them laughing too loudly, clinging to each other in a ridiculous way. "Well, I believe it is. What are the chances of him coming to visit?"

My lips were dry. I tried to swallow, but couldn't.

"Are you all right?" Thomas asked. He was looking at me, and he suddenly moved to me swiftly and grabbed my arms in order to keep me from falling. I felt so dizzy. I could not believe what was happening.

Before I could respond to Thomas, I heard William Knight's voice call out loudly. "Thomas, is that you? I've come with Melanie to ride my horses!"

I had to act fast. I didn't even look in William's direction any longer as I grabbed Thomas and pulled him inside the barn where I shut the door behind us with a force that made the door shake violently.

"What's going on?" Thomas asked me, his eyes wide.

Practically slamming him against the closed stable door in my terror, I whispered with increasing volume and speed, "I must tell you something right this second! I made a bet with this—this creature or demon or something. In the woods, south of Mrs. White's house. Ask Mr. Graham about it. But know this. This demon makes bets with people. The cost is a life if you lose. I made one before, betting Mrs. White's life for the reward of being able to sing." Thomas's eyes were popping and his mouth was open. I continued, "I won the bet, and so Mrs. White lived and I could sing. I made another bet, though. I wanted to be beautiful. The cost was your life if I lost. I would lose by William Knight coming to ride a horse on the fourteenth of September, and that is today. Because he is here, you would die. Unless I were to tell you of everything before the bet was complete. Then I would die." As I spoke, I felt a dull pain spread from my head to my feet.

"What are you talking about?" Thomas asked, grabbing my arms tightly and wildly.

Outside of the barn, William Knight was finally within polite talking distance. "Thomas, are you in there with a girl?" William asked while Melanie giggled annoyingly by his side.

Thomas acted as if no one were there. "Louisa, you're just sick is all. Had a bad dream," he spoke urgently to me as I felt myself lose my strength. He helped me crumple gently to the floor.

"No, it's true. I was beyond selfish, and my only hope was in things. You've taught me that that's not all that matters," I said, and as I did so, my eyesight began to fade as I tried in vain to focus on Thomas. My voice sounded hoarse when I spoke next. "Thomas, you've changed my life. I'm so sorry that I've messed everything up in the end. I could not let you die for me, though, so I had to tell you the truth. I am so sorry."

"Stop it. I'll go find a doctor," he said, and he went to stand up. With the last bit of strength I had, I held onto his arms and kept him near to me.

"No time," I said. Then, as I could feel my heart slow and life stop racing through my body, I whispered, "I love you."

"I love you too," Thomas said, his voice broken. And the last thing I felt before I died was Thomas's tender hand caressing my cheek.

Chapter Nineteen

My body died, but my soul did not. It was as if it knew, or perhaps more accurately it was told, that I wasn't going anywhere just yet. And so I remained for a time where time did not exist. There was nothing to recall, and yet there was no overwhelming blackness. This is not to say that more does not exist after death, but merely that I could not yet be a part of it.

As time did not exist, I simultaneously waited forever and not at all during the period that my earthly life faded and then reappeared.

The first of my five senses to return was touch. I expected to feel the familiar jabbing of straw beneath my back, but instead it felt as if I were lying on a sponge. A cool, soft sponge. Grass and moss, I slowly determined. I became aware of my limbs lying next to my sides in a peaceful resting pose, my mouth shut, but not too tight. I then noticed a chilly breeze moving the strands of my hair. I could hear it too. The soft sound of wind playing with the slightly dying leaves of trees. And water. Not a large, roaring body of it, but the slight clunks of movement in a pond, the noises caused by lively bugs and acorns falling into it from branches above.

My breathing was light, for I did not yet feel the need to inhale deeply. As I gently inhaled and exhaled, though, I caught the living smells of the greenery of a forest and the earthy scent of leaves and twigs accumulated on the ground. Finally, I breathed in deeper, taking in even more scents of a forest as I began to open my eyes. Everything was blurry at first, a ruined watercolor of green and tan and brown. Then, as opposed to seeing what was directly in front of my face, the background came into focus at an excruciatingly slow speed. I saw green feathers swaying above me. I thought of the bright green plumage of Mr. Graham's Elbert immediately. The feathers continued to gain definition as I stared. The feathers turned into leaves, the leaves of a willow tree. And then I saw that the tan and brown blob directly in front of my face was a person peering down at me. My heart jumped with joy as the memory of my death came back to me in full force.

"Thomas," I murmured, my mouth dry like cotton.

"No, it's me," a melodic man's voice responded.

Dark brown hair, darker than Thomas's, and intense dark eyes came into focus, surrounded by healthy, flawless skin. "William Knight?" I whispered, confused.

"Yes," William Knight said triumphantly, taking my shoulders and jerking me to a sitting position. "I am so pleased to see that you are all right."

My head spun with the rapid change in position, and I could feel blood coursing through my body. "What happened? Where is Thomas?" I asked, looking around as quickly as my body would allow before becoming too dizzy. I was in the woods south of Mrs. White's house, under the willow tree and next to the pond that was located directly outside of the demon's cave. Shivering all over as I saw it, I actually began to cry.

"Don't cry," William Knight said, sounding extremely uncomfortable by my show of emotions. "I'll explain everything," he continued, regaining some of the confident control that he almost always showed. "When I arrived at the barn yesterday, I saw you inside—dead."

"That all just happened *yesterday*?"

"Yes. Anyway, Thomas repeated what you had told him right before you died. He was skeptical, but as they were your dying words, I thought we should look into them. So, I picked up your body and took you to Mr. Graham's residence as fast as my horse would move. Thomas came along too. It was horrible, riding with you cold to the touch upon my lap the whole way there. By the time we reached Mr. Graham's, it was very late. We laid you in the parlor with us while we talked to him about the demon you had mentioned.

"As Mr. Graham talked, Thomas seemed increasingly nervous and upset. After Mr. Graham fully explained everything to us and told us where we could find the demon, we set out at once. It was on the way here that Thomas lost complete control of himself."

"What do you mean?" I asked slowly.

"I do believe the poor man went insane," William Knight said, looking pained as he spoke. "I tried to talk with him, comfort him, but all of a sudden he refused to talk. I begged him to say a word to me, but he pointed to his throat and shook his head no. I asked him if he were sick, and he just stared at me with his eyes practically popping out of his head as he refused to make a sound. Finally, after I pleaded with him for

124

almost an hour, he just shook his head like a maniac before he forced his horse to run off into the forest."

"What?" I shrieked. "You must be lying!"

"No, no, no. Calm down, Louisa," William Knight said, actually pressing me back into the grass. "Rest for a minute."

I turned over onto my stomach, away from the man before me as I cried and punched the cushioned ground of wet grass and moss. "It cannot be true."

"It is, my poor, dear Louisa," William Knight said quietly.

I cried until I had no more tears. How could Thomas go insane? It didn't make sense. It made sense that he might try to seek out the demon, but to just leave me with William Knight before he even made it to the cave? And yet, he truly wasn't in the woods with me, but William Knight was. If Thomas were not insane, would he not surely be here with me?

Finally, I threw myself onto my back again, staring up at a patiently waiting William Knight. "What happened next?" I whispered miserably.

William Knight smiled. "I wanted to bring you back to life. I was not about to make a deal with a…with a devil. Especially if it would mean risking another's life. So, I went in there with nothing but a small knife. And I walked to the right."

"You didn't!" I exclaimed, sitting bolt upright. "But I thought he kills people if they walk the wrong way."

"Not if you can kill him first," he said, and he pulled a small knife out of his interior coat pocket. The knife had semi-dried blood still clinging to its blade.

"How?" I asked. Though of course I had never seen the demon, I knew the weight of his incredible power. I could remember the stench of his breath and the smothering feel of his presence.

"I must have taken him unawares, for I merely raced ahead with my knife out in front of me and struck him. He let out a horrible yell. I stabbed again and again," William Knight said, the heat rising to his cheeks as he told his story. "He bit at me. Oh, he didn't go down without a fight, but I dodged him, and in the end, I was victorious. Once I was sure he was dead, I raced out to your body. I don't know why, but I had a feeling that if I were to kill the demon, you might live again once more. And sure enough! As I leaned over you, the color returned to your face and you began to breathe again. Your breath was almost imperceptible at first, but you seemed to become more alive by the second until you eventually opened your eyes, and I knew that you were going to be all right!"

I was struck speechless. I knew that I should have perhaps thrown my arms around my rescuer in thankfulness, weeping tears of joy. Instead my mouth hung open dumbly. What was life without Thomas? What did it matter that I was alive once more if the person to thank was not the young man who had managed to change my entire outlook on life in just a few weeks?"

"Thank you," I finally pushed out.

"You are very welcome," he said. He then took me by the arms as he helped me up off the ground. "Come back to my house with me."

I rode to the Knights' estate, my arms wrapped around William Knight's middle as we made our way there together on his horse. I sourly thought about how less than a month ago if I had been told that William Knight would not only save my life, but whisk me away on his horse like a brave knight in shining armor, I would have fainted from pure elation. Now, though, the whole experience was a meaningless blur.

I don't really remember arriving at the Knights'. Much less do I remember how I ended up sitting in the parlor with a blanket wrapped around my shoulders and a cup of tea in my hands. I was in too much emotional turmoil and distress to pay much attention to anything.

I went over the facts again and again and again. And each time I could not account for Thomas's absence unless I chose to believe William Knight. The only other thing I even considered was that William had somehow harmed Thomas, but why would he do that? The last I had seen William Knight, he had had Melanie Burges glued to his arm. I could see no reason that he would want Thomas out of the way so that he could have me all to himself.

The sun was setting outside the parlor window. I was alone in the room. William had gone upstairs to take a nap while his parents stayed well out of my way, allowing me some silence with which to recuperate. William had told them I had been very ill; I supposed he thought the truth would be too unbelievable.

As the top of the sun dipped below the trees, there was a loud knock on the front door. From my position within the parlor, in the very corner of the room, I had no view of the front door. However, I could hear a timid maid answer and an equally as timid man ask for Mr. William Knight. In a few minutes, I heard William's ever smooth voice as he stepped with authority into his family's foyer.

"Yes, sir?"

"Hello, Mr. Knight. My name is George Perkins. I work for the attorneys Smith and Brown in Philadelphia."

"Oh, yes. I've heard of them, though my mentor, Mr. George Hall, has not yet had the chance to introduce me to Mr. Smith and Mr. Brown."

"Yes. Well, I come to you today on a strange piece of business," Mr. Perkins continued. He sounded like a tiny man, and I wondered if he were intimidated by William Knight's strong presence.

"This arrived today for a Miss Louisa West. The outer note, as you can see, said that she might be found at the Knight Estate," Mr. Perkins said.

"Yes. She is here. Do you need to see her? I must warn you that she has been very ill and is not really in the mood to accept visitors unless absolutely necessary."

"Oh, no. That is fine. Eventually, she will need to come by the offices in Philadelphia and sign some papers, but for now I am just delivering this piece of news. She may read it at her leisure, and if there are any questions, please feel free to send a note to our offices."

"Thank you," William Knight said, and I heard the door shut as the presumably small Mr. Perkins left.

I was sitting in the dark, the maids having even kept their distance from me.

William Knight poked his head into the dark room, saw me in the corner, and then backed out again. He returned in a minute with a maid who scuttled over to the fireplace and began lighting it as quickly as possible. She looked shaken, even in the dark shadows of the parlor, and I wondered if she had been scolded for neglecting the room.

Only after the fire was fully lit and the maid had left did William Knight walk into the room and sit in the chair across from me, close to the fire.

"How are you feeling, Miss West?" he asked formally.

I simply shrugged in response, my shoulders feeling heavy with not only the warm blanket wrapped tightly around my body, but with the depressing reality of my life.

Without another word, William Knight tore open the large envelope in his hands. Inside the envelope, he pulled out yet another envelope. From inside of this, he withdrew a letter, the stiff paper bent in several places.

William Knight's face was serious at first as he read, but the longer he stared at the letter, the more he began to smile. A minute later, he set the letter down on his lap as he stared into my face, beaming.

"Do you want to know what this is?" he asked, excitement breaking through his voice.

"What?" I asked, not exactly interested, but attempting to be polite.

"A letter from your mother and father."

I grew slightly curious, though I knew that it must be a mistake. "That cannot be. My mother and father died some years ago."

"Not years ago. But let me reiterate. This letter is from your *true* mother and father."

"I knew my *true* mother and father, and I can assure you that they have both died."

"You did not know your true mother and father according to this letter." He did not hand it to me, for he was obviously taking great joy in parceling out the details one by one as little treats. "You were stolen from your real parents when you were just a baby by a poor couple. The people you called mother and father had kidnapped you, hoping for ransom. While we might never know exactly why," he continued, fingering the paper as if he might discover more information, "it appears that they never wrote for the ransom. Your parents had contacted the authorities, it seems, and your fake parents may have been afraid of being caught if they risked reaching out for the money."

I thought, now, how could this be? I even looked like my mother. Still, keeping me for ransom in the hope of obtaining money did sound like the kind of desperate measures my parents might have gone to if they had had the opportunity. They longed for money, but there was never any way to possess more of it.

"Still, you are correct in that your parents are dead," William Knight continued. "Even your real parents just recently died according to this letter. Their attorney has forwarded it in a last attempt to find you."

"So, what does any of this mean?" I asked skeptically.

"It means that you inherit their entire fortune, and the good name that comes along with it."

"And what is that inheritance and name?"

"From what I can tell, you will receive a large house in Philadelphia. It appears that they never lived there, but they merely used it for vacations. Their main house was located in Boston. However, that one was sold by their lawyers after their deaths—caused by an illness—before instructions about you were discovered. All of the money made by the sale of their estate and belongings will also go to you and will be left in the house in Philadelphia. That house also comes fully furnished."

"Wonderful," I said flatly.

"You can sound a bit more excited!" William Knight exclaimed. "You must be the luckiest lady in the world. First, you escape death, and then you find out that you are an incredibly rich heir! Speaking of which, your new name is Miss Catherine Collins."

"Even my first name is different?"

"Why, yes. Apparently your fake parents changed your name entirely in order to keep you hidden. The letter was very clear, though, that they just discovered somehow that Miss Louisa West was the false name of their dearest Catherine."

"I see."

"That's really much better," William Knight continued. "Catherine is a name that speaks of class. Louisa is so...ordinary."

"You're not really thinking of calling me Catherine?" I asked, peeling the blanket away from my warm arms, but allowing it to remain wrapped around my legs.

"Why not? It is your real name."

"Perhaps, but it is not the name that I've used for all of my life."

"Yes, but don't you want to embrace who you actually are?" William stood from his chair, throwing the letter behind him and into the seat cushion. He actually sat up on his knees in front of me as he held my hands and spoke earnestly to me. "Louisa West the maid is not who you are. You are Miss Catherine Collins, a great lady with enough wealth to control the city if you wanted. You can afford whatever dresses you like. Your singing can be a talent that only further impresses those you will come in contact with, but it will no longer be a necessary avenue to wealth. All other women will be jealous of you, and they will not be able to compete. Think of the parties you will be able to throw. Everyone will like you, and you'll never hear the word 'no' ever again."

It was everything I had ever wanted. And yet, "I do not desire those things any longer."

"How can you not?" he shouted, more shocked than angry.

I silently sat with my blanket, staring vacantly down at his hands holding mine. Finally, he asked, "What could you *possibly* desire more than what I just told you that you now have? You can literally have *anything* now."

"I cannot have Thomas," I answered.

"My servant?" he shouted once more, and I met his eyes bravely as I nodded yes. "How on earth can you desire my *servant* more than what I have just offered you?"

"He was wonderful. I fell in love with him," I said quietly, though clearly.

As he kept his eyes on mine, William Knight looked as if he were about to be sick. His face turned a pale gray color for a moment as he ran his tongue over his lips. "What is it that you think Thomas has?" he croaked out.

"Kindness, patience, love—," and he cut me off.

"I can offer you those things too," William Knight stated emphatically.

I actually withdrew my hands from his. What was he saying? Obviously he now wanted me, but why? Had he always been interested in me? Was he simply filled with jealousy that I could love his servant and not him? Did he only want my miraculous and unbelievable newly discovered wealth?

William Knight dropped his head for a moment and took a deep breath, his shoulders quivering slightly with the task. He then looked up and cupped my cheeks with his hands. "Louisa," he began with every impression of sincerity, "it is time to be honest with yourself. You died." He let those words sink in for a moment, and I shivered despite the blanket. "However, because I have found you to be so incredibly...wonderful...I risked my own life to win back yours. Now, Thomas was not able to be there for you; he wasn't strong enough. And so he is gone. He is no longer an option for you. He does not possess a stable mind any longer. And so you must let him go. Or are you going to waste the life that I won back for you by pining over an ordinary servant who gave up when we were so close to rescuing you?"

The tears started without my being ready for them. They poured from my eyes as I whimpered in sadness. I then found myself in the embrace of William Knight without even remembering who first reached out for whom. I wanted to be comforted, though I felt that I would never be happy again. How could I lose Thomas? Still, I felt a heavy sense of duty to live for the sake of the man who had rescued me.

"Tomorrow we shall see the lawyer, and it will be the beginning of your new, empowered life," William Knight whispered in my ear as the fire crackled beside us.

Chapter Twenty

"And here is the key," the attorney, Mr. Smith, said, handing it to William Knight who was standing next to me. It was only the day after I had come back to life, and I had just finished signing the necessary papers in Philadelphia in order to claim my inheritance.

"Thank you, Mr. Smith," William Knight said, and he whisked me out of the room and into the warm and breezy early fall day.

William Knight's carriage was waiting for us outside the attorneys' offices. I kept hoping that I would see Thomas driving the carriage, but of course it was a different servant. William Knight gave this servant instructions on finding the house I had inherited, and as soon as we were seated inside the carriage, it took off.

"Aren't you excited to see your new house?" William Knight asked me. Then, before I could answer, "You will have to throw a party there as soon as you feel able. You should invite dear old Mrs. White too. I have sent her word as to your new status and success, by the way."

"Thank you," I mumbled, and I stared out the window.

It took us twenty minutes to reach my new house, formally named Pleasant Hill. It was well within city borders, but in a strictly residential area. As the carriage pulled down the semi-circular driveway, I stared at the ivy climbing up one side of the all-brick house. It was located somewhat close to the neighboring houses, but it was at least double the size of them. Compared to Mrs. White's, the house was only slightly larger, though its size was much more impressive as it was located within the city. In opposition to its name, it was not situated on top of a hill at all, and while it was incredibly stately, it did not have a homey or pleasant quality as far as I could tell from the outside.

William Knight descended from the carriage first and then offered me his hand. I took it, my interest in this new house finally piqued ever so slightly as I stared at its intimidating exterior.

"Well, Miss Collins, what do you think?" William Knight asked, and I cringed as I remembered that he had insisted that I begin using my newer, more respectable name.

"It's very lovely," I said quietly, and William Knight raced toward the front door, still holding my arm, and so I was forced to run to keep up with him.

At the large, wooden double doors, William Knight stopped and took out the key. He unlocked and opened the doors with a great deal of dramatic flair.

I had not really given any thought to the house, so it would seem as if I would not have had any met or failed expectations. However, the sight before us was so absolutely unbelievable that my mouth dropped open in awe. The walls of the foyer were covered with what appeared to be actual gold. Rubies were embedded in the chair rail, and emeralds stood out in the border surrounding the tray ceiling.

We stood in the open doorframe for a good five minutes before either of us spoke. Finally looking at each other, William Knight grabbed both of my hands and said, "Welcome home."

"Thank you," I dazedly replied, and he gallantly escorted me through the rest of the house, each room proving to be more elaborate than the previous.

There was an art room, filled with works by famous artists whom William Knight had heard of. The dining room contained place settings made of gold displayed on a table with intricate, carved vines growing up the legs. The master bedroom contained a golden, four-poster bed with silk and velvet sheets without a speck of dust on them. The fireplace in the bedroom was surrounded by large sapphires, which would surely sparkle in the firelight. The incredibly spacious ballroom, appearing even larger than Mrs. White's, had a piano with smooth and graceful curves. The solid gold walls were enhanced by bright red, lace curtains and impressive, fist-sized rubies cut into diamond shapes and set in the wall between each of the many windows.

Finally finishing with the supersized parlor, I was at first confused by the untidy appearance of the room. There were so many boxes piled inside that it was almost impossible to tell what the actual space looked like. Moving over to one of the boxes, I lifted the already unfastened lid off. Inside, the box was filled with hundreds of gold coins. I opened another box and found the same thing. I opened more and more, becoming dizzy by the sheer amount of money around me. Finally, after the twelfth box, I found something different—seemingly irreplaceable artifacts. One impressively large ruby ring was labeled as having belonged to Queen Elizabeth of England. A diamond necklace was attributed to some royal lady of France whom I was not familiar with. There was a jewelry box filled with pearls, labeled as those of some duchess from the 1700s.

To my right, William Knight was finding similar items in another box. He held a ring in his hand with a stone large enough to sink a person if they were to wear it while swimming. "This is all too incredible for words. Not only is the house absolutely…breathtaking…but there is enough money and items of worth in this one room to live wildly rich for the span of many lifetimes." He had said this all directly to the ring he was holding, but as he finished he turned toward me.

He held out a note in his other hand. "This was with the ring," he said, and I thought I actually saw tears in his eyes.

The note was yellowed just slightly with age. Upon examination, the date explained its weathered appearance, as it had been written almost twenty years before, in 1837.

For our dearest Catherine. Your great-grandmother's wedding ring. To be worn by you once you find a husband, if you so desire.

The cursive was fine, much nicer than any script I could have even attempted to emulate.

As I finished reading the note, William Knight sank down to one knee, still holding the huge ring in his hand. As he held it out to me and spoke, my heart raced. "Miss Catherine Collins, I know I have not known you as long as some couples have known each other. But in the time that I have known you, you have captured my attention through the sweet melodies of your voice and then through the strength of your personality. These things caused me to fight for you, and now I ask that you do me the honor of marrying me and becoming Mrs. William Knight."

My heart continued to beat wildly, and I knew not at first if it was out of fear or excitement. "I—," I began, and my mind raced to Thomas. Everything had only just happened! I had just lost him, even though I had hoped to spare him by giving myself up to death. Now, all I could see was his face!

"Yes," I finally spoke out of the pit of despair. What other option did I have? With Thomas gone, William Knight was a respectable match, and I had, after all, at one time been enamored by him.

"Perfect!" William Knight exclaimed brightly in sharp contrast to the shadowed and cramped parlor in which we stood. He slid the ring onto my finger, and I could not help but notice that it fit perfectly.

At first glance, I had thought that the stone that the ring contained was a sapphire. But upon closer inspection, the knuckle-sized stone glinted in a different fashion—it was a rare blue diamond.

"I am so happy," William Knight said, pulling my dressed hand away from me and kissing it.

I could not truthfully say that I felt the same way, and so I simply tried my best to smile at my new fiancé.

"We shall be married in the spring," he continued. "How about the month of May?"

"Sounds wonderful," I said, and my voice sounded hollow, at least to my own ears. Thankfully, my newly betrothed did not seem to notice as he scanned the room, his smile stretched wide.

"You shall have lots of planning to do, my dear. Tonight, for now, let us go out into the city and celebrate!" he exclaimed.

"Sounds wonderful, Mr.—um…may I simply call you William now?" I asked, as I had always respectfully referred to the young man as Mr. Knight when addressing him.

"At least in private, yes," he said, and we walked out of my new residence.

Chapter Twenty-One

As September came to a close, I was amazed at how I had already spent my time as the soon-to-be Mrs. William Knight. I was honored at a party or large social gathering literally every night. I tasted some of the finest food surely created in the world—sweets that looked as wonderful as they tasted, meats that seemed to melt in my mouth, and fine cheeses that I struggled to acquire a taste for. Somehow, I captured the attention of even more men than I had while I was simply Miss Louisa West, the singer. I was asked to dance by nearly everyone, and I mindlessly obliged despite the increasing size of my dress skirts.

I spent some of my days shopping. I bought gorgeous dresses that made me appear as if I had the most petite waist. There was a forest green one that was shockingly low cut with a striking lace overlay, a rose colored one with ruffles on the off-the-shoulder sleeves, and a tight, everyday yellow one with ivory buttons up the front. I very quickly came to own as many dresses as Mrs. White had, including those she would never fit in again that were kept in trunks.

When I wasn't shopping, I wrote letters to my kind party hosts, and occasionally I read books that I had bought. Reading, though, often depressed me, as I thought of one of the first conversations I had ever had with Thomas about which subjects I most enjoyed reading.

Even though my house was in Philadelphia, I had a large backyard, complete with very tall evergreen trees lining the perimeter. There was also a small stable and carriage house out back, and pansies lined a circular, brick patio directly outside my back door. I did not like to spend much time out there, though, for the clouds all seemed to take on fantastical shapes when I looked at them anymore; the memory of picking out animals from them with Thomas was still far too painful.

In order to avoid painful memories as much as I could, I spent a large portion of my time simply examining my new house. William had set to the task of hiring maids and servants for Pleasant Hill immediately, and so I now had a stable boy, a cook, and five maids. Since I had nothing to clean, I would simply walk from room to room, examining the details of wealth.

Although I had everything I could have ever asked for, materialistically speaking, of course, I walked through life in a haze for the most part. I longed to see Thomas, crazy or not, and then on the first night of October, my wish was fulfilled.

There was no fire in my bedroom fireplace that night, and I slept in the middle of the majestic bed, knowing that I would have to share the space with William come spring. I left the curtains to my bedroom window open. If I had been looking directly out of it, I would have had an almost centered view of my backyard. As I was reclined, though, the only thing I saw was the moon, perfectly round and washing me in cool, blue light.

Though the moonlight unfortunately reminded me of my time outdoors with Thomas, I could not bring myself to shut it out. As I continued to stare, then, I thought I heard a faint noise, like something had hit the side of my house. I brushed it off, too sad to force myself to investigate. A minute later, though, I was shocked into action as the dark silhouette of a man's head appeared at my second-story bedroom window. I strangled off a scream, however, for even backlit as he was, I immediately recognized Thomas. My feet barely hit the floor before I reached the window.

As my windows opened outward, I signaled for Thomas to step down a bit before throwing it open for him. As soon as it was opened, Thomas bounded up the last couple of ladder rungs and into my bedroom.

Before either of us spoke a word, he grabbed my face and brought my mouth to his. I started crying as we kissed, completely overwhelmed with emotion. My face was wet as it brushed up against his, and I wondered if he were crying too.

A minute later, forcing myself away from him so that we could talk, I asked, "What happened?"

But Thomas didn't answer. Still only lit by moonlight, the shadows on his face changed as he flinched. He then lifted his right hand and, seemingly with a great deal of embarrassment, pointed to his throat and shook his head.

"What do you mean?" I asked, beginning to tremble out of concern as opposed to pure joy. "You really cannot talk?"

He shook his head again, and went to embrace me. I hugged him, but continued to quake. William had told me that Thomas had lost his mind along with his ability to speak. So William had indeed told the truth about Thomas's voice. Could Thomas mean me harm then? Of course not—that was silly, I immediately tried to tell myself.

While I fearfully and ashamedly went over what William had told me in conjunction with the evidence that Thomas could truthfully not speak, my bedroom door burst open and additional light entered my room from the candles lit in the hall. Standing in the open doorway was William, rage painted clearly on his face. At the sudden noise of my door being opened, Thomas and I had sprung apart. Still, seeing Thomas in my room, William ran at him, his fist cocked. Thomas did not have time to prepare an attack of his own before William swung at his head, situated slightly above his own. Thomas managed to dodge this first swing as William screamed, "Out of my house, you lunatic!"

Thomas stole a glance at me while I fearfully watched from in front of the side of my bed. Thomas cocked his own first then, prepared to hammer William. I had complete confidence that Thomas would win, being more physically intimidating than William, and that is when I screamed, "Wait!"

Thomas did not throw his punch, but instead used his right arm to partially block one issued by William. "Wait!" I screamed again.

William backed up a step, but he did not look at me while he yelled, "This man is crazy now! He is here to hurt you!" And then to Thomas, "Now leave and never come back or I will call the authorities and have you arrested for trespassing!"

Thomas glanced at me one more time. I looked for a sign of mental instability in his eyes, but saw only a deep sadness. Still, I found that my mouth was dry and I felt choked, and as I did not speak, Thomas turned and quickly climbed out of my window and down the ladder. William watched him depart. He must have only turned toward me once he was satisfied that Thomas had indeed gone.

"What were you thinking?" William finally spat, racing toward me with his hand open. The stinging slap that I received actually did little to shock me further, emotionally stretched as I was. "Answer me! What were you thinking?" he demanded again, raising his voice even louder.

"What do you mean?" I asked. My eyes had been looking at his own while he spoke, but they had not actually been focused on them. At this point, I allowed them to actually see what was in front of me, and I did not like it one bit. William's dark eyes were piercingly black, and for a split second, I fancied that I was staring into the eyes of the now-dead monster from the cave.

"I mean what do you think you were doing, letting a crazy man into your bedroom?"

"It was Thomas!" I cried.

"And he is insane, or do you not believe me?" he shouted. "You saw, he could not talk, could he?"

My cheeks were soaked with tears, and I shamefully shook my head no.

"So you see how very foolish you were. And plus, *I* am your fiancé. Stop thinking about another man! It is not only improper, but it is insulting and sinful. If you are going to behave in this way, I was better off leaving you dead!"

With that, he stomped over to the window and locked it before leaving my bedroom and slamming the door shut behind him.

My body continued to shake as if I were freezing to death. I did not move for a long time, standing in front of my bed. Tears rushed down my cheeks and onto my nightgown.

I could not believe that it was true. Thomas had been in the room with me, so he was indeed alive. And yet, he could not speak to me. Perhaps it was an illness, I thought. But then, what illness would cause one to become mute in the space of a heartbeat without any other symptoms—unless it really was a condition of the brain. William had to be correct, and I grew angry at the thought. The way William had looked at me with those cold eyes. There was anger, but also perhaps something else. Jealousy? I supposed he was not used to struggling for a woman's affections against another man. Still, he was my fiancé now, and so he was right to refer to my actions as insulting and sinful. I felt dirty, but at the same time I longed for Thomas's embrace again, even though he did not seem to be the same Thomas I had known.

My mind continued to swirl in this loop of logic for hours, until my legs shook violently and I finally allowed myself to collapse onto the bed behind me.

If only William had not been in my house at such a late hour. He was still officially living elsewhere until our wedding, though he occasionally slept in one of the other bedrooms if it was late and he was already at the house or in the area.

I did not sleep the entire night. I did not move either, remaining on top of my sheets where I had collapsed backward onto them. My eyes felt puffy and dry after draining my body of tears. Finally, the sun climbed above the horizon, and I sat up.

Walking to my window, I touched the chilled glass and looked below. At first I jumped because I thought that Thomas was below once more, but then I realized that it was a different man, marching around my house.

I threw on a house coat and stepped outside of my bedroom. At this early hour, I was surprised to see that William was also already up and fully dressed, sitting in the parlor with a plate of eggs. "Good morning, Catherine," he spoke pleasantly, no sign of puffiness in his own eyes.

"Good morning, William," I said flatly.

"Please, take a seat," he offered me.

After our initial discovery of the boxes of wealth and valuables, they had been moved to various locations for safekeeping or display, and so the parlor was once again a parlor. The furniture that had been hidden amongst the boxes was very exotic in appearance, and it looked to be from Asia with a satin design featuring storks. The walls were painted a bright teal, like the color of the furniture, making the gold fireplace inlaid with pearls stand out. William was sitting on the sofa, which directly faced the lit fireplace. I chose the adjacent loveseat.

"Catherine," he began calmly, "I would like to put last night's traumatizing events behind us." He paused, and I did not react. "As you could see for yourself, Thomas is not the man he once…might have been."

I frowned as I picked up on the fact that William could not even say "the man he once was," for that would be as if he were confirming that Thomas was once a fine man.

"Anyway, when I asked you to be my fiancée, you did not have to say 'yes,' and yet you did. Therefore, I ask for your respect as a husband and as your rescuer." He then drew his eyes downward as he sullenly said, "It is hurtful to me that you would leave me in a second for a mere servant."

"Tea, Miss Collins?" a servant said from behind the sofa at the parlor door.

"Yes, please," I said, sitting up straighter in order to face her.

When my eyes returned to William, he still had a sad expression glued to his face, and he remained silent so that I was forced to speak. "Very well," I finally said, lowering my own face. "I will try my best to forget Thomas."

"Wonderful," William said, brightening considerably.

"Who is the man outside?" I then questioned.

"Oh, I have simply hired a group of men to monitor the perimeter of the house to make sure that no one else tries to come in," he said.

"How long will they be here?" I asked.

"Until we are married. At that point, we will be in the same room, and I will be here to protect you."

I wondered if the men were present not only so that Thomas might no longer come into my house, but also so that I might not leave it without William finding out.

Chapter Twenty-Two

Despite my reluctant promise to try to forget Thomas, it was clear that
William was still fearful of my leaving him. I always counted at least
one man patrolling my property, and when I went on errands, a servant
or one of these patrolmen always insisted on accompanying me for
safety reasons. When visitors would call on me, I even wondered if they
were scrutinized more carefully by these guards and servants than they
otherwise might have been.

Soon, though, these tagalongs became like shadows, and as I did
not see or hear of Thomas, I came to believe that we would indeed never
see each other again.

In the beginning of December, I was preparing for an elaborate
pre-Christmas party to be thrown at my house, which would also be the
first formal gathering I would host.

The servants scurried about making sure that everything shined
and sparkled, and tantalizing aromas wafted from the kitchen. Garland
was strung around the house, adding a festive and desirable bit of life
around the inorganic stones.

As the hour of the party neared, the maids helped me into an
evergreen-colored dress with two layers of different lengths to the wide
skirt and sleeves that fell off the shoulders, bordered by lace. My coarse
hair was placed in a respectable, low bun, and a deep emerald necklace
hung around my neck.

There were two different staircases in my house. The one went
directly to the front foyer, right outside of the parlor. The other entered
the massive ballroom. And so instead of greeting my guests as they
arrived that night, I waited upstairs until after the party had begun so that
I might be introduced and make a grand entrance.

Placing my hand on the smooth banister at the top of the stairs, I
took a deep breath and slowly descended into the bustling party below.
As soon as my feet were visible, halfway down the stairs, one of my
servants loudly announced, "Miss Catherine Collins."

Everyone grew quiet, and there were murmurs of approval as I
came fully into sight. William was waiting for me below, and as he took
my hand while I was on the last step, my guests actually burst into
applause. I smiled at them, and they applauded even louder. William

then guided me to the dance floor where the band began playing and we danced amongst the other guests.

William was dressed in all black and white, and he looked quite charming, as he had when I first laid eyes on him.

After William and I danced, I spoke with many of my guests: An overly exuberant Mrs. White, who acted as if she had treated me like a daughter for most of my life instead of a servant, a kind Mr. Graham, who politely made no reference at all to my foolish bet with the demon, Melanie Burges, who barely even looked at me while I greeted her, and others from the highest society.

After milling about for a time, the moment arrived for me to sing. Prior to the party, William had requested that I do so as my voice was such a treat. I would sing one song, enough to make my voice useful, but not enough that it would seem as if I were sinking to the position of hired entertainment.

As I sang my song, I actually felt relaxed for a moment. I was the center of all of this attention, the house these guests stood in was mine, and I still had something all my own with which to impress people. Scanning the room, though, I quickly became agitated; my husband-to-be was nowhere to be seen. As I continued with my piece from an Italian opera, a sinking feeling swelled in my stomach—Melanie Burges was also nowhere to be seen.

At the end of my performance, I curtsied and hurried upstairs, mumbling to people who attempted to talk to me that I was going to lie down for just a minute as performing often made me tired.

Upstairs in my bedroom, I paced around. Where was William during my performance? He would not have been with Melanie Burges, surely. But then, confirming my sickening suspicions, I heard high-pitched giggling from my backyard. I hurried to the window and looked out. The glass was frosty at the edges, but I could still clearly see William emerging from one of the closed carriages with Melanie Burges, laughing excitedly with her arm looped tightly through his.

Anger flooded me, and my feet carried me down the staircase that led to the foyer and through the house to the back door. I arrived so quickly that they were just exiting the kitchen at the back of the house as I caught up with them. Seeing me, Melanie's eyes widened, though she still wore a triumphant smile above flushed skin. "You rat!" I shouted at William, and before I could say anything further, William clapped his hand over my mouth as Melanie disappeared back in the direction of the party.

Literally dragging me through the house, as far away from the ballroom as possible and up the front stairs, he finally pulled me into the bedroom that he occasionally used. He had kept one hand over my mouth and one arm around my waist, but as soon as he had me in the room, he let go, standing in front of the door so that I might not exit.

"What do you think you are doing? Dis—sin—dishonoring me like that in my own backyard!" I sputtered. I felt pinpricks of heat along my skin, and I bravely stepped forward and shoved my finger in William's face in accusation. He slapped it away, though, as I continued to speak. "You were with Melanie Burges while your own fiancée was inside with her guests! I should leave you right this second!" I said, and I unsuccessfully tried to push him away from the door.

Though he had remained somewhat stoical as I spoke, he finally must have decided he had had enough because he bolted into action, grabbing me by both arms, spinning me around, and slamming me up against the wall. The action startled me, and I was shocked into stillness for a moment.

"You will not leave me, you understand?" he said menacingly, and there was loathing in his eyes.

"Why not? You obviously don't want to be with me, and…and you know that I had feelings for Thomas that I will never have for you," I shot at him while I tried to twist my body free from his grasp.

"You are like dirt if you would rather have a servant over me, but you listen here. You will not leave me. I will not be disgraced in that way, especially over some lunatic who is probably sleeping somewhere in the streets if he is not dead," he growled.

"You had the audacity to sneak off with another woman on your own fiancée's property," I growled back.

"In less than half a year, thankfully, this will not be *your* property any longer as Mrs. William Knight."

My mouth fell open. "It is all for my money then," I said hoarsely.

"Well, it is certainly not for your looks."

I swallowed. He was still holding me tightly against the wall, but I was no longer struggling. "Why did you go through the trouble to bring me back to life then? I had no money at the time."

William lost his look of anger for a moment as he muttered, "Because I am a good person."

I very strongly wanted to disagree at that moment, but I remained silent.

"You need to know, you *will not* leave me, and you *will* become my wife, and we *will* live here together," he then stated firmly.

"Why don't you become Melanie Burges's husband instead?" I said, rage beginning to creep under my skin once more.

"Because she is not half as wealthy as you are. And while her looks beat yours any day of the week, her looks may fade while your money will definitely not."

"That answers it then. I am leaving you."

"You are not," he said, doubling up his grip on my arms and scaring me with his strength.

"Why not?" I attempted to ask strongly, though it came out as a whimper.

"Because I saved your life. I as good as own you now. You will not leave me out of the need to pay back that debt."

"If this is the life I will have, I would have been better off dead," I said, and he spit in my face as soon as I finished my sentence.

"If you still wish to leave me, know this. I will make your life miserable until the day you die. You forget—even though you are wealthier than I am for now, I come from a long-remembered and respected family. Miss Catherine Collins didn't even exist until a few months ago, and while perhaps she is respectable up north where her family is from, you are a blank slate down here. And I will ruin your reputation. And not only will I ruin all the happiness you could try to wrangle out of life, but I will make sure that you and that lunatic Thomas never even have the satisfaction of knowing that at least you are both alive."

By this point, I was trembling. "What do you mean by that?"

"Just know that I am a man of my word, and I will make good on that promise."

With a sudden, final jolt, he pushed me against the wall that I was already pressed against before storming out of the room.

I couldn't bring myself to return to my party, and so I sent apologies to my guests through one of my maids. I feigned a slight cold and stayed up in my room, my legs bent into my chest as I rocked myself back and forth on the floor in the corner, attempting to soothe my broken spirits and racing heart.

Chapter Twenty-Three

I simply assumed that I would never know happiness ever again. How could I? For the millionth time, I reflected that a year ago, I would have been beyond delighted if someone were to have told me that I would be the richest woman in the area with the voice of an angel and William Knight as my fiancé. I would have never been able to conceive that it would all be a miserable prison from which there was no escape.

I barely even looked at William when he was in my vicinity, let alone did I speak to the cruel man. However, he did not seem to care that I, his future wife, was giving him the cold shoulder. Rather, he simply took my emotional and social absence as permission to carry on with all the benefits of being my fiancé and yet act as if I were not even there. He was absent for long periods of time, and I would occasionally hear female voices echoing up the stairs from the parlor. Only a few days before Christmas, though, I was shocked at his blatant disrespect toward me even more so than I had been.

I was awakened early in the morning by the sound of a door upstairs being opened and hushed voices in the hall. I tiptoed from my bed and slowly and noiselessly opened my bedroom door a crack to peek out into the hallway. The room adjacent to my own was the room William used when he spent the night. And there, in the open doorway, stood William in pants and an untucked, partially unbuttoned shirt kissing a tall, slender woman with silky smooth, dark brown hair. Despite her hair's fine texture, it stood up in a few places, and a button on the front of her dress had been missed and left undone.

A fully detached part of me wondered if Melanie Burges would be outraged as the woman leaving William's temporary bedroom was most definitely not she. A more emotional part of me wanted to slink back into my room unnoticed, but I remained immobile while their lips parted and she whispered "good-bye" before lightly scampering down the steps to the foyer and out the front door.

William stayed still until the front door shut behind the young woman. He then turned and looked directly in my eyes, apparently having sensed my spying presence. I would have thought he would have been ashamed, but he did not even blink. Eventually, I was the one who moved away, shutting myself inside my bedroom for the reminder of the day.

Finally, Christmas arrived, and with it came not happiness, but a bearable atmosphere.

I exited my bedroom that morning in a plain, though finely made, red dress with gold buttons down the front. I did not expect to see anyone about the house with the exception of my servants, and so William's presence in the parlor startled me.

"Good morning, Catherine," he said, and his voice sounded strange to my ears, having not heard it in so long, let alone the soothing tones that he had kept hidden from me. Even when we had gone to others' houses during the preceding weeks, we had not spoken to each other, and so I had only heard his voice speaking to others among the constant din of a party.

"Good morning, Mr. Knight," I said.

His perfect, pale complexion showed no signs of emotional distress, as where I could feel my cheeks burning at having to speak to the man. Then, on the small table to the side of him, I noticed a wrapped gift.

As he was sitting in one of the smooth armchairs, I chose the loveseat, situated opposite him and as far away as possible. I waited for him to be the one to speak again.

He took his time bringing his tea cup to his lips and sipping from it before saying anything further. "Would you like your Christmas present?"

I remained still. "I didn't purchase you anything," I finally said.

"That is fine and expected as we have not exactly been on the best of terms. But we cannot continue to live with such an undercurrent of hostility. Please, open the gift."

Hesitantly, I stepped forward and picked up the gift. Still, I retreated to the safety of the loveseat before tearing open the wrapping. It was a small box, not much bigger than the palm of my hand, and inside there was a long pearl necklace and pearl earrings. "They are beautiful. Thank you," I stated lifelessly, and I wondered if he had bought them for me himself or if he had simply taken them from the jewelry that I had inherited.

"When I saw them in the store, I thought they would suit you," he said, seemingly reading my silent accusation.

"Thank you," I said solemnly, and we were quiet for another minute.

"Catherine—."

"Louisa," I corrected.

"No, Catherine," he counter-corrected. "Catherine, I have been thinking a great deal about our impending marriage and why we are together in the first place. Obviously our current anger is not working, so let us boil down what we expect from each other."

I was listening.

"In May, we are to be married. I will not leave you afterward and abscond with your wealth. Do you understand?"

I sat still, but continued to listen.

"Obviously, we do not love each other." I winced even though it was the truth. "However, I believe that we will still make a lovely pair. We are both from money, and the Knight name is a highly respected one for you to marry into. You have the wonderful ability to sing beautifully, which will only endear you to people further. I, on the other hand, have impressive social skills, if I do say so. So, between the two of us, we have the potential to have the perfect and jealousy-inducing social life."

I swallowed.

"Now, I expect you to at least be kind and dutiful toward me as your husband. Also, before we are married, I will be available to you as you begin to plan our wedding, which I expect you to make a lavish affair. In exchange for your obedience, I will be a good husband to you—."

"Does that mean you will give up the other women?" I cut in.

"No," he answered calmly and immediately. "I cannot give up other women, for I find true pleasure in them. However, out of respect for you and awareness for our family name, I will be beyond discreet about it. I will never again bring any women to our house, and I will have no outward sign of it shown to you."

I was biting down hard on my interior lip, and I startled myself with the taste of blood.

"However, life will be fine for you, and more comfortable than you could have ever imagined growing up. Have we come to an understanding?"

The metallic taste in my mouth was sickening, but I swallowed it expressionlessly. "We have," I answered.

"Good," he said. He then stood up, and as he began to walk out of the room he said, "If you would, I would be honored if you wear the pearls to the Christmas party at the Harmans' tonight. I am going to tell the servants to bring us some breakfast now."

He was already out of my sight and in the foyer when I called, "William."

"Yes?" he inquired pleasantly enough as he backtracked and made eye contact with me.

"Why do those other women bring you pleasure, and yet you don't seem to believe that I could be the one to bring you that pleasure?"

His mouth turned downward into a frown as he ran his eyes over me. "Quite frankly, Catherine, your physical appearance does not attract me to you. It is true that you are not ugly, but you are not of the goddess-like material that I search for in women."

He turned his back to me then, but I continued. "So, you would be happy with me if only I were beautiful?"

He turned around once more and his face spoke of him dealing with new thoughts. He brought his hand up to his chin as he stood examining me. It made me uncomfortable, and I felt the impulse to move out of his gaze, but I waited for his answer. "Yes," he finally said, a glimpse of happiness breaking through his serious demeanor. "If you were beautiful, I suppose I would be more satisfied with our pairing, and I might not need to look elsewhere, or at least as often. I—do not do anything to change your appearance, though. If it is to change, it will come about by my direction and choosing," and he left before I could say anything more to him.

Chapter Twenty-Four

Interactions between William and me were considerably more pleasant and civil after our discussion on Christmas Day. Our conversations stayed surface level, though I certainly did not have the desire to dive into our emotions and hopes and dreams. My dreams would offer William no delightful insights anyhow, as he had no part in them. Still, we were courteous and polite, and so in the middle of February, I went about the business of beginning to plan our wedding.

"So, following the wedding at the church, we will have everyone back here for lunch and then a dinner with music and dancing," I told William at the dining room table while we ate together.

He had been looking quite relaxed as he munched away, but at this sentence, his back straightened as if suddenly tied to a rod. "Music and dancing?" he asked, coughing on his food a bit.

"Yes. Is that a problem?" I asked, confused as I saw his face grow slightly pale.

"No. It is just—I did not know for sure if you wanted to make it such a long affair."

"You had told me that you wanted it to be a lavish, impressive event," I said, gently stabbing a bit of the duck we were eating that night.

"Yes. I only—you see, my dear, I know you are not as used to dancing as others, and so you are not as graceful on your feet as some."

"I believe I have done a fine job with dancing," I replied indignantly.

"Yes, yes. And if you wish to dance at our wedding, then we shall. I just do not wish for you to feel uncomfortable under such scrutiny."

"I will be fine," I insisted.

"Very well then," he said.

"Anyway, I was hoping for lilies for the flowers."

"Lilies? Why lilies?" he asked, and I thought he looked a bit pale still.

"Because I like them," I responded. And also because my preferred choice would have been white roses, but to use them for such a depressing marriage would have been a waste.

"Very well, then. And what of a bridal party?"

"I honestly believe I would prefer to have none," I answered, keeping my eyes on my plate. Out of the things I had considered thus far, this was the one part I had anticipated him having a problem with.

"No bridal party? Why on earth not?"

"Who exactly would you like to be in our bridal party? Neither of us have siblings."

"Well, no, but there is David Proctor perhaps. And his fiancée."

"You're just naming them because they are well-off."

"No. I also think they are delightful. Fine then. What about Elliott Gray? He is a kind gentleman, and not nearly as well-off as David Proctor?"

Elliott Gray. That name sounded familiar to me, and then I remembered. He had been among my original admirers immediately following the acquisition of my singing voice. I snickered into my plate.

"What are you laughing at?" William asked, annoyance creeping into his voice.

"Oh, nothing. But no. I do not believe that Elliott Gray would be a good choice as one of the groomsmen."

"All right, then." He sighed. "You really have no one you would like to be in our wedding party?"

"My closest friend was Caroline," I said after a great deal of thought.

"Caroline who?"

"Caroline Bowen."

He shoved another forkful of duck into his mouth while he contemplated the name. Only after fully swallowing did he say, "I don't believe I've ever heard of her."

"I'm sure you've seen her before. She worked with me at Mrs. White's."

"Wait. You want a *maid* to be in our wedding?" he asked. His brow furrowed and the corner of his lip inched upward in disgust.

"Not necessarily. She was simply the only person who came to mind when I tried to think of an appropriate friend."

He sighed and looked up at the ceiling. "Were you two that close to warrant even bringing up her name and embarrassing yourself?"

"Um...I suppose, truthfully, no. I mean, our personalities matched all right, and she was my friend. Though...I did not know her all that well. We never spoke of anything more than surface topics. There has really only been one…,” and I stopped, for obviously Thomas, though he was the only person I felt that I had actually known in life, could not be in our wedding. If he could, then it would no longer be a wedding between me and William Knight.

Ignoring my explanation, William finally declared, “Well, I suppose we will just have it be the two of us.”

“That is good. It will force all of the attention to be on us then,” I said, hoping that this would endear him more to the idea.

“True,” he agreed, and I saw his color finally begin to return. Perhaps he was not ready to help with wedding preparations as he had promised, I thought, since the entire discussion had been tense.

After dinner, William opted to return to his rented house that night. Whenever he left for the night, I always cynically determined that he must have had a liaison planned with another woman. I never spoke of this, though, so that peace might be maintained.

“Good night, Catherine,” he said at the front door, his coat in his hand.

“Good night, William,” I said, and he kissed me on the cheek and left.

The house seemed unusually quiet after he left, and I ashamedly realized that I actually liked having him around so that I was at least not lonely in such an intimidating house. I walked into the parlor, my feet thudding loudly as I went. Inside the room, a fire was blazing, and I pulled the armchair forward to be closer to it. Swinging my feet under me, there I sat, staring into the crackling fire, grateful for the lively noises that it made.

I had been sitting for a few minutes when I noticed the wind pick up outside. It whistled angrily, pushing at the glass windows in an attempt to slip inside. I shuddered though I was realistically quite toasty by the fire. As the wind continued to push in my direction, I noticed snow flurries begin to come down and then fall faster and faster. And as they fell, the wind took on a different tone—that of haunting sadness, like a woman whose beloved husband had just died. The cry continued, and it penetrated my very being. Meanwhile, as the snowflakes hit the heated window glass, they melted at once, forming the visible tears of the depressed widow, trickling downward in tiny rivers.

A loud and sudden knock at the front door took me completely unawares, and I actually let out a small yelp.

"Are you all right, Miss Collins?" one of the maids poked her head into the parlor before answering the door.

"Yes. It just startled me," I answered from behind my satin, cushioned refuge. I felt like a small child by my outburst, and so I was too ashamed to look in the maid's direction.

"Hello?" the maid questioned.

"Hello," a booming voice greeted her. "My name is Mr. Samuel Howe. I have come to speak with Miss Collins, though I do apologize for the late hour.

I glanced at the clock on the fireplace mantel. It was almost ten o'clock.

"Yes," the maid answered hesitantly. "And may I ask the nature of this visit?"

"I am a poet here in the city. I was told that Miss Collins is a refined woman of such beauty that I wished to merely speak with her in order to possibly obtain some…inspiration for my work. I come at this late hour simply because I find that my creative spirit is more alive at night."

"Very well," the maid said, but I was already standing up and making my way to Mr. Howe.

"Mr. Howe," I said, stepping forward to him where he took my hand and delivered a tiny kiss.

The man was simultaneously classy and wild. He had hair that fell a good half foot below his shoulders, but it appeared freshly combed and silky smooth. In contrast, the hairs from his full beard twisted and turned into each other like the vines growing up the side of my house. He was a short and stout man, like a very masculine Mrs. White. And like her, he too had a hint of jovial mischief in his eyes.

"It is a pleasure to meet you, Miss Collins."

I smiled at him. "Please, join me in the parlor," I said, and he followed me while the maid turned in the opposite direction.

I sat on the loveseat, while he took the liberty of swinging my armchair around so that it faced the loveseat directly.

"Thank you for seeing me at this late hour, Miss West," he said in hushed tones, and my heart skipped a beat before picking up its pace.

"Miss West?" I asked, placing my right hand over my heart in an effort to calm it.

"Yes, though do you prefer Miss Collins now?"

"No. I prefer Louisa West. It is the name I grew up with, and even though it seems that Catherine Collins is a truer name, I do prefer my old one."

"Well, it may not be a truer name after all."

"What do you mean?" I asked, and my heart beat faster still.

He smiled at me gently, as a grandfather might to his grandchild. "I wished to see you only after it was clear that Mr. Knight was not present and not returning. I have remained hidden near your property for a time now, keeping a lookout for the man. Then, I was interrogated as to my identity and the purpose of my visit by a gentleman guarding your house out front."

I had managed to forget about the men who still circled my house at all hours of the day and night, and so it momentarily surprised me to hear of their presence.

"And then your maid seemed a bit hesitant to let me in as well. I am of course glad that they all did, though."

"For what purpose have you come here then?" I asked. The firelight lit our sides, and though that meant that we were also partly in shadows, I felt very comfortable with my mysterious visitor.

"It is true that I am a poet," he said, and then he stopped at once as my maid entered with a tray of cookies and some tea.

"Thank you," I said to her as she politely placed them behind Mr. Howe on the small table and left the room.

"As I was saying," he continued at once, not reaching for the refreshments, "I am a poet. I primarily write of God and angels and the stories of old. However, while I am sure that you will offer me a substantial amount of inspiration as a beautiful creation of the Lord, my primary reason for being here is to act as a messenger for a promising pupil of mine."

With that, he reached into his slightly wrinkled coat and withdrew an even wrinklier letter.

The handwriting on the front of the envelope was incredibly messy. It simply read, '*To Miss Louisa West.*'

I tore open the envelope and tossed it aside, trembling as I held a lengthy letter in my hands.

My Love, Louisa,

It has taken me much time to learn to write to you, though I fear this may be my only hope at communication for the foreseeable future. As you know, I could not write, nor could I read. However, when I lost the use of my voice and could find no way to reach you without risking jail or physical harm for trespassing, which could very well result in having no chance of ever seeing you again, I went about the task of finding a writer. I managed to communicate to dear Mr. Samuel Howe that I could not speak and that I desired to learn to read and write. I practiced what he taught me during every second that I was awake so that I might communicate with you as soon as possible. I can proudly tell you that it is with my own hand that I write this to you. (Though I also must admit that this is a final draft after several with errors that were corrected by Samuel.)

Now on to the true purpose of my letter. I desired that you should know what has happened to us, at least so far as I know.

You died, and it was too awful to describe. I shudder to think of it now, and the memory of it haunts my dreams. However, I also cannot begin to explain how thankful I am, simply knowing that you are alive, even if we are not currently together.

Almost as soon as you died, William Knight burst into the stable with that woman that we saw hanging from his arm. As soon as they saw that you were not breathing, the woman screamed and fainted, so Mr. Knight preoccupied himself with tending to her while I stayed by your side, too stunned and too confused to think clearly. Finally, as the fog drifted from my mind, I sprang into action, determined to follow up on what you had so shockingly told me about the demon and Mr. Graham. With the brief description you had given me, I was already prepared to make a deal with this demon. However, I was still somewhat unsure about the terms regarding a life. And so, out of sight and earshot of his female companion, I begged William Knight to go with me. After making me repeat myself a dozen times on what you had said directly before you died, he finally agreed.

He first accompanied his female companion home, saying that you had not actually died, but that you had merely fallen ill. As soon as he returned to me at the stable, we set off with your body for Mr. Graham's house. The feeling of your lifeless body in my arms was almost too much to bear as we rode all the way there.

Upon arriving, it was very, very late, but we knocked anyway. Mr. Graham kindly met with us, still in his nightwear, for we said the matter was extremely urgent. With your body placed solemnly with us in the parlor, he told us all about his own experience with the monster, and then what he knew of your own. He said he regretted telling you, for it obviously caused both of us unspeakable misery. I then asked if he thought it was possible to make a deal to bring you back to life. He was skeptical, but said we could always ask, and we of course reserved the right to refuse the terms of the demon's bet. However, we should know that, as far as Mr. Graham was aware at least, the monster always chose another person's life as the wager. That is when I officially decided to have William Knight be the one to make the bet, with him only agreeing to use my life as the potential cost. This is the reason I had requested his company in the first place. After all, if I were to go in, I could not bring myself to use another person's life. I love you more than anyone in the world, and yet I could not play God. However, I would gladly sacrifice my own life if there was a chance that I might have you here once more.

After receiving the specific instructions about entering the cave to the left, William Knight and I left for it with you still on my lap.

We reached the cave well after the sun had already begun spreading its morning rays throughout the forest, and so the place actually looked quite peaceful. I climbed from my horse, which I had carefully directed through the woods, and gently laid you down on the moist grass under the willow tree. I stayed by your side while William Knight went into the cave. I have never prayed so hard in my life as I did while he was in there, hopefully making a deal so that your life might be restored.

He emerged about ten minutes later with a smile on his usually serious face. As he could not tell me the specifics of his deal for obvious reasons, he said that we were to simply leave your body under the willow tree and return to our day-to-day lives in the meantime. I hated to leave you there, worried that you would be attacked by wild animals, but William Knight said that the demon ensured the safety of your body in the interim. He then said that he would return to his rented house, and I headed back to the MacIntosh Farm. I flew through Philadelphia, not even looking at people for I was still so distraught even though I had some hope. Then, as soon as I reached the stable, I felt my vocal chords tighten and dry up. I went for a drink of water with which to wet them. They felt perhaps a bit moister, but when I tried to speak, nothing came out. I continued to try all day, but found that I could not make even a sound. I thought perhaps I had simply caught an unusual disease, so I tried resting my voice. But the next day, and then the day after that, I still could not speak. Mrs. MacIntosh even had a doctor in to see me, and the doctor said that I did not appear ill in any way except for the total loss of my voice. By the fifth day, this seemed more than strange, and I wondered if William Knight had been entirely trustworthy in his deal with the demon. So I rode into Philadelphia that day, planning on finding him at his temporary house there. One of his maids, whom I was of course familiar with as one of the Knights' servants, managed to understand what I was there for through my hand signals. She then told me that Mr. Knight had become engaged to a Miss Catherine Collins, a previously unheard of heiress to a fortune so huge that her worth could not even be fathomed. She told me of the place where his fiancée lived, and that was that.

Feeling quite uncomfortable about knocking on his fiancée's door looking for William Knight, especially without a voice, I returned to his rented house each day, but I never could find him. Still, as my voice did not return, I grew increasingly suspicious until I finally determined that, difficult or not, I deserved to know if this was part of a plot. And if it was part of his plot, then where were you? Or did he not even bet for your life at all? A large part of me worried that William Knight had simply lied to me, left your body for wild animals in the woods, and bet something about my voice in exchange for a fiancée richer than anyone could imagine.

When I reached the house of Miss Catherine Collins, I was shocked by the fine quality of the dwelling. This made me even surer that there was something unnatural happening. I waited at the edge of the property for a minute, trying to gather my thoughts and figure out how I was to confront a man without a voice. As I waited, a carriage pulled past me and up to the front door of the house. You were a bit of a distance away, but there was no mistaking your beautiful, healthy, and very much alive figure stepping out of the carriage, your arm resting on William Knight's.

The sight both filled me with joy at seeing you alive and sickened me at seeing you holding William Knight and not looking for me. I was so confused and overwhelmed that I did not knock on the door after all as planned. Instead, I waited out front, hoping to see you if you left the premises once more. In the afternoon, the front door did open, but only William Knight left in the carriage. I then finally decided to knock on the front door. One of the maids answered, but when she saw me and noticed that I could not speak, she shut the door in my face. I can only assume that she had been warned as to my appearance and condition.

And so I tried to think of how I might find you again. If you did not leave before nighttime, I figured you would spend the night at Miss Collins's house. Then, I would gain access to your bedroom where surely no maid would be keeping watch.

Around the back of the house, I waited, staring at the windows, hoping I might see you appear in one of them. Sure enough, I saw you, and the sight was breathtaking. You looked wonderful, just like you did before your death. However, you also looked sad, at least from the small glimpse of you I received before the light was extinguished in your room.

Quickly memorizing which window I had spotted you behind, I entered your carriage house. If you have a full-time

159

stable boy, he must have been home by that point, for I found myself alone with the horses.

Inside your carriage house, I found a ladder. I unlatched it from its spot on the wall and rushed with it to the side of the house, trying to be quiet despite my excitement. As soon as the ladder was firmly situated, I climbed up. You know the next part.

I was overjoyed to see you. That time contained the only few seconds that I did not mind my absent voice, for I could not have spoken even if I had wished to, so happy as I was. Then, when William Knight burst through the door, I was going to fight for you, as he seemed to be attempting to keep you from me. However, you yelled, "Wait," and I did not know whether that was for him or me or both of us. Therefore, I merely dodged William Knight's attack. When the man commanded me to leave, I was not going to. However, the look in your eyes at that point was unsettling. You looked almost fearfully in my direction. Since you did not protest any further, I left, wishing for you to be happy first and foremost. If I were indeed the one making you uncomfortable, then I had to leave.

Despite this depressing event, I could not simply give up on you. I went searching for answers. After reading a piece of his poetry in the newspaper, I managed to find Mr. Howe. I communicated with him at first through simple pictures that I drew, though I can definitively say that I shall never be an artist. He then began to teach me how to read and write. When I was finally able to communicate at least the basics of why I was there and what my goals were, Mr. Howe was able to help me more completely. I asked about you, and he managed to discover that, for whatever reason, my Louisa West was now known as Miss Catherine Collins and you were engaged to William Knight. I will not lie—when I heard this news, my heart broke into a million pieces and I did not remove myself from bed, even to practice writing, for several days. Finally, though, curiosity overcame my sadness, for I needed to discover why you had a different name and had agreed to marry William Knight. And so I continued to learn reading and writing so that I might write you this letter and hopefully hear a response.

I am jittery with excitement to know that I might hear from you soon, and at the same time I am terrified that my heart will once and for all be defeated. I worry that you have indeed loved William Knight all this time, or that you have been tricked into believing that I am him, or something else strange as a result of the bet. Still, you must tell me the truth and spare no detail. I await your response with love,

Thomas

The letter had large wet marks on it, for I could not hold my tears back while I read his words, ringing of truth. I wiped my eyes with my hands, my spirit filled with emotion.

Finally, I looked up and saw Mr. Howe's kind, patient eyes staring at me. "Are you all right, dear?"

"Yes," I said, smiling then, though I tasted salt water as my tears trickled into the corners of my upturned mouth. "I have so many things to tell Thomas. I must see him at once."

"What of the men patrolling your property?" Mr. Howe asked, and my smile faded somewhat. "I'm just guessing, but I believe that if you leave, they will inform Mr. Knight immediately."

I remembered all of the threats that William had promised to deliver if I were to leave him, especially for Thomas.

My smile disappeared entirely then, but my resolve did not. "Could you wait while I write a response that you can deliver to Thomas?"

"Of course," he said, and I moved over to a small desk in the very corner of the room. "As long as you don't take two full days to write one as Mr. Parks did," Mr. Howe added jovially, and I smiled once more as I lit a candle, retrieved stationery, and took a seat.

Chapter Twenty-Five

The muscles in my hand were painfully tight by the time I finished writing my letter. The fire had burned down to just embers, and I wrote primarily by the light of a large candle. Mr. Howe had stayed the entire time and was lightly dozing on the sofa.

I had drawn the curtains partway through writing my letter, and the darkness of night was heavy. Still, I guessed that it had to be incredibly late, definitely closer to morning than evening.

I picked up the several pieces of paper and read them over once more.

Dearest Thomas,

Words cannot do justice in expressing the happiness that your letter has given me.

First, let me assure you that I love you with all of my heart, though I believe we have fallen victim to a most evil plot of deceit.

I awoke in the woods, I believe, the same day that you and William reached the cave. However, when I opened my eyes, you were not around. Now I know that this is because William had tricked you into returning to the stable at MacIntosh Farm. However, William said that it was because you had gone insane on the way to the cave, overcome with grief. You lost the use of your voice, and your sanity with it. I mourned bitterly for you, and I felt unimaginable guilt that even though I had tried to save your life, in the end, I still managed to destroy it.

William Knight then told me how he had gone into the cave, not to make a deal with the monster, but to destroy it in the hope that killing the creature would restore my life. He even showed me a knife with blood on it, which he had used to kill it. The monster's death did in fact cause me to awaken—and I must say awaken, for even though I truly died, it seems my soul was simply waiting, knowing that I would open my eyes on this earth once more.

After I had recovered enough strength to move from under the willow tree—where I now know it was you who had so

162

tenderly placed me—William Knight took me back to his parents' residence where a man delivered a letter to me, explaining that I was the lost child of an unimaginably wealthy couple from Boston and that my true name is Catherine Collins. The very next day, William took me to claim my inheritance. After seeing the grandeur of the home and my new possessions (you can only imagine the sort of wealth I have been living amongst), William Knight immediately proposed. I am ashamed to say that I accepted, not out of love, but out of a sense of duty. After all, at one point I had hoped for such a proposal, and once it was upon me, I determined that since he had saved my life through a heroic and brave act, I should accept his offer to become my husband. Let me repeat that I did not and do not love William Knight, but I merely determined that if I could not have you, I could at least marry him out of respect and as a thank you for rescuing my lost life.

Though I thought that I could at least live with some minor purpose to my new life without you, I must tell you that I have been sadder than I had ever thought was possible. Even before seeing you that one night, I had no true interest in anything really. And then there was that night that I saw you. I must simply say that I am truly, truly sorry. I shouted stop for both of your sakes, unsure of whether you really had gone insane, I must regrettably admit. This lie that I have been fed, of your instability, is what caused that hesitation you spotted in my eyes. I am so sorry to have doubted you, as I should have left through that window with you.

I now say the following not so that you shall feel pity for me, but so that you will be aware of the situation so that we might, together, plan the best course of action. William Knight is a horrible and cruel man. As I write this now, I am also vaguely remembering you telling me something similar about him during our very first conversation. Anyway, it is very true. He plays games with my mind, which torment me day and night. He will act wonderfully engaging and civil toward me, only to flaunt an intimate affair with another woman right in front of my face. And while, I must admit, he has been more secretive about these affairs in the very recent past, it does not mean he has ended these sinful actions.

While I am on this topic, I need to let you know that I do not allow William Knight to kiss or touch me with the exception of a passionless kiss on the cheek, never reciprocated by my own mouth. Though I used to find him intoxicatingly handsome, I am now disgusted by his presence and the way that he so easily lies to me.

William Knight has not only used general intimidation to keep me in line, but he has threatened ruin, and even death, if I should leave him, especially for you. It is for this reason that I do not come to you this very night. If he should use his full resources, I worry that he would indeed have us hunted down out of rage. However, I cannot live without you, and so I wish to know if you have any ideas for how to pull us out of this mess. I am saddened and ashamed by the extreme task I commit to you.

I look forward to your response. It is wonderful to know that you have been working so diligently at reading and writing so that we might contact each other. And even if you never receive your voice again, I will love you just the same.

And now in closing, I cringe as I must acknowledge my most evil and selfish deed. Please, accept my sincerest apologies from a broken heart. I am sorry. And yet simply saying or writing sorry will never be enough, I know. I feel terrible, for I made such an evil deal with a demon, and I am repulsed by my own self when I consider it, which is why I try to keep it out of my consciousness as much as possible. I feel sick that I had risked Mrs. White's life over something so trivial—a singing voice. And I feel literally faint when I think of how I had risked your life in the hope of becoming beautiful just so that I might catch William Knight's eye—a man not deserving of even an ounce of my attention. As I fell in love with you, I realized how truly evil my actions had been. You showed me that the wealth and life I desired were nothing but a fleeting luxury that promised no happiness. And then the night that you first kissed me, you told me I was beautiful. And yet I had made a deal so that I might become beautiful! I felt deep regret, for I was risking your life over absolutely nothing, and it was too late to take it back. Then, even though I determined to die myself for my awful actions, I still caused you unspeakable pain and even the loss of your voice. Forgive my handwriting if it has grown slightly illegible, for I quake as I write this. I have also found myself in a loveless engagement to a horrible, manipulative man, but my pain is nothing compared to what I have done to you. And I have brought this pain on myself, after all. Thomas, please, I beg that you forgive me though my offense is so extreme. I love you, and I am sorry.

Forever in your debt,

Louisa

P.S. Thank you for still calling me Louisa, as I abhor my new name.

I wiped my tears on the sleeve of my dress as I still held the letter, wondering what Thomas's reaction might be. My wonderings finally rested on my postscript, though, and I thought of something I had written. My "new" name. I supposed that I had written something incorrect. My "new" name would be Louisa West, given to me by my false parents. However, Catherine Collins felt like my new name even though it was my old. And then I felt indeed very stupid as it hit me—I was probably truly Louisa West. Just as Thomas suspected that William Knight may have indeed made a deal with the demon to bring me back to life for his own gain and to destroy Thomas's voice in the process, perhaps my newly discovered wealth and identity were part of this monstrous deal as well. My face flushed as I felt embarrassed, even just to myself, that I had not thought of this possibility before. How could being the lost heir of an incredibly rich couple seem more probable than my life as the only child of a poor couple?

I laid the paper back down once more as I added to the bottom:

P.P.S. I feel foolish indeed, but I have just thought of a possibility. William Knight's deal might have very well included not only my life and the destruction of your voice, but my wealth. He may have seen a deal with the demon as the way to create the perfect wife—a woman whose name and wealth would allow him to live in luxury for the rest of his life without fear of ever running out of money and needing to work. And thus, I was created for his purposes. Although he is the embodiment of evil, part of me wishes that the demon were still alive so that we might ask him about the details now that the deal seems to be complete. But then again,

My pen remained poised over the paper as yet another thought occurred to me. I finally gathered the courage to write my next thought as hope filled me.

perhaps your sanity and my wealth are not the only things William Knight has lied about. Perhaps the blood on the knife was simply for show. After all, William could not have both killed the demon and at the same time made a deal with him. I will of course wait to hear from you, but maybe our next move should, instead of stealthily running away together, be to visit that horrible cave once more.

Before I could think on it further, I placed the letter in an envelope, sealed it with the Collins family wax crest, and gently awakened Mr. Howe. He pleasantly and dutifully took the letter from me, promising safe delivery over his dead body.

I watched out the front window as Mr. Howe rode off in his carriage, his progress thankfully unhindered by the hired guards.

The snow had stopped falling, but a fresh blanket of white lit up the night and reflected the moon. The world seemed to reflect my mood, a bit of bright hope in the midst of bleak darkness.

I turned around and faced the fireplace, for I had one unfortunate, painful act to perform before I could turn in for the night. I threw the envelope and Thomas's letter onto the hot embers of the dying fire, which revived the flames temporarily as the letter turned to nothing but ashes. Only after it was fully destroyed and the ashes had been broken up into tiny pieces did I walk upstairs. I felt sick at destroying Thomas's words, but it was better that I kept them in my heart than have them discovered by William Knight.

166

Chapter Twenty-Six

Although I finally fell asleep around four o'clock in the morning, I had difficulty sleeping deeply, and so I rose at six o'clock and dressed. I impatiently spent the morning attempting to read while I waited for a response from Thomas, as I now happily knew him to be all right with the exception of his voice.

Then, around noon, I heard the front door open. I raced to it, hoping that it was the delivery of a letter. Instead, it was William.

"Catherine, how are you doing today?" he said, making a show of embracing me as a couple of the maids passed us on their way up the front stairs.

"I am doing fine. And yourself?" I replied stiffly.

"Just fine," he said. He smelled of perfume, and I imagined that he wasn't lying about his "fine" state of being.

"Have you had lunch yet?" he asked.

"No."

"Good. I'll go instruct the cook," he said, and he walked toward the back of the house.

Feeling most deflated at having found the visitor to be the most dreaded possibility, I walked back into the parlor where I stared out the window. Just as I focused on the street in front of my house, though, a shabby, black carriage came into view and pulled up my driveway, after of course being interrogated by one of the guards. After it came to a stop, I was thrilled upon seeing the unusual figure of Mr. Samuel Howe emerge.

I had already opened the door for him by the time he reached it.

"It is so good to see you again," I said, my knees bouncing my body slightly in happiness.

"And you too, Miss Collins," he said as he bowed over my hand and kissed it. I wondered why he had called me Miss Collins, as he knew my real name, but my question was soon answered as I heard William's voice behind me.

"Hello," William said, waiting for an introduction.

"Mr. Knight, it is a pleasure to meet you," Mr. Howe said without skipping a beat as he stuck out his hand for William to shake. "I am Mr. Samuel Howe. Your lovely fiancée was so kind as to entertain me for a large portion of the night as I am a poet hoping to gain some inspiration from your wife's life and her new status as Miss Catherine Collins."

William was skeptical at first, but he seemed to relax as Mr. Howe continued, "She spoke quite a bit about you as well, you will be pleased to know. She seems to think you have been largely influential on her, which is quite the compliment since she is a very engaging woman."

"Well, thank you, Mr. Howe. That is very kind of you. And what brings you here this early afternoon?" William inquired pleasantly.

"I simply come with the rough draft of the poetry that has been inspired by the discussion with your wife last night. I was hoping that she might run her eyes over it so I might read her reaction to see if I truly captured the essence of her life."

"Of course," William said. "If you'll excuse me, I have some matters to attend to elsewhere, but I should like to be made aware before you depart so that I might see you off."

"Thank you," Mr. Howe said, nodding his round head as his untamed beard vibrated with the motion. As William retreated back in the direction of the kitchen, I slipped into the parlor with Mr. Howe. The second we were alone, Mr. Howe withdrew an envelope from his coat and handed it to me silently. I tore it open and soaked in Thomas's speedy reply.

Dearest Louisa,

    I am so overjoyed that everything that has happened to us since your death is not the result of our love not being strong, but rather the result of outside tampering. Although this is not an easy obstacle to overcome, I believe that together we might rise above and beyond the situation.

    I agree with your final thoughts. Everything that has happened might very well be the result of a bet made by William Knight for his own personal gain. And therefore, we must go back to see the demon ourselves, as I also suspect that he is truly alive.

    If possible, meet me at Mr. Howe's house at 52 Brook Road this afternoon. Send word with Mr. Howe if you will be able to do so. I am grateful that he is very supportive of the two of us and has already proven to be incredibly trustworthy.

With Love,
Thomas

I looked up at Mr. Howe. "This is a wonderful first draft. I agree with everything it says completely."

He caught my secret meaning and actually risked a wink at me as there were no servants in the room with us. "Thank you, Miss Collins. You are too kind."

Then, in case there were a servant about, I politely offered, "Would you like to stay for lunch or some tea?"

"Thank you, dear, but I actually must be going. Thank you for the invitation, though, and for looking over my words."

And with that, I quickly retrieved William, whom I found just about to sit down in the dining room to eat without me. The two of us bid Mr. Howe good-bye, and then I returned to the dining room with William.

Food was brought to me as well, and as I was finishing the last bites of my lunch, I told William, "I believe I'd like to go shopping for a new dress. Miss Phillips is throwing that party next month, and I do believe I have already stepped out in all of the dresses I own."

"That's fine," William said, not really paying any attention to what I was saying.

And so the next minute, I pushed my plate to the side for a servant as I stood and readied myself for a trip in the frigid cold.

A little while later, I was bouncing along the streets of Philadelphia in my carriage, heading toward a dressmaker who kept a shop in the center of the city. Upon exiting my carriage at this initial destination, I instructed my coachman to return to Pleasant Hill. I told him that I was going to meet a friend and spend the rest of the day shopping with her, and afterwards she would accompany me home in her own carriage. My coachman did not seem suspicious in the least, and instead seemed grateful that he could return to my residence and the warmth that it offered. With a brief good-bye, he took off at once while I entered the store.

After indeed being fitted for a dress, so that it might not seem too suspicious if my story's plausibility were probed, I hurried on foot to Brook Road.

Mr. Howe's residence was a good half hour walk from the dressmaker, and I could not feel my face by the time I made it there as a bit of wind had picked up.

Mr. Howe lived in a brick row home, not decrepit, but certainly not a nice one. When I knocked on his door with my half-numb hands, I was not surprised to see Mr. Howe himself answer it.

"Miss Collins, what a pleasant surprise," he said, not sounding surprised at all. "Do come in," he continued with a quick glance at the street outside.

"I come alone," I assured him as I crossed over the threshold.

Inside, I did not have a chance to focus on any of the interior of the house before my eyes met Thomas's. Like we had the night he found my bedroom, we rushed to each other, him holding my frozen cheeks in his warming hands as he bent down to me.

When we parted, I still half-expected him to speak to me, and I cried as no words came from his mouth.

"I am so sorry," I said as Mr. Howe shifted uncomfortably by his front door.

Thomas shook his head strongly, and then he turned around, grabbing a piece of paper and writing utensil from the small table located against the wall. Slowly and carefully, he wrote, "Do not apologize anymore. I forgive you and am actually proud of you for growing so much as a person. I love you."

I continued to weep as I reached for him, and he gave me a comforting hug that warmed not only my body, but my spirits.

When we parted this time, Thomas and I both turned toward Mr. Howe, who was still at the front door. "Are you two ready to leave now?" he asked kindly.

Thomas nodded his head as he stood at his full height, and I felt safe knowing that I would have such a good, brave man with me in the face of potential danger.

"Very well. I shall send my carriage around front for you," he said, and he walked toward the back of his house.

Alone with Thomas, I said, "I wish we could talk." Thomas simply held my hand and threw me an encouraging smile. Squeezing his hand lightly, I said, "It is wonderful just to be with you, though."

We waited in comfortable silence until Mr. Howe's carriage pulled up front. It was driven by a boy, bundled up from head to toe.

With Thomas's arm around me, shielding me from the cold, we stepped outside and into the carriage. It was obviously an older carriage, unfortunately drafty against the winter chill. Nonetheless, it would do for our journey to the cave.

We rode quietly and peacefully, not relinquishing the other's hand even for a moment. Though we occasionally peeped outside in order to assess our progress, most of the time our eyes were locked on each other.

After a while, as the sun was already beginning its descent, the boy stopped the carriage. We stepped outside, and I saw that we were at Geresh's Glen.

"I was told to bring you here, and that you would return to me in roughly four hours."

"Yes," I said, and I shivered against the cold.

"Very well," the boy said, and as we began walking south, he hopped into the carriage himself in an attempt to keep warm.

Thankfully, the evening had not yet seemed to sink dramatically in temperature. Also, even though the light continued to fade as we walked and the moon become increasingly brighter, the white snow that had fallen the night before seemed to serve as a natural torch to our surroundings, standing out bright against the leafless trees all around us.

We kept at a quick pace as we were on an important mission. Still, by the time we reached the cave, all of the sun's light had disappeared, and yet we found its location easily. It stood out as a dark silhouette against the glowing ground and snow-strewn tree limbs.

I turned to look at the willow tree, which had uneven lumps of snow below it that must have fallen from its delicate branches during the course of the day.

The cave mouth seemed as normal as ever. And so together, Thomas and I stepped into the dark and to the left. After carefully walking an appropriate distance, I pulled Thomas to a stop, remembering that this was his first time in the cave. I waited for the monster to walk up behind us immediately, but there was no movement.

"Just wait a minute," I whispered, standing completely still.

Several minutes passed, and there was nothing. Feeling depressingly certain that we were utterly alone, I turned around with Thomas, prepared to leave the cave. Just as I took a step forward, though, I felt the swift movement of air as the familiar, gravelly voice spoke to us, sounding almost pleasantly amused, if such a voice could contain anything resembling pleasantness. "Thought I was actually dead for a moment, did you?"

My heart jumped into my throat. Meanwhile, Thomas's hand squeezed mine so hard in reflex that it actually hurt.

"For a moment," I responded, trying to regain control of my feelings.

"Well, then, you actually believed that I could be defeated with a simple knife?"

"William Knight showed me blood on a knife, claiming that he had killed you."

The monster laughed, making the tiny hairs on my arms stand on edge. "He couldn't even kill a squirrel. He had to find an already dead bird on the ground in order to obtain some blood." He paused. "So you have come to see if I were indeed still alive, so you can't have believed everything William Knight has told you."

"No," I said, noting that the demon was helping me arrive at the point of our visit. "I know you might not be able to tell us anything, but Thomas and I had to come to at least ask."

"Yes, William Knight made a very complex deal," the demon said immediately before I even questioned him. "William Knight is an interesting man, perfect for my bets. He told me that when he heard of me, he was intrigued even though my existence seemed questionable. However, since I was real, he desired that I should make him an offer. I knew he desired wealth and its resulting luxury and relaxation more than anything in the world. And so when I offered it to him, he jumped at the opportunity."

"Can you tell us the details of that deal? Since it is already complete, I assume."

"Of course," the demon continued. "William Knight desired lasting wealth. I told him that the most secure way to have a good life is to marry a woman who will add to his wealth in unimaginable ways, and who will stay with him out of duty. Love can fade, but a sense of obligation might take a bit longer to run out. And so I proposed that I bring you back to life and give you incredible wealth. Therefore, by marrying you, William Knight would become unfathomably wealthy, even when compared to his previous riches. Additionally, you might not

172

be inclined to leave him if you were to hear that it was he who had saved your life."

"Why are you telling us about this then?" I asked.

"Because obviously you have acted out of your own free will and denied a sense of obligation to him, or else you and Mr. Parks would not be standing before me. Shall I continue now?" the demon asked, and though the darkness in the cave was truly impenetrable, I nodded my head, for it seemed that the demon could see us nevertheless.

"Very well. So, after I offered this initial deal, William Knight hesitated. He said it had seemed that in some odd, incomprehensible way, you had fallen in love with his servant, our Mr. Parks."

Thomas squeezed my hand again, but this time in a comforting way.

"So," the monster said, "Mr. Knight was fearful that, even if he were to originally trick you into believing that he was the one who had rescued you, you would still run off with Mr. Parks. He therefore wanted Thomas's death to be part of the deal." My mouth went dry as I thought of how unbelievably evil William had been in his dealings with the demon.

The demon continued, "I told him that killing someone would cost him more than he had to wager. However, I would take away Thomas's voice if William won, allowing him to come up with any story he chose as to what had happened."

"He didn't count on Thomas learning how to read and write," I said, unable to control my pride in Thomas despite the scary situation in which we found ourselves.

"I suppose not," the monster said flatly, clearly not as impressed as I was. "Anyway, the stakes were still incredibly high since it was such a huge deal. On the way back to the stable, Thomas could not speak to anyone. If he did not speak to anyone, William would win, and he would discover that he had won upon your waking under the willow tree. Of course, Thomas did not speak to anyone, upset as he was and in such a hurry to return to his everyday activities in the hope that you would come back to life. However, if Thomas had spoken to someone, both of William's parents would have died."

"He was willing to lose lives that were that close to him?" I cried out, bringing my free hand up to cover my mouth in shock.

"Apparently. I told you, he loves material possessions more than anything."

There was a pause, as the story was complete. "So, there is nothing more that we can do?" I then asked. "He won the bet, so now Thomas will never be able to speak again. I—I do not believe that I can make another bet with you in the hope of winning his voice back. I cannot do that to another person again," I said on the verge of tears, for I had messed up in such an irreparable way. Thomas once again squeezed my hand encouragingly, nonverbally letting me know that he was in full support of what I was saying.

"Of course not. I never expected to make another deal with you again. However, there is still a chance that Thomas will regain his voice," the demon said, that odd sense of evil mischief returning to his words, which I had caught at my previous visits when he was excited about something.

"What do you mean?" I inquired hesitantly.

"I mean that another bet has already been made which might restore his voice."

"Oh," I said, quite taken aback. "If the bet is still in progress, I suppose you cannot elaborate further," I added, and I could feel my hands beginning to sweat with nerves despite the cold in the cave.

"Why couldn't I elaborate further?"

"Because if you did, the person would die since the bet is not complete."

"I'm the one who made that condition. I can say anything of a bet if I wish to. It's only the person who made it who cannot speak of it until it's complete."

I stayed as still as a statue as the monster continued.

"The bet was made once again with Mr. William Knight. He wanted to see if there was any way to make you, Miss West, more physically appealing to him. I thought that he was perhaps a bit harsh, but apparently you do not have the proper curves and perfect skin that he finds desirable in a woman," the demon said. I noticed that Thomas began to shake as his hand held mine firmer. Without being able to see him, I could sense that he was angered at this blatant attack on my beauty, and his anger actually did something to comfort me in an odd way.

"So," the monster said, "I told him I could make you beautiful, but that this might cause you to become even more unfaithful than you already desired to be with Mr. Parks. And so I offered him one additional thing, though I warned him that this deal would come at a heavy price. I told Mr. Knight that I could make you appear still recognizable, but tuned more to his personal tastes, so that his wife might not bore him so. I then told him that I would send a document to him, addressed from me to you, which would state that if you were to cheat on Mr. Knight at any point with anyone, Thomas would die immediately."

"That is terrible," I croaked out.

"Well, he was willing to risk two lives once more," the demon stated matter-of-factly.

"Under what terms?" I asked.

"Ah, and while I *can* tell you that, this is where I will *choose* not to," and the controlled beats of his words punctuated the cruelty behind them.

"You will not tell me anything?" I asked.

"I will not tell you the terms of the actual bet," he said. "And I will only tell you this about a potential loss on William's part. First, to add insult to injury, if William loses, Thomas's voice will be fully restored. Additionally, the two beings he most cares about at that point in time will perish, whoever they might be."

I shuddered, wondering who they could possibly be. His parents again? Perhaps Melanie Burges and that new woman I saw him with.

"It could even be you," the demon interrupted my private speculations.

"Not likely," I said. "I do believe that he hates me."

"Not true. While he does not love you, you *are* the key to all things good for him, and he has additional hope in the future through you for you might become beautiful to him."

My breathing became staggered as I let the demon's words sink in. "I cannot stay with him for even another second. I am merely an object in his eyes—a magic genie of sorts!"

"I don't know that I would leave him," the demon said, and there was an awful smile in his voice.

"Why not?" I asked, feeling out of breath.

"Because what if he loses the bet in part by you leaving him?"

"But what if he loses by me staying with him?"

"It is true, there are a lot of 'ifs' in this situation," the demon said. "But if I were you, I would just carry on in my day-to-day routine and pray that I woke up beautiful instead of dead. And then simply plan on being a faithful wife as opposed to running off with your mute love."

"How do you still manage to hold so much power over me?" I asked, feeling totally defeated and helpless.

The demon's response was darker and more serious than anything else he had ever said to me. "Because I am stronger than you, and I always will be."

Chapter Twenty-Seven

As the late afternoon sun filtered through a crack in my bedroom curtains, I tried to stretch my arms above my head, finding that they were more restrained than usual. Throwing off my bed sheets, I remembered that I had been so tired upon arriving back at my house in the morning after a sleepless night of traveling that I had not even bothered to change out of my semi-constricting dress and into a looser nightgown.

I sat up, still exhausted despite having finally been able to sleep. After visiting the demon with Thomas, I felt trapped. With the demon alive, it seemed there was a good chance that I would die as a result of his second murderous bet with William.

I stretched my arms out to my sides where I was allowed more movement in the dress I was wearing. As I did so, I heard a very faint crinkling noise, and I remembered about the tiny piece of paper Thomas had left with me. I reached into the front of my dress and pulled out the note, written in sloppy handwriting, but with perfect spelling.

The night before, as we returned to Philadelphia, I had told Thomas that I felt hopeless for I was still under the control of the demon and facing further consequences of my previous, horrible decisions. Rather than give in to despair as well, Thomas sat for a while, writing something down:

Likewise the Spirit also helpeth our infirmities: for we know not what we should pray for as we ought: but the Spirit itself maketh intercession for us with groanings which cannot be uttered. And he that searcheth the hearts knoweth what is the mind of the Spirit, because he maketh intercession for the saints according to the will of God. And we know that all things work together for good to them that love God, to them who are the called according to his purpose.

A little space separated the next line:

What shall we then say to these things? If God be for us, who can be against us?

I looked up at him from these somewhat familiar verses as I choked out, "But aren't these only the consequences of my actions? It is too late."

Thomas looked pained, and took the paper back from me. I thought at first that I had made him angry, for he remained looking out the carriage window for several minutes. Finally, though, he seemed to have made up his mind, for beneath the verses he continued writing.

I did not write this because everything will necessarily end as we would have it, but in order to offer you some peace and hope, for which it is certainly not too late if you turn to God.

As I finished reading this explanation, Thomas took my hand and gave it a comforting squeeze. I squeezed his back as a smile lightly grazed my lips. "Did you recently memorize these verses, or have you always known them?" I asked.

He winked at me, and then with a fresh sheet of paper and a smile explained, *Mr. Howe believed the Bible to be a good teacher in more ways than one. I studied and copied verses so that I might learn how to read and write.*

"I'm glad," I declared, rereading the verses. I felt choked with emotion as I once more read the line about the Spirit making intercession for us with groanings which cannot be uttered, and I guessed that this particular line had comforted Thomas following his sudden, cursed silence.

Though I had necessarily destroyed the other writings by Thomas in case William should find them, I kept these verses with me, as the paper did not have Thomas's signature and only a few of his original words.

After looking them over once more in the loneliness of my bedroom, I replaced the verses to the front of my dress and offered up a silent prayer before stepping out into the upstairs hallway.

As I closed my door behind me, the guest bedroom door opened next to me, the suddenness of the motion causing me to jump.

"Well, good morning, Catherine," William said, looking me up and down with no discretion whatsoever.

"Good day, William," I responded.

He wasted no time in arriving at the point of the conversation. Stepping fully out into the hall and closing his bedroom door behind him, he said calmly, "The servants and guards told me that you did not return to the house until early this morning."

I wondered if William had done the same thing. "Yes. I met a woman who invited me back to her house for tea, but she lived a little ways away, and when I went to leave, one of her carriage wheels broke, so she offered that I stay the night while it was repaired."

"She did not have a spare that could be replaced quickly?" William asked skeptically, and I regretted that I was not a very good liar.

"I suppose not, but as I was simply exhausted by that point, I took her up on her offer."

"What is her name?" William asked.

"Leslie Wilson," I said immediately, thankful that I had spit out a reasonable sounding name in a split second.

"And where does Miss Wilson reside?"

"In a large house a couple of hours west of the city," I said, knowing that if I said "east" he would know the area entirely too well.

"I see," William said. He then took a step toward me, and in reflex I stepped backwards, my backside hitting my closed bedroom door lightly. He must have sensed my fear, for rather than interrogate me further, he actually laughed without humor and walked downstairs.

Chapter Twenty-Eight

My life seemed to be in a never-ending cycle of hurt and loneliness. Even as the winter snow began to melt and reveal the fresh life of spring beneath it, I continued to die inside.

I began each day by standing in front of my mirror and examining myself to see if I had been given a cursed beauty. Each day, though, I simply looked like the old me—the me that I wanted so desperately to keep. It was bad enough that I already had a different name, soon to be further desecrated by the addition of a last name that I had come to loathe.

Staring into the mirror, I would sometimes touch my face and stare at each little frizzy strand of my hair. Thomas had found me beautiful, and in that I had a renewed belief in my beauty so that I did not wish it to be changed. In addition, I did not desire to be attractive to my manipulative and selfish fiancé. Part of me was now almost glad each night when he would leave and not return until morning; though these were constant attacks on my self-worth, I determined that it was much better than having me be the object of his deplorable affection.

April finally arrived, and my wedding day was rapidly approaching. Invitations had already been sent out, and the time came for me to try on my wedding dress so final alterations could be made.

As I exited my carriage at the dressmaker's, I scanned the streets for any sign of Thomas. I had neither seen nor heard from him since our journey into the forest together. I had promised that I would send word if my appearance proved altered, though, signaling the end of the bet. Conversely, I asked that he and Mr. Howe keep their eyes and ears open for news of my death, in case William should lose the bet and as a result happen to end my life. Thomas additionally promised to send word if his voice returned, in the chance that my death had not also occurred.

Every day that the bet did not yet seem complete, I fought inwardly with myself. I desired to go back and make another dangerous deal with the demon in the hope of avoiding an impending calamity. But I could no longer see any good, no matter how it might seem at first, coming from such an evil creature. To make yet another deal would surely put me back on the inglorious road upon which I had previously walked.

Inside the dressmaker's shop, the lady who owned it, Mrs. Anna Burton, was quite bubbly.

"Are you excited?" she asked, laying out a large box on the counter of her store.

"Yes," I said, faking a smile for the sake of Mrs. Burton. It was not the kind seamstress's fault that her assuredly beautiful creation would be worn for the ceremony of a loveless marriage.

Excitedly, she removed the top of the box and withdrew her masterpiece from within it.

I suppose that my breath should have caught in my throat at the sight of the dress's complex beading and undeniable beauty. Instead, tears immediately welled up in my eyes. It was over the top, expensive, and admittedly gorgeous, but still I did not want it at all. I wanted to be marrying Thomas in a tasteful and flowing dress out on his family's farm.

Fortunately, Mrs. Burton took my crying as tears of joy.

"Oh, you like it?" she asked, a huge smile spread across her face.

I forced my head to nod.

"Splendid! You will look absolutely breathtaking for your wedding day! Now, let's put you into this to see how it fits!" she proclaimed exuberantly.

It took a full half hour before I was completely secured inside the dress. Mrs. Burton then led me from the back of her store to the front where she told me to stand on top of a stool so that the bottom of the dress could be fully examined as well as the rest of it. I had been facing away from a full-length mirror as she finished situating it perfectly on my body so that, according to Mrs. Burton, seeing it prematurely would not ruin the full impact of the dress on my frame.

Finally, I was permitted to turn around and look in the mirror while Mrs. Burton beamed at me with pride.

The result was indeed stunning, and as I stood there examining myself, I could not help but notice that passersby in the street had actually stopped at the large shop windows to stare.

The dress itself was made of white satin. I had originally asked for a darker color, such as plum. Mrs. Burton had insisted, though, that I should look radiant on my wedding day, and white would accomplish this as it would stand out against the constant blush of my skin and my deep brown hair.

I was slightly shocked to see the incredibly low neckline of the dress, which had been sewn as to give me a considerable amount of cleavage. Around the neckline, there was a bit of lace, as there was around the short sleeves and bottom of the dress.

Though the main material was the white satin, you could not see it clearly at all for it was covered over almost entirely by crystal beading and gold thread designs. The crystal beading formed large decorative swirls or took on the more distinct shapes of lilies, which would indeed be my wedding flower. Most of the beads were sewn tightly onto the dress. However, around the lace sleeves and at the back of the dress, there were sections where they were bunched together in a way that they hung from the dress as a separate material unto themselves. The gold thread used throughout the dress made some of the details pop with the life of color.

Even with my hair in a simple low bun that morning, I could have walked right then and there to my marriage ceremony, with the dress completing my entire appearance in such an exceptional way.

"It is truly a masterpiece," I said, regretting that I still did not want it.

"Thank you, Miss Collins," Mrs. Burton said, honing in on the details.

I spent another half hour in the dress while Mrs. Burton pinned the tiniest places to be hemmed or fixed. "I'll be sure to have this to your house early the morning of your wedding," she said.

"Thank you," I responded before paying her double the amount we had previously agreed upon.

Outside on the street, the gawkers had moved on, changed back into my normal clothing as I was. Still, I noticed with an uncomfortable twinge that my pale green dress was finer than any other clothing in my sight.

As I simply stood outside of Mrs. Burton's shop for a minute, the spring sun began to heat my skin, prickling pleasantly. I could not help but feel a sort of peace as I allowed its warmth to soak through me. With good feelings beginning to infiltrate my mind, I suddenly felt startlingly emboldened. I would risk visiting Thomas that day, to at least see him one last time before my wedding.

I turned purposefully to my right, walking with large, manly strides. I was not paying attention to anything as I walked with single-mindedness toward Mr. Howe's residence. That is why hearing my name being called came as such a shock to me.

"Catherine!" the loud shout struck me as I stopped at once.

I turned around and saw William standing only a few feet away. He was exiting a row home whose owner I was unfamiliar with.

"Catherine," he said, walking up to me now that I had stopped for him. "What are you doing, marching around in such a hurry? I called your name three times before you stopped," he scolded me quietly, lest anyone in our vicinity should hear.

"I just came from Mrs. Burton's where I tried on my wedding dress. I thought that I would like a brief walk now as the day is quite wonderful."

"It is a wonderful day," he agreed in a voice louder than he had previously used. "Would you like me to accompany you?"

"Of course, dear," I said, mentally kicking myself for the necessary acceptance of his invitation.

I would not see Thomas that day as I had so desired.

Chapter Twenty-Nine

My mouth opened in an incredibly wide yawn. I should have covered it with my hand as I stood surrounded by at least a dozen women, but I didn't even bother. After all, I almost rather wished that I were dead on this particular day—my wedding day.

Each morning prior to this one, I had awoken and raced to the mirror, expecting my appearance to be altered. It never was.

Meanwhile, I never received the agreed upon note from Thomas, happily relaying that his voice had been restored.

Just in case, I also tried to keep close tabs on William Knight's parents and the more obvious other women in his life. No one had died that I had heard about, obviously including myself.

And so I awoke on my wedding day, Saturday, the nineteenth of May, 1855, with my life hopelessly unchanged.

In stark contrast to my mood, it was an absolutely gorgeous day, with a sky of rich silky blue and puffy clouds that forced me to remember when life was good with Thomas by my side. I stood on top of a low stool while several women fastened my ornate dress to my body. Meanwhile, a different group of young women readied a bunch of hair pins, waiting to dive down upon my frizzy hair like a group of vultures on their prey. Other women mixed powders, staring at my face in critical thought as they determined the perfect shades of make-up to apply to my blotchy skin.

All of the women around me made such a happy fuss. You would have thought that *they* were all the ones about to be married. On the other hand, I remained rigid and silent.

The women who were helping ready me were supposed to be my friends. And while I knew all of them from parties and get-togethers, I truthfully knew almost nothing about any of them other than their names.

Just as the women who had been dressing me backed out of the way to make room for the girls with the hair items, there was a knock on my bedroom door. One of my maids entered, holding a sealed envelope on a golden tray.

"Miss Collins," she said meekly. "Mr. Samuel Howe, the poet, just arrived, saying that he wished for you to read this brief poem that he

184

wrote for the occasion of your wedding. I would not disturb you with it just now, but Mr. Howe insisted that you should read it beforehand, for reading it after the ceremony would cast bad luck upon your new marriage."

"Thank you," I said, reaching out a shaky hand to read it. Could Thomas have already received his voice, signaling the end of William's wicked bet? If so, I planned on rushing from the room without so much as a good-bye, finding Thomas, and running far away from this place and this cursed life. I was desperate by this point and not at all considerate of William's previous threat if I were to do this.

I was disappointed then that the note did not contain immediate exclamations of joy. However, it was still slightly comforting, for it was from Thomas.

Dear Louisa,

My voice remains unchanged and silent. However, perhaps there is still hope if you have not found yourself altered this morning.

I have thought many times over what is the best course. Should you leave him today before the ceremony? Or would that only seal a horrible fate for someone? I know not what to tell you. I'm inclined to urge you to run, though I could never live with myself if this urging caused your death or the deaths of two innocent people.

I wanted you to know that I will be at the ceremony today, in disguise of course. I do not wish to attend, for it shall surely be a miserable day for us—one where I know I should never hold you in my arms again. However, I want to be there for your sake. To support you, even if this support must come at a distance and at a heavy emotional cost.

Please take comfort in that, even if I am not destined to be with you again, you still hold my heart and I am still near to you.

Your Love Forever,
Thomas

One of my tears spattered directly onto his name, smudging it slightly. "That was beautiful," I said aloud. I then replaced the letter in the envelope and asked my maid to please place it on my nightstand for the time being. As soon as the paper was out of my hands, women swooped down upon my hair and began combing it and pinning it up.

"What was the poem about?" one of the women on the periphery asked as my head was yanked backward by a knot caught in the brush.

"Just a simple, but beautiful poem about weddings," I replied. If she was hoping that I would permit her to read it, she was sorely mistaken.

I turned my gaze from her eyes to outside of my window, attempting to discourage further conversation on the matter. As a bird sang loudly on my windowsill, I frowned slightly as an actual poem came to my mind:

Marry on Monday for health, Tuesday for wealth, Wednesday the best day of all, Thursday for losses, Friday for crosses, and Saturday for no luck at all.

If I was destined to have no luck at all, I would at least pray, and so I silently did so while the women finished with my hair.

The next hour was a blur as my ensemble was completed and I was rushed to a tall, gray stone church in the middle of the city.

As I entered the church foyer, someone must have given a signal, for classical music was suddenly played on the church organ, announcing my entrance. And so, as the sanctuary doors opened, I began walking down the aisle toward the revolting William Knight.

There were audible gasps as our guests beheld me in what had to have been the most beautiful dress ever designed. Although my focus should have remained on my groom-to-be, I found my head swiveling left and right. Like the ladies who had been in my bedroom earlier, I recognized many of the people, but knew almost nothing about them. I was somewhat glad when I spotted Mrs. White's familiar face, though if I had had my way, Caroline, Frank, Amos, and even Laura would have also been in attendance.

Turning my gaze to the pews on the left side of the aisle for the third or fourth time, I spotted Mr. Howe. He looked as grim as I surely did. The man next to him quickly attracted my attention, though. The man was tall and he had a full beard, too bushy for the man's wrinkle-free face. He also had a pronounced gut, though his coat hung off of thin arms. I finally smiled. Even in his over-the-top, utterly ridiculous disguise, I immediately recognized the comforting, clear blue eyes of Thomas. I wanted to laugh, ever so briefly, for the fake beard and presumably pillow-cushioned gut looked completely unconvincing. Still, no one gawked at Thomas, and it was then that my heart sank as I remembered that everyone was looking at me, the beautiful bride.

I had walked too far to keep my eyes from William Knight. Only a few steps in front of him, I was forced to direct my face at his. He looked stern, and I could only imagine the scolding I would receive for not acting my best, as a grateful lover, but instead eyeing the audience. It would only be a scolding from embarrassment instead of hurt, though, and so I could not feel any pity for already treating him coldly on our wedding day.

As I reached the altar, the minister began the ceremony, his voice echoing off the walls of the now music-less room as all eyes remained on me and William.

Even knowing that Thomas was so close to me, I could no longer bring myself to even glance at him. I knew that if I spotted him again, I would surely shirk my responsibilities and run away with him, not caring, at least at first, for the deaths that I might cause by such an action.

William Knight stared dispassionately into my own eyes throughout the ceremony, and before I knew it, the minister was directing William to take his vows. It was at this point that I finally realized that some part of me had never truly expected to end up this far. I had honestly believed that the bet would have been over by this point. Perhaps it was, I madly thought. Perhaps he had lost and the two people who had died had been entirely unknown to me. Though there was still the lack of Thomas's voice, I then remembered.

It was my turn to recite my vows. I spoke monotonously as disgust and despair filled my soul.

Before I could process the reality of my life, the minister pronounced that William may kiss the bride. Without so much as a smile, he leaned in and kissed me as the organ started up again. There was no life to the kiss, no saving magic; I instead felt the venomous bite of a snake. As he escorted me down the aisle, tears stung my eyes, though I probably appeared happily overwhelmed to the casual guest.

Once again, time flew as I detachedly met my guests as they exited the church. I only noted that Thomas must have exited through the back of the church; whether due to emotional turmoil or fear of being discovered by William, he did not pass our way. Then, outside, I had rice rain down upon me under the now cloudless sky.

Finally, just William and I entered my carriage, which was waiting to take us back to the reception at my house.

After the carriage door was shut and it had begun to move gaily down the street, William spoke. "How are you this morning, Catherine?" he requested formally.

"Fine, William. And how are you?"

"Fine," he answered.

After several uncomfortable minutes of silence, he produced a wrapped parcel from the side of his carriage seat. "I purchased you a wedding gift," he said, handing it to me.

I reached for it and unwrapped it emotionlessly and silently. Seeing what was inside, though, I received a bit of a shock as my brain turned back on and feeling returned to my limbs.

Casting the box lid to the floor, I withdrew a long, silk nightgown of dark blue. Objectively, it was quite beautiful, with long flowing sleeves and a wonderfully simple, yet classy tie around the middle. Seeing it reminded me that I was indeed William Knight's wife and that I would necessarily have to share a bedroom with him. More shocking than this unfortunate reminder, though, was a quick assessment of the actual nightgown.

Thankfully, as I held the nightgown up in front of me, I shielded my face from William's, for my eyes and mouth were both opened a suspicious degree. I noticed that the middle of the nightgown looked as if it would fit a waist even tinier than mine. At the same time, the bust on the nightgown, though naturally more flowing and baggier than a regular dress, looked as if it would be too excessive, so as to appear unbecoming on my own smaller bust.

"Thank you, William," I tried to say while suppressing the emotion that wanted to explode from me. "I do fear, though, that this will not fit me, as the waist is so dainty. Also, you flatter me with such excessive fabric in the chest region."

I had dropped the nightgown to my lap, and so I studied William's face for signs of a clue. "Perhaps, but perhaps not. We will see tonight when you try it on," he said, and he actually smiled, though more to himself than to me.

Although he was naturally guarded, secretive, and cold with me, I could still sense something odd in his demeanor—something almost like victory in his smug smile. I wondered, though I dared not verbalize, if he had bought this nightgown in anticipation of my new beauty, which would be present this very night. At this same moment, though his strange smile remained on his face, sweat beaded on his forehead, for which there was no natural excuse; though the sun was out fully above our carriage, it was not a particularly hot day as a cool, light breeze washed the city in natural comfort.

As we neared my house, I had no doubt that William Knight anticipated the completion of his bet with the demon this very day.

Chapter Thirty

"Mr. and Mrs. Knight, we are *so* happy for you," an older woman told us in the ballroom at my house.

"Thank you," William and I said in unison, sounding neither happy nor sad.

After hearing my new name dozens of times within the last two hours during the wedding reception lunch, I was already tired of it. At first, it was frustratingly shocking. Already, though, the name "Mrs. Knight" seemed depressingly dull.

As our plates were cleared from in front of us, the string quartet we had hired took up an energetic tune as opposed to the slower, meal appropriate music with which they had been providing us. Not even ten seconds into this new song, yet another well-wisher approached our table. "Congratulations, Mr. Knight. Mrs. Knight." I had been looking through the person as she spoke, but the tone of the woman's voice had such a sarcastic ring to it that I forced myself to focus on the speaker before me. It was none other than Melanie Burges, sneering at me plainly.

"Thank you," William said as if there had been nothing unusual at all in Melanie's voice.

"Thank you," I followed, quieter.

It was not the first time that day that I had received a dirty look or nasty greeting from a young woman in attendance. I wondered how many mistresses William would continue to keep up with now that we were married.

As Melanie Burges walked away, several young men in the massive ballroom snapped their heads in her direction. I found it strange that in a room with so many eligible bachelors, Melanie only cared for the attentions of William Knight. As this thought hung in my mind, though, it made me feel as if I would be physically sick to my stomach; after all, I had had that same blind infatuation with this man.

"Catherine," William said, and as he was staring directly ahead, it was quite obvious that he had not noticed my discomfort in the slightest. "Do you still wish to proceed with dancing and then dinner and more dancing, as planned?"

"Yes," I said, thankfully catching the comforting eye of Samuel Howe at that moment, though he was located far from me, against the opposite wall. Although Thomas would not be able to gain access to the private reception unnoticed, Mr. Howe had been able to tell me that Thomas would still be nearby my house in case he should be needed.

"Well," William said, heaving a deep sigh, "I suppose we should dance now."

I moved my chair backward slightly so that I would be able to stand. The movement, though, caused my stomach to flip once more, and I actually swallowed a bit of vomit. "Actually," I said, reevaluating exactly what I could handle, "why don't the two of us dance after dinner instead of now? My stomach is not feeling entirely well."

"Very well," William said, not seeming disappointed or disapproving in the slightest. In the meantime, dancers had already begun to gather on the dance floor. Spotting the still-sour Melanie Burges, William made a beeline for her where he immediately escorted her to the dance floor. As he talked to her, she brightened considerably. I could only guess that he was promising continued devotion to her and her picture-perfect figure.

The afternoon dragged before the sunlight penetrated my westward-facing ballroom at harsh angles. As the semi-transparent, red lace curtains were drawn, the gold and scarlet room reminded me of blood, dripping with the reflected light of the massive rubies.

William and I eventually ate and finished our dinner in silence. By the time this day's last meal was cleared, the light had faded completely from outside and dozens of candles had been lit. Though the look of the room was hushed, the party was anything but. Following many drinks, dances, and lively conversations, the party was as busy and awake as ever.

"I'm going to converse with some others," William said, making a move to depart.

"Wait," I stopped him. I naturally put out my hand for his arm in order to gently catch his attention, but as I remembered to whom I was speaking, I recoiled and continued to speak with my hands moved to my lap. "I am willing to dance with you once now if you wish to do so for our guests."

I thought I saw William's face flash anger, though it could have just been the shadows from the many candles. "Very well," he said, and with every show of gallantry, he withdrew my seat for me, took my hand, and led me to the dance floor.

As no one had yet descended upon the dance floor following dinner, we caught all of our guests' attention at once as they quieted and watched us supposed lovebirds. The musicians began a slow piece, and William took my hand in his as he held onto my waist with his other hand. I winced slightly at his touch, but managed to convince myself that I was just going along with what would now be normal as his wife.

As we twirled lifelessly around, I whispered, "It seems our guests are having a nice time."

"Shh. You should pay attention to what you are doing. Everyone is looking at you, after all," he scolded.

I became even more rigid as I focused on my dancing.

Though beautiful, my dress was not exactly made for graceful twirls. The crystal beading and excessive material made the dress somewhat heavy. The skirt portion was large, though not as large as some of the hoop skirts worn by our guests. All of this considered, William was correct in that there truly was a lot to focus on. I kept my arms stiff so that the beaded clusters, concentrated particularly on the sleeves, would not slide out of position.

As I felt the song nearing its end, I was more than ready to return to my secret solemnity and away from the probing eyes of my guests watching me participate in this socially-expected dance with my husband. Feeling relieved that I was almost done this task, I risked a glance at our guests around the dance floor. With no amount of luck, the first eyes that I caught were the burning eyes of Melanie Burges. I found her stare to be so intense and full of hatred that I did what I had tried so hard not to do—I tripped on the skirt of my dress.

William caught me before I actually fell over, but I had still stumbled quite noticeably, and several of our guests murmured around me. I was mentally concluding that this day could not grow any worse when I noticed William's face.

"You are pale," I said. It was not that I had an ounce of tender concern for the man I had come to despise, but his color was so stark, it necessitated comment.

As I spoke, he stopped dancing and just stared at me. His dark eyes penetrated mine and I noticed that he shook slightly.

"What's wrong?" I asked. The intensity of his gaze and the absurdity of his demeanor were actually beginning to frighten me.

"I must sit down," he whispered quietly. I turned to my side, anticipating a return to our seats, when William Knight simply sat where he had been standing on the dance floor.

At this point, several of the male guests who were doctors or colleagues of William's raced forward. "No!" William actually shouted. "Everyone back!"

The musicians stopped playing their music and our guests whispered loudly to each other at a distance, confused by this sudden change in William. I too began to walk away, but he reached up quickly for my arm. I remembered the last time he had touched me so spiritedly. He had hit me during that previous instance, and I involuntarily pulled free from him. Still, I stayed in place, giving him time to say, "Stay here."

Discomfort could not even begin to describe how I felt as I knelt down and peered into the suddenly sickly face of William Knight. As soon as my knees touched the floor beside him, he whispered, "It's me. I cannot believe that it is me." He was breathing heavily.

"What is you?" I asked.

William then looked at me as if I were the only person in the room. He had never, not once, looked at me so directly, and I wondered if he were really only seeing me for the first time.

"Louisa," he said, and a jolt went through me at having heard my real name uttered from his lips. "I made a deal with the demon."

"I know," I said strongly, and I could not conceal all of my disgust for him in my tone.

"What do you mean?" he asked. His eyebrows drew down over his dark eyes and a shot of red entered his pasty cheeks.

"Only that you made a deal in the hope of making me beautiful. The demon told me. He did not tell me what the terms of your bet were, though."

William took a few seconds to soak in my words. He then began to laugh as if something hilarious had just happened. Our guests talked even louder along the edge of the dance floor, no doubt attempting to drown out the haunting sound of William's insane laughter.

"What's so funny?" I asked urgently.

William finally stopped as he began to noticeably perspire. He then grabbed hold of my wrist tightly. "I do not have much time," he whispered seriously and quickly, in harsh contrast to his sudden mood of hilarity. "I have lost the bet."

"How?" I asked.

"The bet was simply that you would not trip if you danced with me at our wedding."

A chill started at the top of my head, traveling down my face and neck. The room spun, but William held me to reality with his mercilessly tight grip on my wrist.

"So it is all my fault," I said as I noticed William's breathing become uneven.

"If you were not so clumsy with your dress then I would not be dying right now."

"Wait. Why are *you* dying if it was your bet?"

Again William laughed, but this time briefly. "My bet was that if I lost, the two people I most cared about would die. I should have realized before now that I was putting my own life in jeopardy with such a bet."

The room kept spinning around me, but I felt no radiating pain, no loss of consciousness. Though William was dying before me, I was certain that I was not.

"Why did you even make such a sinful bet?" I asked, anger boiling out of my voice.

"Because, though by marrying you I would have essentially unlimited money and a license to do as I pleased, I wished that you would be more physically appealing to me if you were to be my wife—a person whose beauty would equal her money."

"Why did you not bet with Melanie Burges?" I asked, though the demon had already given me one explanation. Though I caught her glaring at me, I was thankful that she did not seem to hear anything that was being said, even on the very edge of the crowd as she was.

"Because you were perfect—without a family or a truly concrete background. Also, Melanie Burges would never allow me to visit the other women in my life if she were my wife." William winced in pain and slumped against me then. "I'm almost gone. I just—." He shut his eyes, though he continued to speak. His words were calmer, more measured, and I knew that these were indeed among his last. "You taunted me with your love for a low-life servant. How could you want Thomas when you could have me? I needed to win. If I couldn't win against so simple and stupid a man, then who was I?"

I wasn't able to offer any answer, for his grip on my wrist slackened and his breathing stopped altogether.

Chapter Thirty-One

The gong of the church bells reverberated through the city streets as a crowd of people exited the dreary church graveyard, dressed in black. The day itself even seemed to be aware of the ceremony for the selfish man, as a cold drizzle fell from the completely cloud-filled sky. Still, there was nothing violent or emotional in the attitude of nature—not even a light breeze to play with the black veil covering my face. Rather, it was as if she were bored with the proceedings, and could think of nothing more eventful to do than be sullen. Meanwhile, not a bird sang on this chilly spring day, though I did notice bloomed flowers of yellow and purple in front of the church.

The last few days had seen a fluctuation in my emotions, ranging from the bottom of the ocean to the top of a mountain. Although I certainly had no love invested in the cruel and selfish form of William Knight, his death still brought out many unexpected emotions. Looking back on our wedding day, I determined that it is impossible to be that close to death and not be impacted, no matter the victim. I saw the light forever fade from William's eyes, and there was nothing I could do in that horrible drama before me. Also, even though I had grown to dislike the man with every fiber of my being, there was an awkward sense of remorse for the man himself. After all, at one point, I had desired nothing else in life than to be his wife. Most of all, though, I felt an often overwhelming sense of guilt. If it had not been for me, he would not have made such an unholy deal. Also, more than a day after his death, I still had not discovered the identity of the demon's second victim.

The day immediately following William's death, preparations had been made for the funeral to be held the next morning. Of course, it was lavish for being so solemn an affair, and William was buried in the best attire with minor treasures surrounding him.

Tears had fallen from my eyes occasionally, satisfying the throng of sympathizers who had been constantly in my presence since the wedding. Little did they know, though, that sometimes these were tears of thankfulness and joy.

While I had not exactly wished William Knight dead, I still did have to face the happy fact that I would not be forced to be his miserable wife for the rest of my days. I would not be shamed every time he spent the night with another woman. Also, I would not feel sullied if I had indeed become beautiful to his tastes. I say sullied because he would have indeed only desired me as an object of physical perfection, and he would have cared nothing for the soul dwelling inside. Such an existence, I could assume, would be quickly deadening.

Then, there was the pure and wonderful knowledge of Thomas.

As soon as William died, I was surrounded by the doctors who had been in attendance at our wedding. They worked frantically, trying to revive his already lifeless body. Meanwhile, many of the women ushered me into my parlor and away from the scene as the men reluctantly pronounced William Knight dead. Though I had felt suffocated in so tight a group, somehow Mr. Howe had managed his way to me before I was escorted upstairs to my bedroom.

"Mr. Knight's servant verbally sends his apologies, and though he wishes to be here in person, he believes it wise to stay busy with other necessary tasks until after the funeral of his late master."

"Thank you," I had managed to choke out while I hid my face as several happy tears forced their way from my bloodshot and weary eyes.

Yet further proof that the hideous bet was complete, Mr. Howe had discreetly and wonderfully managed to convey to me that Thomas was back to his normal self. He could speak once more, *verbally* sending me a message, and I rejoiced inside. This result of my past sins had been undone, and I thanked God.

Despite this burst of happiness given through Mr. Howe's words, I had to deal with the fact that Thomas also commanded me to patience. I would not be able to see him until after William's body was committed to the cold ground. Although I did not like this, I understood the wisdom behind such a constraint. If I left with Thomas or even went to see him briefly before the funeral, I would easily attract unwanted attention. And I did not want William's death to seem any more suspicious than it already was. Also, I did not wish to fully dishonor William by fleeing before his body was even cold. And so I forced patience upon myself, knowing that my love would be waiting for me until after I finished the last of my obligations.

"Mrs. Knight," a man said from directly behind me. I had been blankly staring at the flowers in front of the church as my mind came to terms with the true finality of everything following the funeral. I turned and saw my stable boy standing at the side of my carriage.

Though I had only been Mrs. Knight for a space of mere hours, everyone seemed to silently agree that this new name was the most respectful to use. I found it dreadful, but I could scarcely request that they refrain from using it without sounding quite heartless.

"Yes?" I responded to my servant.

"Are you ready to return to Pleasant Hill?"

The question snapped me fully out of my time of quiet contemplation. "No, thank you," I replied. "I am going to go for a walk, I think. You may return home, though."

"But, Mrs. Knight, it is raining and likely to rain harder. You do not want to catch a cold."

"If it rains harder, I shall duck inside a friend's house and have them bring me home in their carriage."

"Very well, Mrs. Knight," my servant responded, and he climbed onto his box seat and departed.

Many of the other mourners were still leaving the church graveyard as well, some climbing into carriages while others turned in different directions to walk home. I saw William's parents climb into one of the more massive carriages present. Although they had spoken with me the night of the wedding before I was taken to my room, our meeting was brief. They merely said, "I am sorry for your loss." I repeated similar sentiments, and then they left. I did not see them again until the funeral, and we did not speak one word to each other. They seemed understandably upset, but not in any mood to foster a relationship with their only momentary daughter-in-law. I was grateful for their snubbing, though, as this would enable me to return to my heart's true partner without the watchful sneering of the older Mr. and Mrs. Knight.

I remained still while the final mourners dispersed. I then crossed the street and continued to the left, in the direction of Mr. Howe's residence.

I walked slowly so as not to attract attention, though my legs were aching to run. I longed to see Thomas right then, but I still had to be patient, especially as, at my current pace, I would not reach Mr. Howe's house for nearly an hour.

A half an hour into my walk, I began to physically shake with excitement as I wondered what Thomas's first words to me would be. I longed to hear his voice again, and tears burst from my eyes as I realized that I had not heard him speak in eight tortuous months. I could not help it—my legs propelled me to a very brisk walk as tears streamed down my face.

Nature seemed to notice the outburst of my emotions and the decisiveness and desperateness to my movements. She matched my mood, and the rain fell in fully formed drops as a breeze picked up.

I finally found myself in a part of town where I no longer had acquaintances. As I previously had noted, Mr. Howe's was not a bad section of Philadelphia, simply one without a budget to be held in comparison to my own.

As I turned onto a street of row homes instead of shops, I actually began to run. The rain once again matched my pace, and I could feel the drops quickly soaking through my heavy black dress as a gust of wind tore my veil from my face. I did not go back for it, and only turned momentarily to see it fly down the street like a little black ghost.

I continued to run down the next street, which was thankfully empty due to the weather. Finally, I made one last turn and Mr. Howe's house was in sight in the middle of the row homes on the opposite side of the road. I ran for it, and while I was still in the middle of the street several houses down, Mr. Howe's front door opened. Out sprinted Thomas, rushing for me as well. We caught each other in the middle of the street and he leaned downward, pressing his lips firmly onto mine. His recently dry hands quickly grew slippery as he held onto my cheek with one hand and my hip with his other. Meanwhile, rainwater from his hair soon began to drip down onto my closed eyes as nature's tears also continued to burst forth, I thought, with happiness.

Just as we parted, we heard a brusque yell to move from behind us, and Thomas quickly pulled me out of the street as a lone carriage and its miserable driver pushed on behind us.

"Let's go inside! You're completely soaked!" Thomas yelled to me through the heavy rain, and I burst into tears all over again to simply hear words from Thomas's mouth.

Inside, as soon as Mr. Howe's door was shut, Thomas again turned me toward him and kissed me as we made a small puddle beneath us on Mr. Howe's worn foyer floor.

"I love you," he said as our lips parted for a moment.

"I love you too."

At least a minute later, our romantic embrace was interrupted by a friendly and familiar voice.

"As a poet, you must know that I am forever a romantic and would generally allow you to continue for years. However, I really must insist that you change before you should catch a cold."

We both turned and smiled at Mr. Howe. As he smiled back, I actually ran to the end of the foyer where he had appeared and gave him a hug.

"Thank you for everything," I said into his long hair.

"You are very welcome, my dear."

I then turned back toward Thomas who happily said, "Come upstairs. I'm afraid we don't have any dresses in the house, but you can wear a clean set of my clothes until yours dry."

Upstairs, he showed me to a trunk in his bedroom, which looked very lived in after months of staying there. There were stacks of paper around the room, and I was again reminded of how much work Thomas had put into learning how to read and write so that he might communicate with me.

He pulled out an old pair of pants and a shirt from the trunk. "Sorry, Louisa. I know it's not exactly appropriate apparel, but you'll only need to be in these until your dress dries."

I took the clothing from his hands, but stopped him before he stepped out of the room so that I could change. "Wait. Could you say what you just said one more time?"

He cocked his head to the side and his brown hair clung to the side of his face as a few more drops of water ran down his cheek from the motion. "You'll only need to wear these until your dress dries?" he asked.

"No, no. You said…sorry, Louisa." I paused only briefly before I hurriedly explained, "It isn't the apology that I wish to hear again. It is simply my name. The only times I have heard my real name over the last many months has been through your couple of letters and when I saw Mr. Howe. William used it once…that is it. I never really used to like my name, but after being Catherine Collins for such a period of time, I long to just be…*me* again. I feel as if I haven't truly existed for more than half a year!"

He looked serious, but there was a great amount of feeling in his next words, "I love you, Louisa West."

He then walked toward me as he brought his large hand up to my cheek once more and held it there as I looked up at him. "I only desire you to be yourself, for that is more than wonderful to me. You will never have to be Catherine Collins, and especially not Catherine Knight, to me. I don't care if you are penniless—actually, I rather liked that you were, for I saw you change before my eyes from someone who longed to be more than Louisa West to someone who was happily content with the more important things in life. I love you, and I am so thankful that you love me."

Thomas leaned down and gave me a soft kiss on my forehead. I closed my eyes and soaked in the feeling of security also planted there.

"Also," he gently continued, and I opened my eyes. "I am glad to see that you are just as beautiful as when we spent the end of last summer together. I would have been...," he swallowed hard as he seemingly had difficulty continuing for a moment. "I would have been devastated had your appearance been altered and defiled in order to fall in line with William Knight's tastes. That desire on his part was truly selfish and awful. I would not like to see even one hair on your head changed in such a dishonest way."

"I am glad that I still look like me too," I agreed. "Still, you do not wish that anything about my looks were different? I have drab, frizzy hair and my eyes are dull and brown. Although I am of an adult age, I often feel as if the body of a woman has eluded me. And my face always seems to be an undesirable, red hue."

"Louisa, I find you beautiful. It is true that your hair tends toward the wild side at times, but that's what I love about it. It is completely natural, and I wouldn't have you any other way. Your eyes are far from drab, but instead I can read your thoughts in them. If you take away the nature of your eyes, you take away my ability to see, at times, into your soul. Your body is delicate with its petite curves, and I find the innate urge to protect you arise when I consider it. However, it is also alluring—please don't fear that I look at you and see a child. Especially after the trials that we have most recently endured and the personal growth I have seen take place in you, I see a radiant woman. And now I feel as if I am forgetting one of your complaints."

"My red cheeks," I said quietly.

"That's right! How could I forget such an outrageous complaint? Louisa, when you died...." Here, he swallowed again hard. "I am sorry," he said. "I still have difficulty thinking of it," and it was my turn to place my hand on his cheek as he dropped his arms. He did not shed tears, though he took several deep breaths before he was able to continue, grabbing my shoulders in an earnest fashion. "Louisa, you were so horribly pale when you were dying. I literally saw the life fade from your face. As I look at your rosy cheeks, I am reminded that that awful nightmare is now nothing but a memory, for you are alive and well."

He then embraced me for a minute as I soaked in a warmth that managed to permeate through his wet body.

Finally, he released me and declared, "Now, you really must change so you can be dry. I'll change after you," he said, and he made it out into the hallway before I called to him one more time.

"Thomas."

He poked his head back into the room.

"You *really* believe that I am beautiful?"

"Louisa, I find you wholly enchanting."

I was too thrilled to smile. Instead, I stared at my love for a moment and considered his features—his lightly pockmarked face, his own brittle hair, the strength in his masculine hands. I too wouldn't change anything about him for the world. "I want you to know that I marvel at you too, Thomas," I said, and he gently shut the door for me, his blue eyes illuminated with peace.

Chapter Thirty-Two

I awoke in my own bed at Pleasant Hill, and for a moment I thought my reunion with Thomas the day before had been a dream. However, I quickly remembered how we had decided that it would be best for me to return to my home that night so that I was not searched for. Thomas and I had reluctantly parted in Mr. Howe's foyer before the kind poet returned me to my house in his carriage.

I was not upset to find myself in my house this day, though, for I knew I would soon see Thomas again. Still, it would not be under the happiest or safest of circumstances that I would see him on this particular day. Rather, we would be on a mission of sorts, and so that morning I put on a simple dress, or as simple as I owned, that was the black color of mourning.

Eating only a light breakfast, I had my carriage readied and I directed it to Mr. Howe's residence. On the way, I left the windows of my carriage open and the curtains pulled back. The rain from the day before had dissipated, leaving white, non-threatening clouds in its stead. I breathed in the air, and although I inhaled quite a bit of city industry, I also smelled spring and all of its promises of life renewed.

Upon arriving at Mr. Howe's, I told my servant that he could return to my house with the carriage; Mr. Howe would be bringing me home that night.

I waited until my servant had already begun to obey my directions before I knocked on Mr. Howe's door. As expected, Thomas answered. "Good morning, Louisa," he said as he let me inside and embraced me. A fresh burst of thankfulness invaded my mind at the sound of his wonderful voice.

"Good morning, Thomas."

He looked seriously into my eyes then. "Are you sure you wish to accompany me? I will gladly investigate it on my own if you are at all nervous."

"I am sure. I will come with you," I said, and Thomas marched off to send Mr. Howe's carriage around, which had already been readied in anticipation of my arrival.

Sitting in Mr. Howe's well-worn carriage with Thomas, I again thought of our conversation from the previous day which had led to our current course of action. Although it seemed that the bet was indeed complete and we were safe from the demon's power over us, it bothered us that we could not discover the second victim. Through our conversation, Thomas fostered an idea, though we had to wait until today to see if it were true, for the necessary destination was not right around the corner by any means.

We traveled for a couple of hours before alighting from our carriage in Geresh's Glen. Arm in arm like picturesque lovers, we passed a few pairs of picnickers on this breezy but warm day before walking into the woods. We stepped over sticks and long dead leaves on the ground. Birds whistled to each other over our heads, hidden amongst the young green leaves sprouting amidst the hardier needles of the evergreens.

A few times we found ourselves sloshing through puddles in the boggy woods, though in the warmth, it did not chill us. And though we still kept a watchful eye out for snakes, it was, overall, an enjoyable day for a walk in the woods.

Finally, we reached our destination—the misleadingly beautiful, miniature lake, enchanting weeping willow tree, and beyond that, the cave of the monster.

We continued toward the cave, hand in hand, suddenly quiet, although we had talked a great deal during our walk.

We called out, but of course there was no answer from within. Then, with our steps synchronized, we walked into the cave. Before we turned to the left, an unusually terrible stench hit our nostrils. Still, we kept on.

We waited in silence, the cold from the cave walls wrapping around us. We waited and waited. I could not tell if my nose had grown more used to the unusual stench, or if it was indeed not as pungent where we stood. Regardless, fifteen minutes must have passed, and there was nothing. No movement, no stale breath. Finally, Thomas led me outside and back into the comforting sunlight.

"What does this mean?" I asked Thomas, and my voice sounded loud to my own ears. He had told me previously that he wished to ask the demon about the identity of the second victim, but his straight and brave posture and his victoriously thoughtful expression spoke of other, secret ideas.

"It means that we no longer have anything to fear," Thomas said strongly. "Stay here for a few minutes."

And shockingly, Thomas began to return to the cave.

"What are you doing?" I said as he continued in at its mouth.

"I am going to the right."

"Are you insane?" I shouted, racing to him at the mouth of the cave. "If you go to the right, the demon will kill you instantly."

"I believe the demon has already met his own death," Thomas said. "Now stay here for just a minute while I investigate."

I was stunned by his bluntly stated hypothesis, though I obeyed his wishes. I waited patiently, praying, and in less than two minutes, he exited the cave. Standing together in the sunlight next to the rippling lake, Thomas announced, "It is as I thought."

"What exactly did you think?"

The corner of his mouth turned up in triumph briefly before he explained. "I couldn't remove the monster's words from my mind—the words he used in discussing the parameters of his bet with William Knight. He said that the two *beings* William Knight most cared about would perish if William lost the bet. He never said humans."

"So, are you saying the monster died because William cared more about him than anyone else in the whole world?" I exclaimed, any happiness evident on my face wiped away by shock and disgust.

"It makes sense," Thomas continued. "William Knight was an incredibly selfish man. He really only cared about his own personal gain. So, with that in mind, it follows that he would be one of the two people to die under the specific bet that he made. However, the monster, a *being* even though he was not a *human* being, was the second most important to William because it was through the monster that William's dreams were being realized, or at least that is how he would have perceived the situation. Although the monster was indeed clever, this just shows that he underestimated William's true nature; I'm sure the monster would have never thought that he was betting on his own life."

My mouth was agape as I thought of the ludicrousness and yet apparent reality of what Thomas said. "I guess that means the monster was indeed alive and capable of death then," I said.

"It would seem so," Thomas agreed. "When I went into the right side of the cave, I, um, tripped on a large carcass. Hence the overwhelming scent of rot in there."

Unfortunately confirming Thomas's story, he smelled quite disgusting. Nevertheless, I found myself hugging him. "It's really over then?"

"It's really over," Thomas said, smoothing my brittle hair around my cheeks.

"What now?" I questioned.

"That's up to you, Miss West," he said with a smile. He completely covered both of my hands in his large ones. "You would honor me greatly if you would marry me, Louisa."

The scene was far from romantically perfect with us standing next to a spooky cave with a large, rotting carcass inside, and the smell trapped in Thomas's clothing to boot. Still, I found it to be perfect for us. We were standing victorious on ground that once more belonged to God's magnificent nature. The day was beautiful, and as the birds continued to sing around us, I answered, "I would be honored to be your wife, Thomas."

He smiled, and keeping one of my hands in his, we began walking briskly back in the direction of the road and Geresh's Glen.

"Just one thing," I added as we passed next to the willow tree.

"Yes?" Thomas inquired seriously.

"You think you might consider washing off in that pond? Poor Mr. Howe's little servant is going to pass out when he receives a whiff of you."

Thomas smiled playfully and retraced his steps to the peaceful lake where he jumped in with all of his clothing on. Upon coming out of the water, he at least smelled wild as opposed to foul.

Walking through the woods once more, we heard a very unique bird call. It almost sounded like the notes of a flute caught in the wind, oddly breathy as it was. Just for fun, I tried to imitate the bird's musical noise. I matched it perfectly when an oddly depressing thought occurred to me.

Seeing my face fall, Thomas immediately inquired, "What's wrong?"

"It's just...I realized that I can still sing. Even though the monster is dead, the results of his bets—of my bets—are still in effect."

Thomas cocked his head, though clearly more out of frustration than out of a lack of understanding. He knew what was bothering me; I wished to be rid of all ties with the evil creature, and yet I was still stuck with the results, good as they might seem.

"Did you enjoy singing before the bet?" Thomas finally asked.

"Only very occasionally," I answered.

"Then only do so when you desire to sing. Just because you now have the ability to sing does not mean that you must, or should for that matter, use it. However, perhaps you can take what was originally done through evil and make it good. Sing when you wish to, and I shall enjoy it, but never value it as one of the things that makes you marvelous."

I nodded bravely. I was not happy to have to carry around this reminder of my sins, beautiful as it was. Still, I knew that it was a minor price to pay for my transgressions. However, it was not the only reminder of my involvement with the demon.

"What about my house and new belongings?" I asked.

Thomas stopped walking and looked at me. "What do you believe is right?"

I considered for a moment before answering. "My parents were my real parents. Although they did not truly prepare me for satisfaction and peace in a world of poverty, it would be a dishonor to them to own new, fake parents and claim that my real ones were kidnappers."

"Then, specifically, we must determine what is the best thing to do."

Chapter Thirty-Three

It took a week, but preparations were finally complete.

It was the end of May, and I dressed that day with my windows open. I slipped on yet another black dress, this one of silk with ruffles at the bottom. Although I had been dressing in black simply out of respect for William Knight, it had also proved prudent for I had received sympathizers each day that I was at home. Most of them were couples, though every once in a while I would receive a single man who would come in poor taste to try to secure an early advantage for when I would be ready and permitted to be sought after once more. Of course, little did they know that I was already engaged.

At my window, I gazed down at the young man who worked in my carriage house. He was riding one of my horses around, giving the strong animal some exercise.

When I turned again into my bedroom, my eyes took a moment to adjust, blazing as the sun was on this particular day. Picking up a hair pin, I placed it somewhat sloppily into my hair before quitting my bedroom for a bit. I stepped into the hallway, walking past spare bedrooms that I had never used. As I walked down the front stairs, I touched the golden banister softly. Before turning into the parlor, I stared once more at the golden walls and ruby- and emerald-studded foyer.

Standing in the parlor, I remembered the extreme number of boxes I had first encountered there. Now, of course, the long parlor walls were noticeable with blue sapphires and diamonds running along the center of the walls horizontally, as a noble divider. I stepped over to the mahogany desk in the corner of the room, remembering the letter I wrote in response to Thomas's.

Exiting the parlor, I visited the ballroom. Though objectively impressive, the sight made my stomach turn, and I continued on to the other rooms I owned, attempting to soak in their beauty.

After my final tour, I was completely ready to quit this house forever. Each room might have been gorgeous, but I could never have felt that they were truly mine.

I returned to my bedroom where I withdrew two fabric bundles from beneath my bed. Each bundle contained two of my simpler dresses, unfortunately pressed flat in a way so that the resulting wrinkles would surely remain for quite some time. Holding one in each hand, I walked down the main staircase, through my house, and out the back door. Though several of my servants saw me, they did not ask any questions as I carefully avoided eye contact.

Outside, I advanced to my carriage house where my servant had gone inside once more.

"Good morning," I called to him, entering through the already open door of the stable portion.

"Good morning, Mrs. Knight," he said, straightening himself up as if I were royalty. He almost always acted in this fashion toward me, my wealth seemingly overwhelming to him. "What can I do for you?" he continued.

"If you could ready my carriage, I have somewhere I wish to go today."

"Yes, Mrs. Knight," he said, and he jumped to work.

"Oh, and one specific request."

He stopped moving.

"If you could harness all four horses as opposed to only two to pull the carriage, that would be wonderful. Are you able to do that?" I asked. Indeed, I knew that he was able to do so for I had snuck into the carriage house the other day while he was out and saw that he had the appropriate equipment.

"Yes, Mrs. Knight," he said, and without any questions asked, he busied himself with the preparations.

Meanwhile, I plopped down on the fresh grass in my backyard, an unusual oasis in the middle of the city.

Once the carriage had been brought out, I climbed inside and immediately drew back the curtains and opened the windows.

"Where to, Mrs. Knight?" my servant asked before climbing to his proper seat.

"Please head toward the late Mr. Snyder's house," I instructed him. "Do you know how to find it?"

"Oh, yes, Mrs. Knight. Ever since his terrible suicide, news of that scandal has spread like wildfire."

I grimaced slightly as this brought back terrible memories of being one of the last people to see the grief-stricken man alive. And of

209

course this encounter is what led to Mr. Graham telling me of his experience with the demon in the woods.

My servant did not sense my discomfort, though, and he began the journey.

An hour into traveling, the road began to grow less crowded and the woods shot up thicker and thicker. I waited another hour before calling out to my servant once more.

"Yes, Mrs. Knight?" he inquired, alighting from his seat and coming to the carriage side to see me.

"I see the edge of the Snyder property from here, and this is where I wish for you to stop."

It was only then that I realized that the young man had been holding his breath. He heaved a great sigh and said, "Good. It is rumored that the Snyders' ghosts still roam this area, and I was a bit uncomfortable with the idea of riding right up to the front door."

"Yes, do not worry. However, I do have two more strange requests for you, though nothing that should alarm you," I said, opening the carriage door and hopping from its interior before my servant could assist me. Leaning back inside, I withdrew my two bundles and then stood before him. "I wish you to undo the first two horses from the carriage. But first, look ahead of us, along the road."

He obeyed.

"See that carriage?" I asked. Of course he would be able to see it, as it was only a minute's walk ahead of us, stopped along the opposite side of the road from the overgrown path that led to the Snyder residence. "That carriage is there for our use. You may use whatever you need from it. If you need to use that harness and equipment, set up for two horses, then you may. Also, there is riding gear located inside of the carriage with which I would like you to equip two horses that you will give to me. Then, with my carriage and the remaining two horses, I wish you to return home and say nothing to anybody about where you have left me. Understand?"

The young man was obviously confused, but he obeyed, pulling my carriage up alongside the other one and readying each horse in the requested way. I stood by and watched, holding my two bundles while my servant used what I knew to be Mr. Howe's old carriage and parts. Although, simply due to its old nature, the carriage gave the appearance that it had been abandoned for at least a month, I knew the reality;

Thomas and Mr. Howe had brought it just that morning, pulled by two horses. After detaching the horses, Mr. Howe had taken both of them back to his house in Philadelphia, leaving the equipment that my servant would need. I also knew that Thomas would be watching our proceedings from the woods.

My servant finished as quickly as possible, and I did not know if it was because he desired to be out of the vicinity of the Snyder residence, or if it was because his confusion somehow hastened his actions. Either way, as soon as he had his two horses secured, he pulled away, bidding me an awkward farewell. I stood along the roadside, holding the reins of the two remaining horses with saddles and bridles fully equipped. I watched my servant depart for several minutes until he was fully out of sight behind the trees and then some distance still. Finally, I heard the snapping of twigs to my side, and Thomas emerged from the woods.

"Are you ready?" he asked, his smile stretched wide.

"Yes," I said, and we climbed atop the two horses, with only a mile to go until the first part of our journey would be complete.

We had chosen the road by the Snyder property as a good meeting location because it was out of the city, and thus out of sight of the people in the city. Also, this section of road was not frequently traveled, especially due to the lore surrounding the mysterious and horrifying deaths of the Snyders. As being there did make me uncomfortable, however, I was thankful that we were moving on quickly, in the direction of our true destination.

In less than a quarter of an hour, I silently signaled Thomas to stop. He then followed my lead as we both climbed from our horses. Finding an appropriate tree out of sight from the main road, we tethered them to it. Although I had tied both of my bundles to the sides of my horse's riding gear, I untied one partially then and withdrew from it a single letter, sealed in an envelope.

Walking forward, we reached the manicured edge of Mrs. White's property. The front door seemed a long way off, and bush and tree cover was scarce. I took a minute to reflect on the landscape before whispering in Thomas's ear, "Use those flowering bushes at the corner of her house."

Thomas nodded, and we launched into our plan.

Risking A Life

Cautiously looking about to make sure we were not seen,
Thomas crept down behind the bushes while I continued, crawling under
the windows in the front of the house and then to the front door. I was
thankful that there did not seem to be any guests right then, as there was
no carriage pulled in front of Mrs. White's house. Still, I had to be
quick. I laid the letter on Mrs. White's doorstep and then, standing up, I
knocked loudly and raced back to the flowering bush and Thomas.
Thankfully, I managed to duck behind it just before the front door
opened. Watching through a tiny hole between the flowers of the bush, I
identified Caroline as the maid who answered the door. She looked
about her for a few seconds, and then, spotting the envelope, she knelt
down, picked it up, and took it inside.

The letter was addressed to Mrs. White, and Caroline would take
it to her at once. As soon as we saw that the letter had been retrieved and
would surely not be lost, Thomas and I bolted from behind the bush and
returned to our horses in the woods. As soon as we untied them, we rode
quickly away from Mrs. White's house.

"How do you feel?" Thomas asked me after we were several
minutes away with our horses traveling at double the speed that we had
pushed them before arriving at Mrs. White's.

"I feel wonderful," I said. "And free."

Thomas's eyes flashed playfully before he continued, "And you
are really all right with having so loose a plan now?"

I smiled and looked up at the blue sky and puffy clouds above us,
visible only directly above the road as the trees rose high on either side
of us. "Our plan, and even the absence of one, is absolutely perfect." I
looked back at him, "I can't wait to see your family again. I really
enjoyed their company."

"As I wholeheartedly believe they enjoyed yours."

We had discussed everything over the last few days. We would
travel from Mrs. White's directly to the Parks' farm. There, we planned
to be wed. I was giddy with excitement as I remembered the dancing and
festivities I had enjoyed at Thomas's family's farm before. I was thrilled
that Thomas and I would be able to repeat such an enjoyable event, and
this time in honor of our wedding! After that, our plan was open-ended.
We both longed for the simple life that Thomas's family seemed to
have, and so we figured it would be good to start there. We would have
to work hard, we knew, to provide for ourselves. However, my

memories kept returning to the time I had spent on the MacIntosh Farm with Thomas, and I found that I was actually excited for the hard work of the future, knowing it would be with Thomas by my side.

Though Mr. Howe had wisely counseled us not to make our romance public so soon after William Knight's death, we all agreed that by traveling so far out of Philadelphia after hiding our actions and plans so carefully, no one would come looking for me there—and they would definitely not conceive of a notion where I, the wealthiest woman any had ever known, would run off with a poor servant.

"Is it just me, or does that cloud up there look just like a dog?" Thomas asked randomly. I looked up and could, in fact, immediately pick out the cloud to which Thomas referred.

"It does!" I happily agreed.

I fully relaxed then, knowing that everything was taken care of so that Thomas and I could start our new life together. I peacefully reflected, once more, on what the letter that I had left for Mrs. White contained, and I imagined the state of euphoria that most likely enveloped the entire household at this moment:

Dear Mrs. White,

This letter is one of the strangest I have ever had to write. And yet, I pray that you keep an open mind regarding its contents, as I hope this letter will reveal wonderful news to you.

First, I must apologize to you out of a sincere heart for repentance. Though you were completely unaware of it at the time, I selfishly put your life in jeopardy for my own gain. What I offer you in return can never truly atone for that sin, but I still humbly ask for your forgiveness.

Now, on to matters of the present, I must inform you that I am going away. I leave you this letter on the stoop of your door not out of trickery, but out of a desire to be made away unseen and unquestioned, as these decisions I have written about are final.

As a way of apology for risking your life and also as a thank you for the interest you showed in me upon discovering my vocal talents, I am giving to you the entirety of my earthly wealth, with small exceptions. Once again, this, I know, cannot make up for the evil sin I committed against you, but I do wish you to have this gift nonetheless.

You may have my house and most of the precious treasures and wealth associated with it. Although you are a very fine woman indeed, this should buy you any luxuries you feel you might have been lacking. I only ask that you reflect sometimes on the true meaning of happiness, as I have found that it does not lie in material possessions; rather, material possessions are only here for temporary enjoyment, but not for the giving of true identities or for pulling meaning out of life.

I ask that you give a portion of my wealth to Caroline, Frank, Amos, and Laura. While I leave the specific amounts up to you, I would ask that you give each of these servants enough so that they may pursue other enterprises aside from servitude if they wish. (If all of them leave for other enterprises, you already have a fully staffed house in Philadelphia. These servants, in the months I have known them, have proven to be hardworking. Pay them well, and try to take an interest in their lives, which is something I have failed in miserably.) Back to the four people I have so far named, I additionally ask that you pay closer attention to Caroline. Like me, she has no family, and she would greatly benefit, I believe, from the personal attentions of a kind lady like yourself. Please learn about her life, especially as you have no children of your own. You should find Caroline humble, kind, and pleasant. I also ask that you pay specific attention to helping her make a match with a respectable young gentleman of her choosing.

I would also like a share of your wealth to be given to Mr. Samuel Howe of Philadelphia, the poet. He has been a warm and generous man to me during the last several months. Aside from the request of generic wealth, I also ask that you purchase for him a new carriage and horses.

Finally, I request that you give some of your wealth to Mr. Jasper Graham. He has always been kind to me and noticed me, even when I was a simple servant.

I have placed a letter with the attorneys Smith and Brown in Philadelphia. In that letter, I have simply stated that the majority of my wealth should go to you, with the exceptions named in this letter. I have also included with Smith and Brown an exact list of where my items of worth are all located. The letter with these attorneys will not be opened until you have arrived at their offices, so please know that you are still the first person to discover and control my intentions. I have written these extra, official directions for the attorneys so that you might keep this letter for your eyes only and so that the legality of my wishes will be carried out properly and not questioned.

The contents of this letter may come as a shock to you, but I assure you that I am making these decisions entirely of my own free will. Although I anticipate living for quite some time still, I am more than willing to part with these material possessions. Though I have been through trying times over the last year, some the result of my own doing and some more indirect, I am thankful for the lessons I have learned. I have been shown the changing forms of clouds and the exhilarating power of lightning. The dances of lightning bugs and bonfires have made lasting impressions on my senses. The romance of nature has made itself known to me, and I have discovered peace in poverty. I wish now to make a clean break from my past mistakes, and I hope you can be happy for me. For I can assure you, I see a happy future for myself, surrounded by love and true joy—things that I pray I shall never overlook again.

Though I have signed the instructions I left with the attorneys with the legal signature of Catherine Knight, I instead leave for you a truer identity, one closer to my heart.

Your humble servant,
Louisa West

Acknowledgments

A huge thank you to Sam Varney of Metal Lunchbox Publishing for your hard work and enthusiasm. I am grateful to have you as my publisher.

Thanks to my wonderful unofficial editors—Claudia Cuddy, Al, and Jess. Your insights are greatly appreciated.

I am truly blessed to have such wonderful family and friends, encouraging me and helping me in many ways.

And in everything, may God, the ultimate Author, have the glory.

About the Author

Ellen Parry Lewis is the author of the young adult novels *Avenging Her Father*, *An Unremarkable Girl*, and *Future Vision*. Before turning to fiction full-time, Ellen was a freelance reporter for several newspapers. Ellen lives in New Jersey with her husband, daughter, son, and two dachshunds.

Risking A Life

Made in the USA
Charleston, SC
02 June 2016